Lilian Jackson Braun composed her first poem at the age of two. She began writing her *Cat Who . . .* mysteries when one of her own Siamese cats mysteriously fell to its death from her apartment block. Since then twelve *Cat Who . . .* novels have been published, all featuring the very talented Koko and Yum Yum, Siamese cats with a bent for detection. She is currently working on the next novel in the series and divides her time between her two homes in Michigan and North Carolina.

Also by Lilian Jackson Braun

The Cat Who Knew a Cardinal

Lilian Jackson Braun

headline

First published in Great Britain in 1991
by HEADLINE BOOK PUBLISHING

5

ISBN 0 7472 3788 3

Printed and bound in Great Britain by
Mackays of Chatham PLC, Chatham, Kent
Reproduced from a previously printed copy.

HEADLINE BOOK PUBLISHING
A division of Hodder Headline
338 Euston Road
London NW1 3BH

Dedicated to
Earl Bettinger, the husband who . . .

The Cat Who Knew a Cardinal

One

September promised to be a quiet month in Moose County, that summer vacation paradise 400 miles north of everywhere. After Labor Day the tourists returned to urban turmoil in the cities Down Below; the black fly season ended; children went reluctantly back to school; and everyday life cranked down to its normal, sleepy pace. This year the siesta was short-lived, however. Within a week the community was jolted by news of the Orchard Incident, as it was headlined by the local newspaper.

Prior to the Orchard Incident there was only one item of scandal on the gossip circuit in Pickax City, the county seat (population 3,000). Jim Qwilleran, semi-retired journalist and heir to the vast Klingenschoen fortune, was living in a barn! An apple barn! Oh, well, the townfolk conceded with shrugs and wagging heads, Mr. Q was entitled to a few eccentricities, being the richest man in the county and a free-wheeling philanthropist.

"Apple barn's better'n a pig barn," they chortled over coffee mugs in the cafés. After four years they had become accustomed to the sight of Mr. Q's oversize moustache with its melancholy droop. They no longer questioned the unorthodox *W* in the spelling of Qwilleran. And most of them now accepted the fact that the middle-aged divorced bachelor chose to live alone—with two cats!

Actually the facts were these: After twenty-five years of chasing the news in the capitals of the United States and Europe, Qwilleran had succumbed to the attractions of rural living, and he was captivated by barns, particularly an octagonal structure on the Klingenschoen property. The hundred-year-old fieldstone foundation was still intact, and its shingled siding was weathered to a silvery gray. Rising majestically as high as a four-story building, it overlooked a field of grotesque skeletons—the tortured remains of what was once a thriving apple orchard. Now it was of interest only to birds, including one that whistled an inquisitive *who-it? who-it? who-it?*

Qwilleran had first discovered the barn during his rambles about the Klingenschoen estate, which extended from the main thoroughfare of Pickax to Trevelyan Road, almost a half mile distant. The mansion of the notorious Klingenschoens, facing Main Street, had been converted into a theatre for stage productions, with the extensive gardens in the rear paved for parking. Beyond was a high, ornamental fence of wrought iron. Then came a dense patch of woods that concealed the barn and the orchard. After that, the lane leading to Trevelyan Road was hardly more than a dirt trail, winding through overgrown pastureland and past the foundations of old cottages once occupied by tenant farmers. If anyone remembered the lane at all, it was known as Trevelyan Trail. At the end of it an outsize, rural mailbox on a post was identified with the letter *Q*.

Originally the barn had been used for storing apples, pressing cider, and making apple butter. In recent years, all that remained was a wealth of empty space rising cathedral-like to the octagonal roof. Drastic renovation was required to make it habitable, but after Mr. Q moved in he was pleased to learn that the interior—on a warm and humid day—still exuded the aroma of Winesaps and Jonathans.

On a certain warm and humid day in September—the tenth of the month, to be exact—Qwilleran's housemates continually raised noses to sniff a scent they could not identify. They were a pair of Siamese—strictly indoor cats—and it was partly for their benefit that the barn had been converted to its present design. With ramps and cat-walks spiraling upward around the interior walls, with balconies floating on three levels, and with a system of massive beams radiating under the roof, the design allowed this acrobatic couple to race wildly, leap recklessly, and wrestle precariously on timbers thirty or forty feet overhead. For their quiet moments there were window-walls through which they could watch the flight of a bird, the fall of a leaf, and the ballet of wind-swept grasses in the orchard.

Qwilleran himself, having lived for two years in an apartment above the Klingenschoen garage, was awed by the spatial magnificence of his new residence. He was a big man in his comfort-loving fifties, with wide shoulders and long legs, and nature had not intended him to live in cramped quarters. On that warm and humid Saturday evening he strode about his domain enjoying the feeling of spaciousness and the dramatic perspectives, all the while stroking his bushy salt-and-pepper moustache with satisfaction. The last rays of the sunset slanted into the interior through high triangular windows, so shaped to preserve the symmetry of beams and braces.

"This time we got it right," he said to the cats, who were following him, strutting elegantly on long slender legs. "This is where we belong!" The three of them had lived at several addresses—sometimes happily, sometimes disastrously. "This is the last time we're going to move, you'll be glad to hear."

"Yow!" was the male cat's reply in a minor key; one could almost detect a note of skepticism.

Qwilleran made it a policy to converse with the Siamese, and the male responded as if he understood human speech. "We have Dennis to thank for all of this," he went on. "I only wish Mrs. Cobb could see it." Chuckling over a private reminiscence, he added, "She'd be tickled pink, wouldn't she?"

"Yow," said Koko in a soft, regretful tone as if he remembered Mrs. Cobb's superlative meatloaf.

The renovation had been designed and engineered by the son of Qwilleran's former housekeeper. Dennis Hough was his name, pronounced *Huff,* and his arrival in Pickax from St. Louis had created a stir for three reasons: The barn project was a sensation; the young builder had given his construction firm a whimsical name that delighted the locals; and the man himself had a mesmerizing effect on the women of Moose County. It was Qwilleran who had urged Dennis Hough to relocate, giving him the barn as his first commission and arranging Klingenschoen funds to back his new venture.

On this quiet Saturday evening the three barn dwellers were on a lofty catwalk high under the roof, and Qwilleran was reveling in the bird's-eye view of the comfortably furnished main floor when a piercingly loud demand from Yum Yum, the female, told him she cared more about food than architecture.

"Sorry," he apologized with a swift glance at his watch. "We're running a little late. Let's go down and see what we can find in the freezer."

The Siamese turned and scampered down the ramp,

shoulder to shoulder, until they reached the lower balcony. From there they swooped down to the main floor like flying squirrels, landing in a deep-cushioned chair with two soft thuds—a shortcut they had been swift to discover. Qwilleran took a more conventional route down a circular metal stairway to the kitchen.

Although he had been a bachelor for many years, he had never learned to cook even the simplest survival food for himself. His culinary skills were limited to thawing and coffeemaking. Now he dropped two frozen Alaska king crablegs into boiling water, then carefully removed the meat from the shells, diced it, and placed a plateful on the floor. The Siamese responded by circling the dish dubiously, first clockwise and then counterclockwise, before consenting to nibble.

"I suppose you'd prefer breast of pheasant tonight," Qwilleran said.

If he indulged them it was because they were an important two-thirds of his life. He had no other family. Yum Yum was a lovable pet who liked to sit on his lap and reach out a paw to touch his moustache wonderingly; Koko was a remarkably intelligent animal in whom the natural feline instincts were developed to a supranormal degree. Yum Yum knew when Qwilleran wore something new or served the food on a different plate, but Koko's twitching nose and bristling whiskers could sense danger and uncover hidden truths. Yum Yum had a larcenous paw that pilfered small objects of significance, but Qwilleran was convinced that Koko craftily planted the idea in her head. Together they were a wily pair of accomplices.

"Those devils!" he had recently remarked to his friend Polly. "I believe they have the Mungojerry-Rumpelteazer franchise for Moose County."

Tonight, as the cats nosed their way through the crabmeat without enthusiasm, the man observed the disapproving posture of the fawn-furred bodies, the critical tilt of the brown ears, and the reproachful contour of the brown tails. He was beginning to read their body language—especially their tail language. His concentration was interrupted when the telephone rang and there was no one on the line. Thinking nothing of it, he proceeded to thaw a pouch of beef stew for his own dinner.

Ordinarily, Saturday evening would have found him dining at the Old Stone Mill with Polly Duncan, the chief librarian in Pickax and the chief woman in his life. She was out of town, however, and he gulped down the beef stew without tasting it, after which he retired to his studio to write his "Straight from the Qwill Pen" column for the local newspaper. His upbeat topic was the success of an unusual experiment in Pickax. On that very evening the Theatre Club was presenting the final performance of *The Famous History of the Life of King Henry the Eighth*. It had been a controversial choice of play. Even devotees of Shakespeare predicted there would be more persons on the stage than in the audience. Yet, the production had achieved the longest run in Pickax theatre history: twelve performances over a period of four weekends, with virtually no empty seats.

Qwilleran had attended opening night in the company of Polly Duncan, fifth row on the aisle, after which he wrote a justifiably favorable review. Now that the final box office results were known, he wrote a wrap-up piece commending the audiences for their discerning appreciation of serious drama and complimenting the small-town performers for their believable portrayals of sixteenth-century English nobility. It was not entirely accidental that he neglected to mention the director until the last paragraph. Hilary VanBrook had offended Qwilleran's journalistic pride by refusing to be profiled in the "Qwill Pen" column—an opportunity that the rest of Pickax equated with winning the lottery. Now the journalist was getting the last word, so to speak, by relegating the director to the last paragraph.

Pleased with his handiwork, he concocted a cup of coffee in a computerized machine, thawed a doughnut, and prepared to relax with a book he had bought secondhand. Qwilleran was thrifty by temperament, and despite his new financial status he retained many of his old habits of frugality. He drove a preowned car, gassed up at the self-serve pump, winced when he looked at pricetags, and always sought out bargains in used books.

After getting into pajamas and his comfortable old threadbare plaid robe, he put a match to some dry twigs and applewood logs in the fireplace and was about to stretch out in an oversized armchair when the telephone rang again. Once more he heard an abrupt click-off followed by a dial tone, and this time he questioned it. In the cities where he had lived and worked Down Below, the incident would suggest a burglar lurking in a phone booth down at the corner. In Moose County, where break-ins were rare, he could suspect only curiosity-seekers. There had been so much gossip about Qwilleran's apple barn (where a fruit grower had hanged himself from the rafters in 1920) that townfolk had been prowling about the premises and peering in the windows.

Putting the phone call out of his mind, he settled down in his big chair with his feet propped on the ottoman. Immediately, the Siamese came running in anticipation of a reading session. He often read aloud to them. They seemed to appreciate the sound of his voice, whether he was reciting from his secondhand Walt Whitman or reading the major league scores in the newspapers from Down

Below. He had a richly timbred delivery—the result of his diction classes while dabbling in college drama—and the acoustics of the barn added to its resonance.

As he opened Audubon's *Birds of America*—the so-called Popular Edition of the nineteenth-century best-seller—his audience arranged themselves in comfortable bundles of attention, Yum Yum on his lap and Koko at his elbow on the arm of the chair. Ornithology was not one of Qwilleran's interests, but Polly had given him binoculars for his birthday and was trying to convert him to bird watching. Moreover, a book with two hundred colorplates was an irresistible bargain at a dollar.

"It's mostly pictures," he explained to the attentive animals as he turned the pages. "Who thinks up these absurd names? Black-bellied plover! Loggerhead shrike! Pied-billed grebe! Don't you think they're absurd?"

"Yow," Koko agreed.

"Here's a handsome one! It's your friend, the cardinal. The book says it resides in thickets, tangles, and gardens as far north as Canada."

Koko, an experienced pigeon watcher from Down Below, now spent hours every day at the windows on the various levels of the barn, sighting myriad small birds in the blighted orchard. Recently he had struck up an acquaintance with a visitor distinguished by red plumage, a royal crown, and a patrician beak, who whistled a continual question: *who-it?*

As Qwilleran turned the page to the rose-breasted grosbeak, both cats suddenly stretched to attention and craned their necks in the direction of the front door. Qwilleran also sat up and listened. He could hear a menacing rumble in the orchard that sounded alarmingly like army tanks, and he could see lights approaching the barn. He jumped to his feet and switched on the yardlights. Peering down the Trevelyan Trail he could see them coming—a column of headlights, weaving and bouncing as vehicles maneuvered through the ruts of the dirt road.

"What the deuce is this?" he barked, palming his moustache in perplexity. "An invasion?" The alarming tone of his voice sent both cats bounding out of sight; they had no intention of being caught in the line of fire.

One by one the vehicles turned out of the lane and parked in the tall grasses between the old apple trees. Headlights disappeared, and dark figures piled out of dark cars and trucks, converging on the barn. Only when they reached the pool of light in the yard did Qwilleran recognize them as the cast and crew of *Henry VIII.* They were carrying six-packs, coolers, brown paper bags, and pizza boxes.

His first thought was: Dammit! They've caught me in my pajamas and old robe! His second thought was: They look like hoboes themselves. It was true. The troupe wore backstage attire: tattered jeans, faded sweatshirts, washed out plaids, bedraggled sweaters, and grimy sneakers—a drastic change from the court finery of an hour before.

"Happy barn warming!" they shouted when they saw Qwilleran in the doorway. He reached around the doorjamb and threw a master switch that illuminated the entire interior. Uplights and downlights were concealed artfully in timbers and under balconies. Then he stepped aside and let them file into the barn—all forty of them!

If their eyes popped and their jaws dropped, it was for good reason. The walls of the main floor were the original stone foundation, a random stack of boulders held together by hidden mortar—craggy as a grotto. Overhead were massive pine timbers, some of them twelve inches square. Sandblasted to their original honey color, they contrasted softly with the newly insulated walls, painted white. And in the center of it all stood the contemporary fireplace, a huge white cube with three chubby cylindrical white flues rising to the center of the roof.

For the first time in anyone's memory the members of the Pickax Theatre Club were speechless. They wandered about the main level in a trance, gazing upward at the interlocking braces and beams, then downward at the earthen tile floor where furniture was arranged in conversation groups on Moroccan rugs. Then they collected their wits and all talked at once.

"Do you actually *live here,* Qwill?"

"I utterly don't believe it!"

"Neat! Really neat! Must've cost plenty!"

"Did Dennis do all of this? He's a genius!"

"Man, there's room for three grand pianos and two billiard tables."

"Look at the size of those beams! They don't grow trees like that any more."

"Swell place for a hanging."

"Qwill, darling, it's shattering! Would you like to time-share?"

Qwilleran had met the entire troupe at one time or another, and some of them were his favorite acquaintances in Pickax:

Larry Lanspeak, owner of the local department store, for one. He had auditioned for Cardinal Wolsey but landed the King Henry role, and his slight build required fifteen pounds of padding to match the girth of the well-fed monarch.

Fran Brodie, Qwilleran's interior designer and also daughter of the police chief. She auditioned for Queen Katharine but was ultimately cast as the beauteous Anne Boleyn. Perfect casting, Qwilleran thought. During the coronation scene he had been unable to take his eyes from her, and he was afraid Polly would hear his heavy breathing.

Carol Lanspeak, president of the club and everyone's friend. She was another capable aspirant for Queen Katharine and was deeply disappointed when director VanBrook picked her as his assistant and understudy for the queen.

Susan Exbridge, antique dealer and recent divorcée. She looked younger than her forty years and desperately wanted to play Anne Boleyn. When the director assigned her to do the Old Lady, she was furious but quickly recovered upon learning that the Old Lady had some bawdy lines that might steal the show.

Derek Cuttlebrink, busboy at the Old Stone Mill. He played five minor roles and was outstanding—not for his acting but for his bean-pole stature. Derek was six feet seven and still growing. Each time he made an entrance as another character, the audience whispered, "Here he comes again."

Dennis Hough, building contractor and new man in town. He, too, wanted to play Cardinal Wolsey but had to settle for a lesser role. Nevertheless, as the Duke of Buckingham, unjustly sentenced to death, he made a farewell speech that plunged the audience into tears night after night.

Eddington Smith, dealer in used books. This shy little old man played Cardinal Campeius, although no one could hear a word he said. It hardly mattered, because Cardinal Wolsey had all the best lines.

Hixie Rice, advertising manager for the local newspaper. As volunteer publicist for the club, she sold enough ads in the playbill to defray the cost of the sumptuous court costumes.

Wally Toddwhistle, the talented young taxidermist. He

built stage sets for Theatre Club productions, and for *Henry VIII* he worked miracles with used lumber, spray paint, and bedsheets.

Also present was the director, Hilary VanBrook, who wandered about by himself and had little or nothing to say. The rest of the company was sky-high after the heady experience of closing night: the standing ovation, the flowers, and the general relief that the whole thing was over. Now they were reacting noisily. The Siamese watched the crowd from a catwalk and twitched noses in recognition of the cheese, pepperoni, and anchovy wafting upward. The troupe appeared to be starved. They wolfed the pizza and washed it down with cold drinks and a strong brew from Qwilleran's computerized coffeemaker, all the while talking nonstop:

"Somebody missed the light cue, and I had to say my lines in the dark! I could have killed the jerk at the lightboard!"

"When Katharine had her vision tonight, the angels dropped the garland on her head. I could hardly keep a straight face."

"Everything goes haywire on the last night, but the audience doesn't know the difference."

"I was supposed to carry a gold scepter in the procession, you know, and tonight nobody could find the blasted thing!"

"At least nobody stepped on my train this time, thank God. For these small mercies we are grateful."

"Halfway through the treason trial he went up like a kite, and I had to ad-lib. That's tough to do in Elizabethan English."

"The audience was really with us tonight, weren't they? The Old Lady even got some belly laughs from the balcony."

"Why not? She played it like the side of a barn!"

Qwilleran moved hospitably through the group, jingling the ice in his glass of Squunk water. (It looked like vodka on the rocks, but everyone knew it was mineral water from a flowing well at Squunk Corners.) He was not surprised to see Dennis Hough surrounded by women. Among them were Susan Exbridge, her dark hair still sleek after wearing the Old Lady's wig . . . and Hixie Rice, tossing her asymetrical page-boy cut, which was auburn this week . . . and Fran Brodie, whose soft, strawberry blond curls contrasted surprisingly with her steely gray eyes.

Carol Lanspeak nudged Qwilleran's elbow slyly. "Look at Dennis with his groupies. Too bad I'm happily married to Larry; I'd join the pack."

Qwilleran said, "Dennis is a good-looking guy."

"And he has an interesting quality," Carol said. "Masculine and yet sensitive. He looks cool, but he's wired to a very short fuse. There were quite a few blowups during rehearsals."

"He's impulsive, but I overlooked his mood swings when we were working on the barn because he was doing such a great job. He was on his way to be a registered architect, you know, before he went into the construction business. Notice how he incorporated the old loft ladders into the design." As he spoke, the lanky busboy was halfway up a ladder, waving an arm and leg at those below. "The catwalks are for washing the high windows. We're going to hang tapestries from the railings."

"You could hang quilts," said Carol, whose taste ran to country coziness.

"No quilts!" Qwilleran said sternly. "Fran has ordered some contemporary hangings. They should be here any day now."

"Everyone in town is aching to see this place, Qwill."

"That's why we're having a public open house. The admission charge to benefit the library was Polly's idea."

"Serve refreshments and the library will clean up! We have a very hungry population." Then casually she inquired, with the licensed nosiness of a Pickax native, "Where's Polly tonight?"

Everyone knew that the Klingenschoen heir and the chief librarian spent weekends together. During bull sessions at the Dimsdale Diner one of the men usually asked, "Do you think he'll ever marry her?" And women drinking coffee at Lois's Luncheonette always brought up the topic: "Wonder why she doesn't marry him?"

To answer Carol's question Qwilleran explained, "Polly's in Lockmaster, attending a wedding. The librarian down there has a son who's going off the deep end."

"Who's taking care of Bootsie?" Another well-known fact in Pickax was the librarian's obsessive concern for her young cat.

"I went over there tonight to feed him, and I'll go again tomorrow morning to fill up his four hollow legs and police his commode. I never saw a cat eat so much!"

"He's still growing," Carol said.

"Polly will be home in the late afternoon to tell me what the bride wore and who caught the bouquet and all that guff. I don't know why you women are so wild about weddings."

"You talk like a grouchy old bachelor, Qwill."

"I'd rather go to a ballgame. Do you realize that I haven't seen a major league game in four years? And I was born a Cub fan in Chicago."

"It's your own fault, Qwill. You know very well that Larry would love to fly you down to Chicago or Minneapolis. He's bought a new four-seater. Polly and I could go along for a shopping binge. Or maybe she'd like to see the game, too."

"Polly—does—not—like—baseball!" Qwilleran said with emphasis. Nor shopping, either, he thought, reflecting on her limited wardrobe assembled haphazardly at Lanspeak's Department Store during sales.

Carol's husband joined them. "Did I hear my services being volunteered?"

At first glance the Lanspeaks were a plain-looking middle-aged couple, but they had a youthful source of energy that made them civic leaders and genial company as well as excellent actors. Qwilleran often wondered what they ate for breakfast. He said, "Larry, you were great onstage! The kingliest Henry I've ever seen!"

"Thanks, fella. Let me tell you, it's good to be thin again. Besides navigating Henry's belly around the stage, I had to *think fat!* That's quite an adjustment! And then there was that damned itchy beard! I shaved it off as soon as the final curtain fell."

Carol asked, "How did Polly like the play?"

"She gave it raves, and we both thought the crowd scenes were tremendously effective. How did you manage all those kids?"

"It wasn't easy—getting them into costume, keeping them quiet backstage, pushing them out on cue. They dressed at the school, you know, and we transported them on school buses. *Trauma time!* Fortunately, Hilary had directed the play before and knew all the tricks. As his assistant I learned a lot; I won't deny that." She turned her back to the other guests and lowered her voice. "But as president of the club and wife of the president of the school board, I wish to go on record as saying *I can't stand the man!*"

A large percentage of the Pickax population entertained

a loathing for Hilary VanBrook, principal of the high school. At fault was his abrasive personality and unbearable conceit. The public even resented the turtlenecks he wore to school. In Moose County there was something subversive about an administrator who wore black turtlenecks instead of the expected white shirt and quiet tie. But chiefly annoying was his habit of being eminently successful at everything he proposed, no matter how preposterous it appeared to parents, teachers, the superintendent of schools, and the school board.

Principal-bashing, therefore, was a favorite pastime. He was an unattractive man, and behind his back he was called Horseface. Yet, everyone remained in awe of his capabilities and self-assurance. It was because of his brilliant record as a school administrator and his reputation as a brain that the Theatre Club had allowed him to mount a play that was considered too dull, on a stage that was too small, with a cast that was too large. And now *Henry VIII* was going into the books as another triumph for Horseface.

"Yes," Larry said grudgingly in a low voice, "that scurvy knave has done it again! Ticket sales were so good we actually made a profit. With all those kids in the cast, you know, the hall was filled with their relatives, friends, and classmates." He glanced to left and right to ascertain the director's whereabouts and continued in a stage whisper. "He made two political mistakes. He should certainly *not* have played Cardinal Wolsey himself, and he should definitely *not* have brought someone from the next county to play Queen Katharine. We have plenty of talent right here in Moose County."

Qwilleran scanned the scattered groups of guests. "What happened to the queen? I don't see her here tonight."

Carol said, "She left right after the curtain. Got out of

makeup in a hurry and didn't even say goodbye to the cast."

"Well, we weren't very cordial to her, I'm afraid," Larry confessed, "although we told her about the party and how to get here, and she wrote it down. I thought she'd show up. Of course, she lives in Lockmaster, and that's a sixty mile drive, so I guess she can be excused."

Carol squeezed her husband's arm. "How do you like the barn, honey?"

"Fantastic! What condition was it in, Qwill, before you started?"

"Structurally solid, but filthy! For years it had been a motel for birds, cats, bats, and even skunks. Fran hung those German prints as an apology to the dispossessed bats." He pointed to a group of four framed zoological prints of flying mammals, dated 1824.

"You should have the barn photographed, Qwill, for a magazine."

"Yes, I'd like to see it published—for Dennis's sake. And Fran did a great job with the furnishings, considering I'm not the easiest client to get along with. John Bushland is coming up from Lockmaster to shoot some pictures for insurance purposes. I'm curious to know how everything looks on film."

"Don't we have a good photographer here?" Larry asked sharply. There had been jealous rivalry between Pickax and Lockmaster for a century or more.

"No one with Bushy's talent and experience and equipment."

"You're right. He's good," Larry acknowledged.

Someone shouted "Last call for pizza!" and the crowd swarmed to the kitchen snack bar—all except Hilary VanBrook. While the others had mingled in shifting clusters, the director had stayed on the periphery. In his bottle-green corduroy sports coat and red turtleneck he was clearly the best-dressed individual in the largely raggle-taggle assemblage. With shoulders hunched, hands in pockets, and a saturnine expression on his gaunt and homely face, he appeared to be studying—with a critical eye—the handhewn and woodpegged framework of the building, the design of the fireplace, the zoological prints, and the printer's typecase half filled with engraved metal plates mounted on wooden blocks.

He was standing in front of a pine wardrobe, seven feet high, when Qwilleran approached and said, "That's a Pennsylvania German *schrank* dating 1850 or earlier."

"More likely Austrian," the director corrected him. "You can see the piece had painted decoration originally. It's been stripped and refinished, which lessens its value, as you probably know."

Qwilleran devoutly wished that Dennis's mother had been present to refute the man's pronouncement. Van-Brook delivered it without looking at his listener. He had a disconcerting habit of rolling his eyes around the room while discoursing. Exercising admirable restraint, Qwilleran replied, "Be that as it may, let me congratulate you on the success of the play."

The director flashed a glance at the frayed lapels of Qwilleran's old plaid robe. "Its success came as no surprise to me. When I proposed doing the play, the opposition came from persons with little theatre experience or understanding of Shakespeare. A dull play, they labeled it. With competent direction there are no dull plays. Furthermore, *Henry VIII* addresses problems that are rife in our society today. I insist that our senior students study *Henry VIII.*"

Qwilleran said, "I understand there was no Shakespeare taught in Pickax before you took the helm."

"Regrettably true. Now our freshmen are exposed to *Romeo and Juliet*, sophomores read *Macbeth*, and juniors study *Julius Caesar*. Not only do they read the plays; they speak the lines. Shakespeare is meant to be spoken."

Listening to VanBrook's theatrical voice and looking past his shoulder, Qwilleran could see the ramp leading down from the balcony. Koko was descending the slope to investigate, walking with a purposeful gait, his eyes fixed on the principal. Effortlessly and silently the cat rose to the top of the *schrank* and assumed a position above the man's head, gazing down with a peculiar stare. Qwilleran, hoping that Koko had no intentions that might prove embarrassing, gave the cat a stern glance and cleared his throat pointedly before inquiring of VanBrook, "What do you think of the job Dennis did with this great barn of a place?"

"Derivative, of course," VanBrook said with a lofty display of design acumen.

"According to Dennis, ramps are in keeping with barn vernacular. Any resemblance to the Guggenheim Museum is purely coincidental. Those ladders," Qwilleran went on, "are the original loft ladders; the rungs are lashed to the siderails with leather thongs."

Apparently the director could feel Koko's stare at the top of his head, and he passed his hand over his hairpiece. (That hairpiece was a topic of much discussion in Pickax, where men were expected to have the real thing or none at all.) Then VanBrook turned abruptly and looked at the top of the *schrank*.

Hastily Qwilleran said, "This is our male Siamese, Kao K'o Kung, named after a thirteenth-century Chinese artist."

"Yow!" said Koko, who knew his name when he heard it.

"The Yuan dynasty," the principal said with a superior nod. "He was also a noted poet, although that is not generally known by Westerners. His name means 'worthy of respect' or words to that effect. An exact translation is difficult." He turned his back to the Pennsylvania German *schrank,* which had suddenly become Austrian, and Qwilleran was glad that the cat staring at the hairpiece was Koko and not his accomplice. Yum Yum the Paw would snatch it with a lightning-fast grab and carry it up the ramp to the bedroom, where she would hide it under the bed or, worse still, slam-dunk it in the toilet.

VanBrook was saying, "Appreciation of all the arts is something I have introduced into the curriculum here, as I did when I was principal of Lockmaster High School. It is my contention that graduates who play instruments badly or draw still lifes poorly contribute nothing to the cultural climate of the community. The essence of a true education is an *appreciation* of art, music, literature, and architecture." He gazed about the barn speculatively. "I should like to bring grades nine to twelve over here, one class at a time, on field trips in the next few weeks."

Qwilleran blinked at the man's audacity, but before he could formulate a reply there was a murmur on top of the *schrank,* a shifting of paws, and a furry body swooped over the principal's head and landed on a rug ten feet away, after which Koko yowled loudly and imperiously.

Larry Lanspeak heard him and interpreted the message. "C'mon, you guys," he called out. "Chugalug! Qwill's cats need to get some sleep."

Reluctantly the guests started gathering paper plates and napkins, collecting empties, straightening chairs. Gradually they drifted out into the night, clowning and uttering war whoops.

As Fran gave Qwilleran a theatrical goodnight kiss, he

said to her, "Was this party your idea? Did you ring my phone a couple of times and hang up?"

"We had to be sure you were here, Qwill. We thought you might be out with Polly. Where is Polly tonight?"

"In Lockmaster at a wedding."

"Oh, really? Why didn't you go?" she asked slyly. "Afraid you'd catch the bouquet?"

"Don't be cheeky, young lady," he warned her. "I haven't paid your bill yet." He watched her leave—a good designer, easy to like, half his age and refreshingly impudent, stunning even in grubby rehearsal togs. Dennis walked out with Susan, the two of them sharing a secret joke. Eddington Smith tagged along with the Lanspeaks, who were giving him a ride home.

VanBrook lingered long enough to say, "I'll have my assistant contact you about the student tours."

This time Qwilleran was ready with a reply. "An excellent idea," he said, "but I must make one stipulation. I insist that Dennis conduct the tours and explain the design and construction methods. If you will take the initiative and line him up, I'll consent gladly." He knew that the principal and the builder had been at odds during rehearsals.

VanBrook rolled his eyes around the interior once more, said a curt goodnight, and followed the others who were trooping to their parked cars, all of them laughing and shouting, reliving the play, hitching rides, making dates. Headlights were turned on and motors turned over, some of them purring and others backfiring or roaring like jets. Qwilleran watched the taillights bounce and weave as they followed the rutted lane to the highway.

Closing the door, he turned off the yardlights and most of the interior lights, then gave the Siamese a bedtime treat. "You two characters behaved very well. I'm glad you sent them home, Koko. Do you realize what time it is?"

The Siamese gloated over their morsel of food as if it were a five-course meal, and as Qwilleran watched them his mind wandered to his recent visitors. He envied them the experience of rehearsing, performing, bowing to applause, grieving over roles that got away, complaining about the director, agonizing over miscues and lost props. For a short time he had been an active member of the club, but Polly had convinced him that learning lines and attending rehearsals would rob him of time better spent on serious writing. Actually, he suspected, the middle-aged librarian who wore size sixteen was jealous of the svelte and exuberant young actresses in the club. Polly was an intelligent woman and a loving companion who shared his interest in literature, but she had one fault. Jealousy caused her to be overpossessive.

The Siamese, having licked their empty plate for several minutes, were now laving their brown masks and white whiskers with moistened brown paws, as well as swiping long pink tongues over their nearly white breasts. Then, in the midst of a swipe, they both stopped and posed like waxworks with tongues extended. Abruptly, Koko broke away and trotted to the front door, where he peered through the side windows into the darkness. Qwilleran followed, and Yum Yum padded along behind. As he stared into the blackness of the orchard he could see the last set of taillights disappearing down the trail and turning into Trevelyan Road.

The spill of light from the barn also picked up a metallic reflection that had no business being in the orchard. A car without lights was still parked among the trees.

He huffed into his moustache. "Can you beat that?" he said aloud. "I'll bet it's Dennis and Susan . . . Why don't they go to his place or her place?"

"Yow," Koko agreed.

Dennis's wife and child were still in St. Louis, and he had not seen them for several months, owing to the barn project and the play rehearsals.

"Oh, well, live and let live," Qwilleran said as he turned out yardlights and remembered his own reckless youth. "Let's screen the fireplace and go to bed."

He turned away from the front door and followed Yum Yum, who was scampering up the ramp, but Koko remained stubbornly at his post, a determined voyeur, his body taut and his tail pointed stiffly. Qwilleran heard a low rumble. Was it a growl?

"Cut that out," he called to him. "Just mind your own business and turn in. It's three o'clock."

Still the cat growled, and the rumble that came from his lower depths ended in a falsetto shriek. It was an ominous pronouncement that Koko never made without reason. Qwilleran picked up a jacket and a flashlight and started out the door, pushing the excited cat aside with a persuasive toe and shouting a stern "No!" when he tried to follow.

"Hey, you down there!" he called out as he crossed the barnyard, swinging the flashlight in arcs. "Any trouble?"

The night was silent. There was no traffic noise from Main Street at that hour. No wind whistled through the dying apple trees. And there was no movement in the vehicle, a well-kept late-model car. No one turned on the ignition or switched on the headlights.

Qwilleran flashed his light on the surrounding ground and between the trees. Then he beamed it into the car at an oblique angle to avoid reflections in the window glass. Only the driver could be seen, and he was slumped over the wheel.

Heart attack, Qwilleran thought in alarm. Only when he hurried to the other side of the car did he see the blood and the bullethole in the back of the head.

Two

Qwilleran's hand hovered over the phone for an instant before he lifted the handset and reported the homicide. As a hard-headed journalist Down Below he would have notified his newspaper first and then the police, but there was a sense of intimacy in a town the size of Pickax, and his loyalties had changed. He knew the victim, and the police chief was a personal friend. Without further hesitation he called Chief Brodie at home.

"Brodie!" was the gruff answer from a man who was accustomed to being roused from sleep at 3 A.M.

"Andy, this is Qwill, reporting a homicide in your precinct."

"Where?"

"In my orchard."

"Who?"

"Hilary VanBrook."

There was a momentary pause. "What was he doing in your orchard?"

"There was a party here for the Theatre Club, and he was the last to leave. He was shot before he had a chance to start his car."

Brodie shifted from gruff lawman to concerned parent. "Was Fran there?"

"The whole club was here."

"Be right over."

"Hold it, Andy! The driveway is probably full of tire tracks and footprints, if that concerns you. Come in the other way, through the theatre parking lot. I'll meet you there and unlock the gate."

Brodie grunted and hung up.

Qwilleran pulled pants and a sweater over his pajamas, picked up the flashlight once more, and headed at a run toward Main Street. The road through the woods had been freshly graded and graveled, and it was only a few hundred yards to the fence. Even so, when he arrived at the gate headlights were already illuminating the theatre parking lot. In a town the size of Pickax, everything was five minutes away from everything else.

He jumped into Chief Brodie's car and pointed the way through the woods, while other vehicles with flashing lights followed. He explained, "We've had trespassers lately, so I lock the gate at night."

"How'd you find out about VanBrook?" Brodie snapped.

"After everyone left the orchard, there was still one car parked among the trees. Then that cat of mine started howling suspiciously. I went out to investigate and found VanBrook slumped over the steering wheel."

"He wasn't a happy individual. No wife. No family. Could be suicide."

"Not with a bullethole in the back of his head," Qwilleran said. "It blew his hairpiece off." They had reached the rear of the barn. "Park here. All the activity was on the other side."

A Pickax prowl car and a state police vehicle pulled alongside, leaving room for the ambulance, which arrived immediately, and the medical examiner.

"Anything I can do?" Qwilleran asked.

"Stay indoors till we need you," Brodie ordered. "Leave the house lights on."

Qwilleran threw the master switch once more, and the entire barn glowed like a beacon, the light spilling out to illuminate the surrounding grounds.

The Siamese were nervous. They knew something was wrong. Strangers were milling about the yard, and police spotlights were turning the misshapen trees into frightening giants. Qwilleran picked up the cats and climbed the ramp with one squirming animal under each arm. In their own apartment on the top balcony there were comforting carpets and cushions, useful baskets and perches, a scratching post, and TV. Slipping a video of birdlife into the VCR to calm them, he returned to the main level, feeling mildly guilty; he had not yet called the newspaper.

He notified the night desk, asking if they had a reporter available. Yes, they said, Roger was subbing for Dave.

"Tell him to use the Main Street entrance," Qwilleran said.

Then he tried to reach Larry Lanspeak; as president of the school board Larry deserved to be notified immediately. It appeared, however, that the Lanspeaks had not yet arrived home. They lived in the country; Larry was a cautious driver; and they always drove Eddington Smith home first. Qwilleran gave them another fifteen minutes to reach the affluent suburb of West Middle Hummock before he punched their number again.

Larry answered on the tenth ring. "Just walked in the door, Qwill. What's up?"

"I have bad news for you, Larry. You'll have to shop around for another high school principal."

"What do you mean?"

"VanBrook has been killed."

"What happened? Car accident?"

"You won't believe this, Larry, but someone put a bullet through his skull. The police are here, combing the orchard with their spotlights."

"How did you find out? Did you hear the shot?"

"Didn't hear a thing, except someone's jalopy backfiring. After the gang pulled out, there was one car left. I went out to check it."

"This is a mess, Qwill. The police will assume it was one of us."

"I don't know what they'll assume, but we'd better be prepared to answer questions tomorrow."

Larry volunteered to call the superintendent of schools and alert him. "Otherwise he'll hear it on the radio, or the cops will bang on his door. I can't believe this is happening!"

A chugging motor in the yard caught Qwilleran's ear. "Excuse me, Larry. Another car just drove in. I think it's a reporter. I'll talk with you later."

The car parked alongside the police vehicles, and Qwilleran recognized Roger MacGillivray's ten-year-old boneshaker. He went out to meet the bearded young man who had given up teaching history in order to report living history for the local paper.

"What happened?" asked the reporter, slinging two cameras over his shoulder.

"We had a Theatre Club party here after the final performance, and at three o'clock everyone drove away except the director. That's all I know. If you want details, you'll have to get them from Brodie. He's down there where it happened."

Qwilleran watched the scene as Roger approached the chief and said a few words. Brodie turned and threw a scowl at the barn, then answered some questions tersely.

before jerking his thumb over his shoulder. Roger snapped a couple of quick shots before retreating to the barn.

"How come you're working tonight?" Qwilleran asked as he opened the door.

"Dave had to go to a wedding in Lockmaster, so I switched with him," Roger explained. "Hey, this place is fabulous! Sharon would love to see it!"

"Bring her down here for a drink some evening. Bring Mildred, too."

"One of us will have to baby-sit, so I'll send the girls alone. Don't let my mother-in-law drink too much. She's been hitting the bottle since Stan died. I don't know why. She's one hundred percent better off without him, but . . . you know how women are!"

"How will Sharon and Mildred react when they hear about their principal's sudden demise?"

"They'll go into shock, but they won't be sorry. VanBrook did some good things for the curriculum and the school's academic standing, and they admired him in a grudging way, but none of the teachers liked the guy, and that included me. He treated us like kids. And then there were his meetings! Teachers don't like meetings anyway—they're nonproductive—and Horseface chaired meetings that were just boring ego trips. That's the chief reason I quit and went to work for the paper. After that, whenever I went to the school to cover a story, VanBrook made me feel like the plumber who'd come to fix the latrines . . . Any idea who shot him? It had to be one of your guests. Right?"

"I'm not hazarding any guesses, Roger, and certainly not for the rapacious press. Would you like a beer?"

"Might as well. Okay if I look around?"

"Go ahead. On the first balcony I have a sleeping room and writing studio. You can open the door and look in, but don't expect it to be tidy. On the second balcony is the guestroom. The cats have the third level. Don't disturb them; they've had a harrowing night."

"Don't worry. You know me and cats! Sharon says I'm an ailurophobe."

The phone rang, and it was Qwilleran's old friend on the line. Arch Riker, fellow journalist from Down Below, was now editor and publisher of the local newspaper. "What's going on there?" he demanded. "The night desk tipped me off. Why didn't you let me know?"

"There's nothing you can do, Arch. Go back to bed. Roger's here. You'll read about it on your front page Monday."

"Any suspects?"

"You can ask Roger."

"Put him on."

The reporter's remarks on the phone revealed that he had learned nothing from Brodie. After hanging up he said to Qwilleran, "How about telling me who was here at the party?"

"That information may be crucial to the investigation. I can't discuss it at this time," Qwilleran recited in a monotone.

"Whose side are you on, anyway?"

Before Qwilleran could answer there was an authoritative knock on the door, and Brodie was standing there with orders for Roger to clear out. The reporter made a routine protest but shouldered his cameras and drove away.

"Want a cup of coffee?" Qwilleran asked the chief.

"Hell, I wouldn't take my life in my hands by drinking the stuff you brew!" He strode into the barn with a lumbering swagger. Off duty he was a genial Scot who wore a kilt and played the bagpipe. Tonight he was the gruff, grumbling investigator, taking in the scene with a veteran's eye.

"Any clues out there?" Qwilleran asked. "Any evidence?"

"I'm here to ask questions, friend—not answer them." Brodie scanned the contemporary furniture upholstered in pale tweeds and leathers. "Got anything to sit on? Like kitchen chairs?"

Qwilleran led the way to the snack bar.

"I smell pizza," said the chief.

"Actors get hungry. You should know that, Andy. You've been feeding one."

"Not any more," said Brodie with a frown. "Fran's moved out. Wanted her own place. Don't know why. She had it comfortable at home." He looked troubled— a north-country father who thought daughters should either marry and settle down or live at home with the folks.

Qwilleran said, "It's normal for a young career woman to want her own apartment, Andy."

Brodie snapped out of his fatherly role. "Who was here tonight?"

"I happen to have a printed guestlist." He handed the chief one of the playbills, listing the cast of characters in order of appearance.

Brodie ran a thumb down the righthand side of the page. "Were all these people here?"

"All except the woman from Lockmaster who played the queen. And of course the spear carriers left on the school bus right after the coronation scene. You saw the show, didn't you?"

Brodie grunted an affirmative. "What were they all doing here besides eating pizza?"

"Drinking beer and soft drinks and coffee . . . hashing

over the run of the play . . . celebrating its success . . . making a lot of noise."

"Were they smoking anything they shouldn't?"

"No. Carol puts the clamps on that. She runs a tight ship. Fran can tell you."

"Any arguments? Any brawls?"

"Nothing like that. Everyone was in a good humor."

"Did you see anybody hanging around the orchard that didn't belong?"

"Not tonight, but we've had curiosity-seekers prowling around ever since we moved in."

"How come VanBrook honored the party with his presence? He was an unsociable cuss."

"He had an ulterior motive," said Qwilleran. "He wanted to bring the entire student body tramping through my barn on field trips. He didn't ask me; he told me!"

"That sounds like him, all right. How popular was he in the club?"

"Ask Fran about that. I'm not an active member."

"Did you hear gunfire in the orchard?"

"No, but the cats heard something, and when I looked out the window I saw the taillights of a car pulling onto the highway."

"Which way did it go?"

"Turned right."

"Notice anything about the taillights?"

"Now that you mention it, Andy, they weren't the horizontal ones you see on passenger cars. They were vertical and set wide apart, like those on a van or truck."

"How long has your mailbox been knocked over?"

"It was okay when I picked up my Saturday mail."

"Well, somebody sideswiped it and bent the post."

"That should make your job easier," Qwilleran said, thinking, Somewhere there is a vehicle with a damaged fender over the right front wheel.

Brodie stood up. "No need to keep you up all night. I'll get back to you in the morning."

"Not too early—please!"

The chief walked to the door and turned to give the interior a final scowling appraisal. "I climbed many a ladder like that when I was a kid. What are the three white things that look like smokestacks?"

"Smokestacks. It's a contemporary idea for venting a fireplace. Bring your wife over some evening. She'll enjoy seeing Fran's work."

"Did my daughter pick out all this furniture?" Brodie asked, more in dismay than admiration.

"She gets all the credit. She has a good eye and good taste."

Brodie grunted and turned to leave, but he lingered with his hand on the doorhandle. "This fella that did over your barn—Dennis what's-his-name . . ."

"H-o-u-g-h, pronounced Huff. He's Iris Cobb's son."

"I hear Fran is kinda thick with him." He searched Qwilleran's face for verification. "He's married, you know."

"Don't worry," said Qwilleran. "All the women in town go for Dennis, but he dotes on his family, and when they move up here, the fringe element will cool off. Meanwhile, Fran and Dennis have merely collaborated on this project."

"I hope you're right . . . Well, good night. We've got the driveway blockaded at the far end, and we're leaving a man on duty. The crime lab is coming up from Down Below." Brodie walked away a few steps and added, "Something tells me this'll be an easy case to solve."

Qwilleran turned out the houselights and climbed the ramp to his bedroom, but he was in no mood to sleep. He perused a playbill and tried to imagine each actor with a smoking gun in hand. In each case it looked like bad

casting. He wondered how soon Brodie would start ringing doorbells and rousing the party goers from their beds
for interrogation. The chief would undoubtedly start with
his own daughter, who lived in Indian Village, a popular
apartment complex for singles. Susan, Dennis, and Hixie
also had apartments there. The Lanspeaks lived farther
out in a rambling country house. Poor Eddington Smith
holed up downtown in the bookbinding workshop behind
his bookstore. Other members of the club came from surrounding towns: bustling Kennebeck, quaint Sawdust
City, ramshackle Wildcat, and as far away as the resort
town of Mooseville. Only Wildcat lay to the south of
Pickax; a driver heading for Wildcat would turn right on
Trevelyan Road upon leaving Trevelyan Trail.

Lying there awake he remembered his houseman's prediction when he first saw the renovated barn. The white-
haired and highly respected Pat O'Dell had been custodian
of the Pickax high school before retiring and starting his
own janitorial service. He gazed up at the lofty beams and
said in a fearful voice, "Will yourself be livin' here?"

"Yes, I enjoy lots of space, Mr. O'Dell, and I'm counting on you and Mrs. Fulgrove to handle the maintenance
as you did in my old apartment."

"The divil himself would be hard up to clean the windows way up there, I'm thinkin', or sweep the cobwebs
down."

"That's one reason we built the catwalks. I hope you're
not leery about heights."

Mr. O'Dell shook his head with foreboding. "An old
farmer, they're tellin', was after puttin' a rope around his
neck and swingin' from one of those rafters. It were seventy year since. Sure an' that's when a blight fell on the
apple trees. It's troubled I'd be, Mr. Q, to live here."

"But life must go on, Mr. O'Dell. Let me show you

where we hide the key, in case you want to work when I'm not here. Mrs. Fulgrove will do the light cleaning on Wednesdays."

"Saints preserve us!" was the janitor's parting remark as he ventured a final apprehensive look at the superstructure. That had been two weeks ago, and now Mr. O'Dell would be saying, "Sure an' I told you so."

When at last Qwilleran managed to doze off on Sunday morning, it seemed a mere fifteen minutes before he was jolted awake by the telephone, its ring sounding more urgent than usual.

Fran Brodie was on the line. "Dad just called and broke the news! This is terrible! What does it mean?"

"It means we'll all be questioned," Qwilleran replied sleepily.

"No one in the club would do such a thing, do you think? Dad refused to tell me if they had a suspect or if they found any evidence. He can be so exasperating when he's playing the cop. It must have been turmoil in your orchard last night."

"It was, and I've had about fifteen minutes' sleep."

"Sorry I woke you, Qwill. Go back to sleep. I'm going to call some of the others now."

Qwilleran looked at his bedside clock. In five minutes WPKX would feature the Orchard Incident on the eight o'clock newscast. He steeled himself for another misleading bulletin, WPKX style, with inflated prepositions and pretentious pauses:

"Hilary VanBrook, principal of Pickax High School, was found dead early this morning IN . . . a parked . . . car. Police say VanBrook was shot in the head AFTER . . . an all-night party held AT . . . a barn . . . occupied BY . . . James Qwilleran. Suicide has been ruled out, and robbery was apparently not the motive according TO . . .

Police Chief . . . Andrew . . . Brodie. No further details are available AT . . . this . . . hour."

Qwilleran muttered, "I could punch that announcer IN . . . the teeth!" The reference to "a parked car" and "all-night party" would have tongues wagging all over the county, he predicted. It was Sunday. He could imagine the buzzing among church goers. Telephone lines would be jammed; restaurants would be crowded with folks who never dined out as a rule; neighbors who disliked yard-work would be raking leaves and spreading rumors across back fences. Immediately Qwilleran's own phone started to ring.

Larry Lanspeak was the first to call. "Heard anything more, Qwill?"

"Not a word."

"Okay if I drop in for a few minutes before church?"

"Sure. Come along."

"Carol's on the altar committee, so I'll have to drop her off at ten o'clock with a trunkful of mums."

"Come through the theatre parking lot," Qwilleran instructed him. "The lane's blockaded."

Next Eddington Smith called, speaking in the same trembling voice that had made him inaudible as Cardinal Campeius. "Do you think they'll suspect me?" he asked. "I've got a handgun in my workshop. Do you think I should get rid of it?"

"Has it been fired recently?" Qwilleran asked, knowing that Edd had never bought any ammunition.

"No, but it has my fingerprints. Maybe I should wipe them off."

"Don't do anything, Edd, and don't worry. The police wouldn't suspect you in a million years."

Shortly afterward, Susan Exbridge telephoned, opening with the brazen banter that she had affected since her divorce. "Qwill, darling, why don't you confess? With those sexy eyelids and that sinister moustache you look exactly like a killer."

In contrast, the next caller was frantically serious. It was Wally Toddwhistle's mother. "Oh, Mr. Q, I'm worried sick," she cried. "Do you think they'll suspect Wally?"

"Is there any reason why they should?"

"Well, he got into trouble in his last year of high school, and Horseface gave him a rotten deal. Don't you know about it?"

"No. What happened?"

"It was only a prank that the kids dreamed up. It wasn't even Wally's idea, but he took the blame and wouldn't tell on the others, and that damned principal expelled him a few weeks before graduation! I went to school and raised hell, but it didn't do any good. Wally never got his diploma. His dad was ill during all this trouble, and I think that's what killed him."

"Did you or Wally make any threats at that time?"

"Wally wouldn't threaten a fly! I guess I said a few things I shouldn't've, though. I speak my mind, but Wally is a sweet boy. He takes after his dad."

"When did this happen?"

"Two years ago last May."

"If you were going to shoot Mr. VanBrook, Mrs. Toddwhistle, you would have done it before this. Put your mind at ease."

She wanted to talk longer, but Larry Lanspeak arrived, and Qwilleran asked to be excused.

Larry, looking immaculate in his custom-tailored suit and highly polished wingtips, said, "Don't let me stay more than twenty minutes. I'm ushering today." The Lanspeaks attended the Old Stone Church across the park from the Klingenschoen Theatre—the largest, oldest, wealthiest congregation in town. He dropped into a chair in an attitude of dejection, saying, "I worry about this situation."

"Did Hilary attend your church?" Qwilleran asked as he poured coffee.

"I don't think he had church affiliations anywhere, but he seemed to be knowledgeable about Eastern religions."

"From what I observed, he seemed to be knowledgeable about everything."

"You can say that again! I remember seeing his résumé when we hired him. He'd spent quite some time in Asia and claimed to read and write Chinese—as well as Japanese, which he claimed to speak fluently. His housekeeper told our housekeeper that he had a lot of Oriental stuff around the house . . . But that's not all! According to the résumé, he had studied architecture and horticulture; he had been an Equity actor in New York; and he had assorted degrees in education. I suppose you can do all that if you're not tied down with a family and don't spend any time socializing. He never attended athletic events or any other school function, which is a faux pas in a small community. In fact, he was conspicuously invisible on Saturdays and Sundays, although a couple of persons reported seeing him driving south on Friday nights—toward Lockmaster, you know."

"Where he spent the weekend smoking opium and reading Chinese poetry, no doubt," Qwilleran quipped.

"He was shot in the head, according to the radio," Larry said. "Doesn't that sound like a Chinese execution?"

"Or someone was hiding in the backseat, waiting for him to get behind the wheel. That's how they do it in the movies."

"Don't take this too lightly, Qwill. It certainly looks as if the shooter was one of us."

"Or someone who wanted to make it look like one of us."

"I'll tell you one thing—straight. I've never seen a rehearsal period with so much antagonism . . . On the other hand, could it be some kind of drug connection?"

"I thought Moose County was free of influences from Down Below," Qwilleran said. "There are no fast-food chains. Not even garage sales!"

"But they're going to creep in," Larry predicted, "now that we've started promoting tourism."

Qwilleran refilled the coffee cups. "Were you able to reach the superintendent?"

"Yes, I woke Lyle around four o'clock this morning and broke the news."

"What was his reaction?"

"Well, you know Lyle Compton! He never minces words! He said he'd often felt like braining Hilary himself. That'll be the general reaction around town, believe me! We'll have enough collective guilt in Pickax to sink a battleship."

Qwilleran said, "I just heard that VanBrook expelled Wally Toddwhistle a few weeks short of graduation because of some schoolboy escapade."

"True. And it was a crime on Hilary's part. Wally is a nice quiet kid, and he was a pretty good student. As for the nature of the prank, most people around town got a kick out of it."

"What was the offense?"

"Well, it was like this. Wally's father was a taxidermist, you know, and Wally brought a stuffed skunk to school. Somehow it turned up on the principal's chair. Wally looked like the obvious culprit, although he swore he didn't do it. The whole school board went to bat for him, but VanBrook threw him out. He told the board he'd run the school his way or tear up his contract. Lyle was afraid to cross him."

"It seems like draconian punishment."

"Wally didn't really suffer, though. He'd been working with his father ever since he was a kid, so he just took over the taxidermy shop, and he's doing okay without a diploma. He's simply talented. Hunters all over the Midwest send him their skins."

"More coffee, Larry?"

"No, thanks. This is potent stuff. I'll be waltzing up the center aisle and spilling the offering plate." He looked at his watch. "I hear church bells. I'll talk to you later." On the way out he stopped to say, "Wait till Lockmaster hears about this! The people down there think we're barbarians, and this will confirm their opinion."

As Larry drove away, answering the summons from the tower of the Old Stone Church, another kind of summons could be heard from the third balcony, where the Siamese had been sleeping off the excitement of the night before. Qwilleran released them from their apartment and was feeding them when Polly Duncan telephoned. He assumed she had heard the shocking news on the air, but her greeting was unexpectedly blithe.

"Dearest," she said, "I'm still in Lockmaster. It was a lovely wedding, and we celebrated into the wee hours. Did you give Bootsie his breakfast this morning?"

"Uh—yes," he said, knowing when it was advisable to bend the truth a little. Under the circumstances he had forgotten Bootsie completely.

"How is my little darling? Did he eat well? Did you talk to him?"

"Yes, indeed. We had a stimulating discussion about American foreign policy and the value of the dollar. When will you be home? Don't forget we have a reservation for dinner at Tipsy's."

"That's why I'm calling, dear. I've been invited to brunch at the Palomino Paddock, and I think I should accept. It's a four-star restaurant, and I've never been there. Do you mind? We can dine at Tipsy's next Sunday." She sounded unusually elated.

"I don't mind at all," Qwilleran said stiffly.

"I'll be home in time to give Bootsie his dinner, and I'll call you then."

"By the way," he said, "obviously you haven't listened to the radio. We've had an unfortunate incident up here."

"No, I haven't heard. What happened?"

"Hilary VanBrook has been murdered."

"Murdered! Incredible! Who did it? Where did it happen?"

"I'll tell you when you return," Qwilleran said. "Enjoy your brunch."

As a point of honor he never broke a social engagement, and Polly's defection irked him considerably. She had been partying all night with that Lockmaster crowd; why did she need to stay down there for a mere brunch? If she wanted to eat at a four-star restaurant, *he* could take her there.

"What do you think of that development?" he asked Koko.

The cat murmured an ambiguous reply, his attention fixed on the berry bushes outside the window, where the cardinal usually made his morning call.

"I'd better hike over to the boulevard and feed the monster," Qwilleran said.

He walked briskly to Goodwinter Boulevard, where Polly's apartment occupied the second floor of a carriage house behind an austere stone mansion. All the houses on the street were built of stone—the coldly impressive castles of nineteenth-century mining tycoons and lumber barons. One such house had been leased by VanBrook, and

Qwilleran wondered why the man had needed such grandiose living quarters with fifteen or twenty rooms. As he passed it he noticed that the draperies were drawn on all the windows.

Arriving at Polly's carriage house he unlocked the downstairs door and climbed the stairs to her apartment, where a yearling Siamese was complaining about his tardy breakfast.

"*Mea culpa! Mea culpa!*" said Qwilleran. "I've been involved in extraordinary circumstances. Here's an extra spoonful." He gave Bootsie fresh water and a quick brushing and then hurried back to the barn in time to catch the phone ringing.

The exuberant voice of Hixie Rice said, "Isn't this exciting, Qwill? We'll all be interrogated! I'm going to invent some lurid details—nothing incriminating—just something to add zest and color to the investigation and attract the media Down Below."

Hixie—a transplant from Down Below, where she worked in advertising and publicity—took pleasure in manipulating the media, both print and electronic.

Qwilleran said sternly, "I suggest you curb your creative impulse in this case, Hixie. We're all faced with a serious situation. Stick to the facts, and don't spread any false rumors to confuse the constabulary or entertain the local residents."

"I love it when you're playing uncle," she laughed.

Relenting he said, "Would you like to discuss the matter over dinner? I have a table reserved at Tipsy's."

She made the obvious reply. "Where's Polly?"

"Out of town."

"Good! I'll have you all to myself. Shall I meet you at the restaurant?"

The place called Tipsy's Tavern was located in the town

of Kennebeck northeast of Pickax. Driving there to meet his guest, Qwilleran passed through countryside that had seemed wild and mysterious four years before, when he was a transplanted city dweller. Now he felt comfortable with the Moose County scene: stony pastures, potato farms and sheep ranches . . . dark patches of woods providing habitat for thousands of white-tailed deer . . . dry autumn cornfields from which clouds of blackbirds rose and swirled in close-order formation as he passed . . . the rotting shafthouses of abandoned mines, now fenced and posted as dangerous.

The first sign of Kennebeck was a towering grain elevator in the distance, the skyscraper of the north country. Then the watertower came into view, freshly painted with the town symbol. Some enterprising artist, not afraid of heights, had canvassed the county, decorating watertowers. Every community flaunted its symbol: a pickax, a fish, a sailboat, an antlered buck, a happy face, a pine tree. Kennebeck's tower, like the welcome sign at the town limits, bore the silhouette of a cat. It was a prosperous community with a wide main street and curbstones, plus senior housing, condominiums, and other signs of the times. Yet, in the 1930s Kennebeck had been in danger of becoming a ghost town.

Then, providentially, a blind pig operator from Down Below, hurt by the repeal of Prohibition, returned to his hometown of Kennebeck to open a legitimate bar and steakhouse. He brought with him a white cat with a deformed foot (it made her stagger) and a comical black patch on her head, like a hat slipping down over one eye. Appropriately her name was Tipsy. Her boozy antics and agreeable disposition made customers smile and attracted diners from far and wide. Tipsy's personality, along with the good steaks, put Kennebeck back on the map.

The original restaurant in a log cabin had been enlarged many times during the intervening years, but it still offered casual dining in a rustic setting, and Qwilleran's favorite table was in the main dining room within sight of a larger-than-life oil painting of the founding cat.

He arrived before Hixie and sat at the bar, sipping Squunk water with a twist of lemon. He was on his third drink when his guest arrived, looking harried and tossing her pageboy nervously.

"Quick! I need a martini!" she said. "Make it a double. Then I'll apologize for being late."

The bartender looked questioningly at Qwilleran, then at Hixie, then at Qwilleran again, as if to say, "Where's Mrs. Duncan?"

"You'll never believe this, Qwill," she said in her usual tragicomic style, "but I was driving out Ittibittiwassee Road with not a car in sight—anywhere! And I got in a two-car accident!"

"That's not easy to do."

"Let me tell you how it happened. When I reached Mayfus Road, a car came out of *nowhere* and ran the stop sign! There were only two of us within ten square miles—and we collided! Why do these crazy things happen to me?"

"You're disaster-prone, Hixie," Qwilleran said sympathetically. She had a long history of getting locked in restrooms, setting her hair on fire, picking the wrong men, and more. "It's fortunate you weren't hurt."

"I had my seat belt fastened, but the passenger side was wrecked, and I waited for Gippel's towtruck to come from Pickax."

"How did you get here?"

"The sheriff dropped me off. He was a real sweetheart, and I adore those brimmed hats they wear! After dinner you'll have to drive me to Gippel's, and they'll give me a loaner."

They sat at Qwilleran's table under the friendly eye of Tipsy and ordered from the no-nonsense menu chalked on a blackboard: steak or fish, take it or leave it. The soup of the day was the soup of the year: bean. The vegetable was always boiled carrots, but they were homegrown, small and sweet. The tiny Moose County potatoes, boiled in their skins, had an Irish flavor, and the steak always tasted like honest meat.

"Have the police knocked on your door?" Qwilleran asked.

"Not yet. Have you talked to anyone?"

"Larry. He worries that someone in the club is guilty, but I think he's wrong." Qwilleran patted his moustache.

"Do you know something that the rest of us don't know?"

"I have a hunch, that's all."

Qwilleran's hunches were always accompanied by a tingling in the roots of his moustache, something he could not explain and refused to discuss. His years on the police beat Down Below, coupled with a natural curiosity, had given him an interest in criminal investigation, and when he was on the right scent there was always that reassuring sensation on his upper lip.

At Tipsy's the food was served by plump, bustling, jolly, gray-haired women who admonished diners to eat everything on their plates.

Qwilleran said to Hixie, "Where do they get all these clones to wait on table? I suppose they advertise: WANTED: Plump, jolly, gray-haired waitpersons with bustling experience. Grandmothers preferred."

They ordered steak—and whatever happened to come

with it. Over the bean soup Hixie said, "I have something exciting to discuss."

"Okay. Let's have it." Hixie's ideas were always novel and usually successful, except when they involved Koko; he declined to do TV commercials or endorse a line of frozen gourmet catfoods. It was she, however, who delighted local readers by naming the new newspaper the *Moose County Something,* and it was Hixie who convinced Dennis Hough to advertise his new construction firm as "Huff & Puff Construction Associates."

"First, have you seen the announcement of my new contest?" she asked.

"Yes. What gave you the idea?"

"Well, you see, Qwill, I drive around the county selling ads, and I see black-and-white cats by the thousand! People seem to think they're all descended from Tipsy. So I thought, Why not a Tipsy Look-Alike Contest? The Kennebeck Chamber of Commerce jumped at the opportunity! They're printing posters and T-shirts."

"And the *Something* is selling some extra advertising space," Qwilleran added.

"Of course! We have a good slogan. The original Tipsy, you know, was a very sweet cat as well as comic-looking, so our slogan is 'Sweeter and Funnier.' How do you like it?"

"It may be just what this county needs. Are you getting any entries?"

"Hundreds!"

The steaks arrived, and the conversation switched to food—also office gossip at the *Something* and the open house at Qwilleran's barn.

When the waitress served the bread pudding, he said, "One thing puzzles me. How will you judge the Tipsy contest?"

"Glad you asked, Qwill. People are sending in snapshots of their cats, and we'll narrow them down to the fifty best look-alikes. They'll come to Kennebeck for the final judging, and I'm hoping you'll be one of the judges."

"Hold on, Hixie!" he said. "You know I like to cooperate, but I would rather not have to judge fifty live cats."

"Your name on the panel will add a lot of prestige to the contest," she said, "and Lyle Compton has agreed to judge."

"Our school superintendent will do anything for public exposure. He might want to run for governor some day. Who else is on the panel?"

"Mildred Hanstable."

Qwilleran smoothed his moustache. Roger MacGillivray's newly widowed mother-in-law was one of his favorite women—and an excellent cook. He said, "All right. It's a foul prospect, but I'll do it."

Over the coffee, Hixie broached the subject of the murder again. "Hilary was infuriatingly uncooperative when I was trying to get publicity for *Henry VIII*. And everyone I talk to harbors some grudge against the guy."

"He's hurt someone more deeply than we know," Qwilleran said. "There are dark corners of his life that he's kept secret."

"Do you think it could be drug-related?"

"Not likely, although I'm sure the idea of a high school principal as drug dealer appeals to your imagination. Moose County has always been pretty clean; that's one advantage to living in the boondocks. We have an alcohol problem, but that's all—as yet."

"The sheriff's helicopter is always hovering over those desolate stretches between Chipmunk and Purple Point."

"They're looking for poachers, not marijuana plantings.

What does Gary Pratt think about it? Do you still see a lot of Gary?"

"Not lately," Hixie said. "He's such a hairy ape, and since meeting Dennis I realize I go for clean-cut."

Qwilleran assumed his uncle role again. "I hope you know Dennis is happily married, Hixie. Don't walk into any more disappointments. He has a bright two-year-old who looks just like him, and his wife's trying to sell the house in St. Louis so the family can be together up here."

"She's not trying very hard," was Hixie's flippant retort. "Dennis says she doesn't want to live four hundred miles north of everywhere." She turned serious. "I don't know whether this means anything, Qwill, but . . . I tried to call Dennis this morning after I heard the news on the radio, and he wasn't there. I got a recorded message."

"He was probably sleeping and didn't want to be disturbed," Qwilleran suggested. "None of us got much sleep last night."

"But I looked out the window at the carport, and his assigned parking space was empty."

"He might have gone home with someone. Did that occur to you?"

"I don't think he did. This afternoon, when his van was still missing, I mentioned it to the manager, and this is what she told me: According to the nightman at the gate, Dennis left before daybreak, right after he came in. He didn't say anything, but he looked worried, and he drove away from the gate very fast and turned onto the highway with tires squealing."

Three

Returning home from Tipsy's restaurant Sunday night, Qwilleran stepped on a small object in the foyer and kicked another one in front of the *schrank*. A third turned up under a rug. They were metal engravings mounted on wooden blocks—printing memorabilia that he had started to collect. In embarking on a new hobby, he had also provided a pastime for the Siamese: stealing typeblocks from the typecase where they were displayed. This time they had filched small cuts of a fish, a rabbit, and a rooster. Either the subject matter was appealing, or the blocks were the right size for a playful paw.

As Qwilleran entered the barn, the light on his answering machine was flashing, and he pressed the button to hear a brief recorded message from Polly: "Qwill, I arrived home from Lockmaster later than I planned. Don't call me back tonight. I'm very tired, and I'm going to bed early."

There were no intimate expressions of affection included in the message; Polly, he concluded, must be very tired, indeed. After brunch at the Palomino Paddock what else had she been doing?

He himself felt in high gear despite his fifteen minutes

of sleep the night before. He was stimulated by the puzzle confronting Chief Brodie, although he had no intention of meddling in the case. His friend would not appreciate suggestions from an amateur investigator. While working the police beat Down Below Qwilleran had written a book on urban crime, now out of print, but it hardly entitled him to advise a pro like Brodie.

He prepared a cup of coffee and carried it to a comfortable chair, propping his feet on an ottoman. Yum Yum promptly took possession of his lap, and Koko assumed an attentive position at his feet. They were ready for some quality time.

"Well," he began, "what we have here is the kind of criminal case that is solved immediately—or never. What's your guess?"

Koko blinked his eyes, a signal that Qwilleran interpreted as "no opinion." Cats, he recalled, were never interested in generalities.

"I don't buy the theory that it was an inside job," he went on, grooming his moustache, "although I don't know why I feel that way. If Brodie expends too much time and effort in hounding the members of the club, he's wasting his time."

"Yow," said Koko.

"I'm glad you agree. The one individual he should be investigating is the victim himself. Who was he—really? Where did he get a name like Hilary VanBrook? We know he came here from Lockmaster, but where did he operate before that? He was obviously not a native of the north country, so why did this brilliant man with a cosmopolitan background and impressive credentials choose to live in the outback? Where did he disappear on weekends? Why did he need that large house on Goodwinter Boulevard?"

Qwilleran had forgotten that he himself was indirectly responsible for bringing the principal to Pickax. Four years before—four long and eventful years—Qwilleran had arrived in Moose County as the reluctant heir to the Klingenschoen fortune, reluctant because he had no desire for wealth. He was a dedicated journalist who enjoyed hacking a living on the crime beat. He was content with a one-room apartment, no car, and a meagre wardrobe that packed in a jiffy when his newspaper sent him off on assignment. Finding himself suddenly encumbered with millions—yet with no interest in financial matters—he solved the problem very simply: He established the Klingenschoen Memorial Fund to give the money away. Immediately a board of trustees started awarding grants, scholarships, and loans to benefit the community.

In direst need, it so happened, was the local school system, known to operate on the lowest per-pupil expenditure in the state. As the Klingenschoen Fund poured money into school facilities and teacher salaries, this cornucopia of largesse gave superintendent Lyle Compton an idea: Money might lure the celebrated Hilary VanBrook away from Lockmaster High School where he had accomplished wonders in a few years. Although Lockmaster considered Moose County a primitive wilderness populated by savages who could not even win a football game, VanBrook accepted the Pickax challenge—and the lucrative contract. Under his leadership the Pickax high school earned accreditation, the curriculum was expanded, and more graduates went on to college. Although the athletic teams did no better, faculty and parents considered the new principal a miracle-worker—while loathing his overweening personality and heartless policies.

A few months before his murder VanBrook wrote a typically curt and scornful letter to the Theatre Club, proposing a Shakespeare production as a change from the light comedies, musicals, and mysteries favored by local audiences. He volunteered to direct it himself. The play he proposed was *The Famous History of the Life of King Henry the Eighth,* and the officers of the Theatre Club uttered a unanimous groan.

Carol Lanspeak called Qwilleran for his opinion. "I'm consulting you," she said, "because the K Fund may have to bail us out if it's a flop. No one likes the idea, and yet Horseface has a reputation as a no-fail genius. We're asking him to meet with our board of directors for further discussion, and we're inviting you to audit the meeting. You can bring your tape recorder if you wish; it might make a subject for the 'Qwill Pen' column—that is, if we decide to cut our throats."

It was a dinner meeting held in a private room at the New Pickax Hotel, built in 1935, the year its predecessor burned down. After a dinner of meatloaf and scalloped potatoes (the hotel was not noted for its imaginative cuisine), the board waited for the guest of honor to arrive. VanBrook had declined to join them for dinner, a pointedly unfriendly gesture. When he finally arrived—late, without apology—Carol called the meeting to order and invited the principal to elucidate on his proposal. As if the board were composed of illiterates, he responded by reading a copy of the same letter he had mailed to them, spitting out the phrases with obvious disdain.

Qwilleran heard someone whisper, "Isn't he a pill?" Yet, the man had a rich, well-modulated voice; it was easy to believe he had been a professional actor. The principal finished reading and rolled his eyes at the walls and ceiling.

Officers and board members exchanged looks of dismay. The first to find nerve enough to speak was Scott

Gippel, car dealer and treasurer of the club, whose girth was so enormous that he required two chairs. "The public won't go for that heavy stuff," he said.

Carol Lanspeak spoke up. "Since receiving Mr. Van-Brook's letter I've read the play twice, and I regret to say that I can't find a single memorable or quotable line except the first one: *I come no more to make you laugh.*"

"That's when half the audience gets up and walks out," said Gippel good-naturedly, his not-too-solid flesh quivering with mirth over his own quip.

The chairman of the play-reading committee, a retired teacher of English, commented, "Mr. VanBrook has a point; it's time we attempted Shakespeare, but is this the right play for us? There is even some doubt that Shakespeare wrote *Henry VIII.* It reads—if you will pardon my candor—as if it were written by a committee."

Qwilleran stole a look at VanBrook, who was listening in supercilious silence, gazing at the ceiling and rolling his eyes as if searching for cracks in the plaster.

Fran Brodie said, "I'd like to make another objection. *Henry VIII* calls for a large cast, and we have limited space backstage and very few dressing rooms. The theatre was not designed for large productions."

"The cost of all those costumes will be prohibitive," Gippel added.

"And there are so few roles for women," Carol objected.

"If you ask me, it's too dull and too long," said Junior Goodwinter, the young managing editor of the *Moose County Something*. "And the last scene is a let-down, like the last half of the ninth in a 14–0 ballgame."

VanBrook rose to his feet. "May I speak?"

"Of course. Please do," said Carol with an artificial smile. She frowned at her husband, who had not opened his mouth during the objections. As president of the board of education he had helped convince VanBrook to leave Lockmaster, and he joined Lyle Compton in humoring the principal—who was doing so much good, and who was known to be temperamental, and whose contract was coming up for renewal. If VanBrook failed to sign again, he would undoubtedly return to the Lockmaster school system, and the good folk of Pickax would be left drowning in chagrin.

In a condescending manner VanBrook began. "*Henry VIII* is no longer than *Romeo and Juliet,* and it is shorter by far than *Hamlet* and *Richard III.* So much for *too long.*" He darted a contemptuous glance at the editor. "As for *too dull,* the play has been captivating audiences for three centuries with its color and pageantry. Furthermore, it addresses such contemporary concerns as corruption, greed, power politics, and the abuse of women. As a morality play it deplores *the vain pomp and glory of this world* . . . Is everyone still with me?" His listeners wriggled uncomfortably, and he went on. "You say there are too few roles for women, and yet one of the strongest roles Shakespeare ever wrote for a woman is Katharine of Aragon, Queen of England. Anne Boleyn is another coveted role, and even the Old Lady is a small gem of a part. For those who fancy themselves in period costumes there are plenty of ladies-in-waiting sweeping on and off the stage. And if you think *Henry VIII* lacks great scenes, let me draw your attention to Buckingham's arrest, his unjust condemnation as a traitor, the roisterous party that King Henry crashes in disguise, the queen's court trial, her later confrontation with Cardinal Wolsey, Wolsey's repentant leave-taking, the coronation of Queen Anne, and the heart-rending death of Katharine."

He flashed a triumphant glance around the conference

room and continued. "It so happens that I have staged this play before, and there are certain techniques that can be employed—notably the use of students as supernumeraries, to be costumed at the school and transported to the theatre in school buses. The Klingenschoen garage at the rear of the theatre can provide dressing rooms for actors playing small roles and making infrequent entrances."

Qwilleran thought, Wait a minute, bub! I'm still living in the garage!

"As for the final scene," VanBrook said, "this purely political indulgence was tacked on to flatter the monarchy, and let me assure you that it will be omitted. *Henry VIII* will end with Katharine's death scene, which has been called the glory of the play."

Everyone was silent until Carol said, "Thank you, Mr. VanBrook, for your enlightening explanation . . . Shall we make a decision now?" she asked the board. "Or do we need time to mull it over?"

Larry spoke up for the first time. "I move that we mount *Henry VIII* as our first fall show."

Fran Brodie seconded the motion. "Let's take a gamble on it," she said, and Qwilleran could imagine visions of Queen Katharine dancing in her steely gray eyes.

"Okay, I'll go along," said Gippel, "and hope to God we sell some tickets. There'll be more flesh on the stage than in the audience—that's my guess."

Hixie Rice said, "It has great publicity possibilities, with all those high school kids carrying spears."

Junior Goodwinter capitulated. "Count me in, so long as you lop off the last scene."

And so *The Famous History of the Life of King Henry the Eighth* went into production. Qwilleran was not further involved, although he knew that Carol and Fran were auditioning for Queen Katharine, and Larry and Dennis wanted to read for Cardinal Wolsey. Everyone assumed that Larry would get the choice role.

On the evening following the last audition, Qwilleran was going to a late dinner at the Old Stone Mill as the Lanspeaks were leaving. He intercepted them in the restaurant parking lot, saying to Larry, "I suppose I'm expected to kiss your ring."

"Oh, hell! I missed out on Wolsey," the actor said with a disappointed smirk. "Hilary wants me to play King Henry. Isn't that a bummer? I'll have to grow a beard if I don't want to use spirit gum. Scott should be doing Henry; he wouldn't need any padding."

Carol said, "Scott could never learn the lines. The only line he ever remembers is at the bottom of the page."

"So I suppose Dennis is doing Wolsey?" Qwilleran asked.

"NO!" Larry thundered in disgust. "Hilary's doing it himself! Of course, it's expedient, because he's done it before. He's also bringing a woman from Lockmaster to play Katharine. He directed her in the production down there a few years ago."

"When do rehearsals start? I might drop in some evening."

"Next Monday," Carol said. "Five nights a week, starting at six-thirty. We've always started at seven to give working people time to eat a decent meal, but Horseface has decreed six-thirty. He wants me as assistant director and understudy for Katharine. Since she lives sixty miles away, she'll come up only two nights a week, so I'll have to read her lines the rest of the time." She raised her eyebrows in a gesture of resignation. "I don't expect to enjoy it, but if I learn something, it won't be a total loss."

Qwilleran said, "I wanted to do a profile on VanBrook for my column, but he refused flatly. Wouldn't give a reason."

"Typical," said Larry with a shrug. "Where's Polly tonight?"

"Hosting a dinner meeting of the library board. What did you have to eat?"

"Red snapper—very good! And try the blue plum buckle—if they have any left. It's going fast."

The Lanspeaks went to their car, and Qwilleran entered the restaurant that had been converted from an old stone grist mill. The hostess seated him at his favorite table, and Derek Cuttlebrink filled his water glass and delivered the bread basket with a flourish. Although Derek was the busboy, his six-foot-seven stature and sociable manner caused new customers to mistake him for the owner.

"I'm playing five parts," he announced. "I get my name in the program five times—for Wolsey's servant, the court crier, the executioner, the mayor of London, and a messenger. I like the executioner best; I get to carry the axe and wear a hood."

"You're going to be a busy boy with all those costume changes," Qwilleran said.

"I figure I can wear the same pants and just change the coat and hat."

"In Shakespeare they're called breeches, Derek."

"I've been thinking it over," said the busboy. "I've decided I'd like to be an actor instead of a cop. It would be more fun. You stay up all night and sleep late."

The waitress appeared, and Derek drifted away to clear some tables. Qwilleran ordered the red snapper. "And save me a piece of plum buckle if you have any left."

During the following week the number of cars in the theatre parking lot every evening indicated that rehearsals were in full swing, and one evening Qwilleran slipped into the auditorium to observe, thinking he might pick up some material for a "Qwill Pen" column. It was six-thirty when he took an aisle seat at the rear. The entire cast was on hand, except for the woman from Lockmaster; it was her off-night. The director had not yet made an appearance.

At six forty-five Carol said, "No point in wasting valuable time. Let's go over the scenes that Hilary blocked last night. We'll skip the prologue and start with the first scene as far as the dirty-look episode. Let's have the Duke of Buckingham, the Duke of Norfolk, and Lord Abergavenny on stage. Norfolk enters first, stage left. The others, stage right."

Three actors, carrying scripts and looking far from aristocratic in their rehearsal clothes, made their entrance.

Carol called out from the third row, "Norfolk, take a longer, more deliberate stride. You're a duke! . . . That's better! And Abergav'ny, show respect for your father-in-law but don't hide behind him. Let's do that entrance again and take it from *Good morrow and well met.*" As the scene progressed, Carol made notes and occasionally interrupted. "Norfolk, don't just look at the speaker, listen to what he's saying. It'll show in your face . . . And Abergavenny, keep your chin up . . . Buckingham, take a couple of steps downstage when you say *O you go far.*"

When Dennis reached Buckingham's clever line—*No man's pie is freed from his ambitious finger*—he stopped and laughed. "That's my favorite line."

There was a ripple of amusement as the actors in the front rows looked at each other with understanding.

Carol said, "Okay, take it again. And Norfolk, use your upstage hand so you don't hide your face."

When they reached the dirty-look episode and Van-Brook had not yet arrived, Carol read Cardinal Wolsey's lines and walked through the scene with the others. Suddenly the doors at the rear of the auditorium burst open.

"What's going on here?" came the director's stentorian demand. Starting down the aisle in his green turtleneck jersey, he caught sight of Qwilleran. "What are you doing here?"

"Waiting for the six-thirty rehearsal to begin," said Qwilleran with a pointed look at his wristwatch.

"Out! Out!" VanBrook pointed to the door.

Dennis Hough walked to the stage apron and boomed, "He can stay, for God's sake! He owns the damned theatre!"

"Out! Out!"

Qwilleran obligingly left the auditorium, walked upstairs, and slipped into the dark balcony, while VanBrook proceeded without apology or explanation. Whatever had delayed him had also annoyed him, and he was impatient with everyone.

Brusquely he said, "Archbishop, stop looking at your wristwatch! This is the sixteenth century . . . You—the Old Lady—we're doing *Henry VIII*, not Uncle Wiggley! You're carrying your hands like a rabbit . . . Who's giggling backstage? Keep quiet or go home! . . . Suffolk, there are four syllables in 'coronation.' It's the crowning of a monarch, not something from the florist." None of this was said in good-natured jest; it was pure acrimony. "Campeius, can you act more like a Roman cardinal and less like a mouse?"

The actors waiting for their scenes glanced at each other uneasily. Eddington Smith, playing Cardinal Campeius, was a shy little old fellow who was always treated gently by members of the club, no matter how inadequate his performance.

When VanBrook told Anne Boleyn to stop simpering like an idiot, the flashing of Fran's steely gray eyes could be seen even from the balcony. As for Dennis, his square jaw was clenched most of the time. At one point Dave Landrum, who was playing Suffolk, threw his script at the director and walked out. Qwilleran doubted that any-one would return for rehearsal the following night. He doubted, moreover, that *Henry VIII* would ever open.

Nevertheless, the rehearsals stumbled along with a new Suffolk, and Qwilleran received reports on the play's progress from Larry, with whom he had coffee at the Dimsdale Diner twice a week.

Larry, whose royal beard was growing nicely, said, "Hilary's always picking on poor Edd Smith, who wouldn't be in the club at all if Dr. Halifax hadn't ordered it as therapy. Edd still doesn't project, even though Carol coaches him. He shouts the first two words, then trails off into a whisper. Dennis has come to his defense a couple of times. There's a real personality clash flaring up be-tween Dennis and Hilary."

"How is Carol taking it?"

"She's being a saint! She puts up with Hilary because she hopes to learn something. If you ask me, she's learning what *not* to do while directing a group of amateurs. He works hard with some and ignores others. He butters up the woman from Lockmaster and insults everyone else."

"Is she good?"

"Sure, she's good, but Carol or Fran could have done as well."

"Who is she, anyway?" Qwilleran asked.

"Her name is Fiona Stucker. I don't know anything about her except that she played Katharine in the Lock-master production of *Henry* five years ago."

"How are the student extras coming along?"

"Carol is working hard with the kids, getting them to walk like sixteenth-century nobles instead of couch pota-toes. I think Derek, with his five roles and great height, is going to provide the comic relief in this play. He's so con-spicuous that the audience will recognize him as the executioner even with a black hood over his head. And I'm afraid he's going to get a laugh during Katharine's death scene. When he enters as a messenger toward the end of the play—his fifth role, bear in mind—Katharine's line is *This fellow, let me ne'er see again.* We all have to struggle to keep a straight face, and the audience is going to crack up!"

"The play can use some comic relief," Qwilleran said.

"Yes, but not during Katharine's death scene."

On opening night the audience made all the right responses. They wept over Buckingham's noble farewell, gasped at the magnificence of the coronation, and suppressed their tittering over Derek's frequent entrances. There was a rumble of excitement during the crowd scenes, when their teenage sons and daughters paraded down the center aisle as guards with halberds, standard bearers with banners, officers with tipstaffs, noblemen with swords, countesses with coronets, and vergers with silver wands.

Onstage there were only two miscues and one fluff—not bad for opening night. Qwilleran, fifth row on the aisle with Polly Duncan as his guest, cheered inwardly when Dennis delivered his poignant speech, cringed when Eddington mouthed words that could not be heard, felt his blood pressure rising when Fran appeared as the beauteous Anne, and waited fearfully for Derek to ruin Katharine's death scene. Fortunately the director had deleted the lines that would get an inappropriate guffaw.

The next time Qwilleran met Larry for coffee, the actor said, "I have to admit that Hilary's good as the cardinal. Despite his built-in arrogance he manages to make Wolsey's repentance convincing. But I have a feeling that he resents the public's adoration of Buckingham. When they flock backstage after the show, it's Dennis they want to see. And when Dennis makes his first entrance and says *Good morning and well met*, you can hear the hearts palpitating in the auditorium."

Qwilleran said, "Your Henry is perfect, Larry—straight out of the Holbein portrait."

"That's what Hilary wanted." He rubbed his chin. "I'll tell you one thing: I'll be glad when I can shave off this beard."

Three weeks later he had shaved off the beard, Van-Brook was dead, and Dennis had disappeared without explanation.

Four

The Monday following the Orchard Incident, as it came to be labeled by the *Moose County Something*, was a gloomy day suitable for the grim police business taking place in the barnyard. The comings and goings of officialdom ruined Koko's morning bird watch. He liked to take his post at the window-wall overlooking the orchard, from which he could see red, yellow, gray, blue, and brown birds flitting in the branches of the old trees and scrubby berry bushes, once cultivated but now growing wild.

Koko's particular favorite was the male cardinal who called every morning and evening in company with his soberly dressed mate. With his red plumage, kingly crown, and black face patch emphasizing his patrician beak, he conducted himself like a monarch of birds. There appeared to be mutual appreciation between the cardinal and the aristocratic cat. Koko sat almost motionless, with the last three inches of his tail fluttering to match the fluttering of the bird's tail feathers.

At one point during the overcast morning a van pulled into the yard, and a photographer unloading camera cases, lights, and tripods was challenged by the police. Qwilleran assured them that this was John Bushland, commercial photographer from Lockmaster, who had an appointment to shoot the interior of the barn.

Bushy, as he was called, was an agile, enthusiastic, outgoing young man who joked about losing his hair early. *"Hair Today; Gone Tomorrow"* was the slogan on his sweatshirt. Seriously he said to Qwilleran, "I heard about the trouble. What's the latest?"

"Police are investigating. That's all I know. What's the reaction in Lockmaster?"

"To tell the truth, everyone's relieved. They were afraid he'd get tired of Pickax, and they'd get him back again. Got any idea who shot him?"

"I suspect it was someone from Lockmaster trying to make it look like someone from Pickax. Did you know VanBrook when he was principal down there?"

"Not personally. Not having kids, Vicki and I weren't involved in that scene."

Bushy regarded the octagonal mass of stone and silvery shingles with awe. "I like those triangular windows around the top. We should do some exteriors, but not while the police cars are here."

"Sorry it's not a sunny day," Qwilleran said.

"All the better for interiors. We won't have to contend with the glare."

"Come on in. Ready for a cup of coffee?"

"Not right now. I want to work first." When they carried the gear indoors, Bushy was amazed by the lightness of the interior. "I expected it to be dark. All these white walls, all this light-colored wood—it makes my job a lot easier."

"That's what I wanted—a minimum of dark corners and shadows. It's too easy for cats to make themselves invisible in a dark environment, and I like to know where they are at all times. Otherwise I worry." He handed Bushy the binoculars. "Up there on one of those radiating beams you can see the mark of the original builder: J. Mayfus & Son, 1881. I'd like you to get a close-up of that if possible. Shall I lock the cats up in their loft?"

"It won't be necessary. Who did the furnishings?"

"Fran Brodie. I didn't want anything rustic, and she said that contemporary furniture would accentuate the antiquity of the structure."

In the lounge there were two sofas and an oversized chair upholstered in oatmeal tweed—all boldly designed, square-cut pieces. The tables were off-white lacquered cubes.

"You don't see anything like this in Lockmaster," Bushy said.

Qwilleran pointed out certain items that he wanted included in the pictures: the pine wardrobe, the bat prints, the printer's typecase, and the Mackintosh coat of arms. "My mother was a Mackintosh," he remarked.

"Sure. No problem. Anything you want." Bushy was wandering about, checking camera angles. "Everywhere you look, it's a picture! And there are lots of places to spot a light under a balcony or behind a beam if I want to light a corner."

"What can I do to help?"

"Nothing. You've got plenty of electric outlets, I see. I might have to move some of the furniture slightly."

"So if you don't need me, Bushy, I'll go out and do a few errands. Help yourself to cold drinks in the fridge. For coffee just press the Brew button. See you later! If the phone rings, my answering machine will pick it up. Be sure the cats don't run outdoors."

Leaving the barn, Qwilleran was intercepted by Brodie. "Where's Dennis Hough?" he demanded. He pronounced it *Howe*.

"I don't know," Qwilleran said. "I haven't been in touch

with him since Saturday. Now that the barn's finished he
won't be coming around any more."

"He hasn't been home since the party."

"Probably drove to St. Louis to see his family. Doesn't
Fran know where he went?"

Brodie grunted unintelligibly. "This company called
Huff & Puff doesn't even have an office."

Qwilleran explained patiently, "My barn was his first
job. All he needed was a phone for lining up workmen
and supplies, so he worked out of his apartment."

"Do you know how to reach him in St. Louis?"

"No, but I'm sure directory assistance can tell you. His
name is pronounced *Huff,* but it's spelled H-o-u-g-h. Give
him time to get down there; it's a long drive."

Qwilleran walked downtown. Most of Pickax was
within walking distance, and he was accustomed to using
his legs, being a former pavement pounder from the Con-
crete Belt. The rest of Pickax depended on wheels.

En route to Lois's Luncheonette for breakfast he stopped
at the used bookstore, an establishment he could never
pass without entering. This time he had a mission. Eddington Smith had recently acquired a large library from
an estate, and Qwilleran was hoping to find a copy of his
own best-selling book written eighteen years before. During the ups and downs of his life following those halcyon
days he had not salvaged a single copy, but now that his
fortunes had changed, he was always on the lookout for
City of Brotherly Crime by James M. Qwilleran. He had
used a middle initial in those days. Professional book de-
tectives had been unable to unearth the book; public li-
braries no longer had the title in the stacks or in the
catalogue. Yet, doggedly he continued the hopeless hunt,
like a parent searching for a lost child.

The store called Edd's Editions was a gloomy cave filled

with gray, dusty, musty hardcover books as well as paperbacks with torn covers and yellowed edges. Eddington materialized from the shadows at the rear of the store.

"Find my book?" Qwilleran asked.

"Not so far, but I haven't unpacked everything yet," said the conscientious old bookseller. "Did the police find any evidence?"

"You know as much as I do, Edd."

"I couldn't sleep last night. 'Other sins only speak; murder shrieks out.' " Eddington amazed his customers by having a quotation for every occasion.

"Who said that?"

"Webster, I think."

"Which one?"

"I don't know. How many are there?"

At that moment a smoky Persian, whose voluminous tail dusted the books, walked sedately toward Qwilleran and sat down on a biography of Sir Edmund Backhouse.

"Am I to consider that a recommendation?" Qwilleran asked. "Or is Winston just resting?"

"It looks like an interesting book," said the bookseller. "He was a British orientalist and sort of a mystery man."

"I'll take it," said Qwilleran, who could never walk out of a bookstore without making a purchase.

At Lois's Luncheonette he sat at the counter and ordered eggs over lightly, country fries extra crisp, rye toast dry, and coffee right away; no cream.

"Whatcha think of the murder, Mr. Q?" asked the waitress, whose nametag read Alvola.

" 'Other sins only speak; murder shrieks out,' " he recited with declamatory effect.

"Is that Shakespeare?" she asked. Thanks to *Henry VIII*, the Bard was the fad of the month among young people in Pickax. In October it would be a rock star or comic strip hero. "It sounds like Shakespeare," said Alvola knowledgeably.

"No, it was some other dude," Qwilleran said as he buried his nose in his book. Actually he was listening to the conversation at nearby tables. No one was mourning the principal; all were fearful that the killer might prove to be a well-known citizen, or a student, or a friend, or a neighbor. It was fear mixed with excitement, expressed with a certain amount of relish. Qwilleran thought, This case will never be solved; no one in Moose County wants it to be solved.

His next stop was Amanda's Design Studio, where he dropped in to see Fran Brodie. On the job she wore three-inch heels, and her skirts rose higher than most Pickax hemlines—facts that were not lost on her client. "Where's your boss?" he asked.

"Amanda's gone to a design center Down Below. Is anything happening at the barn?"

"Various authorities are there, doing their duty. No one is talking, of course. I keep my nose out of it."

"Dad told Mother that they found traces of foam rubber in the car, meaning it had been used as a silencer."

"But the cats heard it. They can hear a leaf fall."

"Want to hear something ironic?" the designer asked. "Hilary ordered custom-made treatments for twenty windows—the whole main floor—and they arrived by motor freight this morning. *This morning!* I called Amanda, and she had a fit."

"What does his house look like?"

"It's one of those stone houses on Goodwinter Boulevard, you know. The main floor is done in Japanese; he did it himself. The window treatments we ordered for him last month are shoji screens. I've never been upstairs, but he told me the bedrooms are filled with books."

Thinking of *City of Brotherly Crime* Qwilleran said, "I wouldn't mind seeing that place."

"I have the key, and Amanda wants the screens to be on the premises when we file our claim on the estate. Would you like to help me deliver them?"

"When?" he asked with unusual eagerness.

"I'll have to let you know, but it'll be soon."

As he was leaving the studio he said, "We've got to do something about the fish-bowl effect at the barn. The Peeping Toms are having a field day." What had once been the huge barn door was now a huge wall of glass.

"Mini-blinds would solve the problem," the designer said. "I'll drop in and measure the windows. I still have your key."

Qwilleran's planned destination was the public library, a building that looked like a Greek temple except for the bicycle rack and the book-drop receptacle near the front steps. As he walked through the vestibule he automatically turned his head to the left, where a chalkboard displayed the Shakespeare quotation of the day—one of Polly's pet ideas. He expected to see *Murder most foul*. Instead, he read: *Love is a smoke raised with the fume of sighs*. The wedding in Lockmaster had put her in a romantic mood.

In the main hall the clerks gave him the bright greeting due the richest man in the county who was also their supervisor's companion of choice. To delude them he first browsed through the new-book shelves and punched a few keys on the computer catalogue before sauntering up the stairs to the mezzanine. Here the daily papers were scattered on tables in the reading room, and here Polly presided over the library operation in a glass-enclosed office. She was seated behind her desk, wearing her usual gray suit and white blouse, but she was looking radiant, and her graying hair still showed the special attention it had received in preparation for the wedding.

"You are looking . . . especially well!" he greeted her. "Evidently you enjoyed your weekend." He took a seat in one of the hard oak armchairs that had come with the building in 1904.

"Thank you, Qwill," she said. "It was an absolutely wonderful weekend, but strenuous. I'm not conditioned to all that partying. That's why I left the message not to call me. The wedding ceremony was absolutely beautiful! The bride wore her grandmother's lace dress with a six-foot train, and everyone was terribly emotional. The reception was held at the Riding and Hunt Club, and I danced with the bridegroom and the bride's father and—simply everyone!"

Qwilleran and Polly never danced. The opportunity seldom arose, and he was unaware that she liked to dance. "How many guests were there?" he asked.

"Three hundred, Shirley said. Her son made a handsome groom. He's just out of law school and has a job with the best law firm in Lockmaster. You've never met Shirley, have you? She's the one who had the litter of kittens and gave me Bootsie. We've been friends for twenty years. Her husband is in real estate. His name is Alan, spelled A-l-a-n."

She's chattering, Qwilleran thought; why is she chattering? Polly's manner of speech was usually reserved and often pedantic; she made a brief, pithy statement and waited for her listener's reaction. Today her speech bubbled with the exuberance of a younger woman—one who has been out on the town for the first time. He combed his moustache with his fingers. "So you had brunch at the Paddock! Do you consider it as good as its reputation?"

"Absolutely!" she said. "It's a marvelous restaurant, and I stayed longer than I anticipated."

He wondered about that "absolutely." It was not Polly's kind of word, and yet she had used it three times. Ordinarily she would say "definitely" or "without doubt," but never "absolutely."

"But tell me about Hilary VanBrook," she was saying. "Everyone is shocked—and worried about what the police will uncover."

"May I shut the door?" he asked. There were a few loiterers in the reading room, and everyone in Pickax had big ears.

"I heard on the radio," Polly said, "that you gave an all-night party!" She regarded him accusingly.

"WPKX has a talent for garbling the news to give the wrong impression," he said. "Actually the entire cast and crew of *Henry VIII* descended on me around midnight and stayed until 3 A.M. After they had left, Koko started creating a disturbance that aroused my curiosity. I went out and found the body. The shooter had used a silencer, and yet that cat heard the shot. Or perhaps he knew by instinct that something was wrong. During the party he was on top of the *schrank,* staring down at VanBrook's head, and I thought Koko recognized a hairpiece. He can always tell the difference between real and false. But now I believe he knew something was going to happen to the man—and that *he was going to get it in the back of the head!*"

"Oh, Qwill! Isn't that a trifle extreme? I know cats have a sixth sense, but I can't believe they're prescient."

"Koko is not your average cat."

"Weren't you surprised that Mr. VanBrook attended the party? He has a reputation for being asocial."

"He had an ulterior motive, Polly. He expected to line

up a field trip for the entire student body, marching grades nine to twelve through my barn! A lot of nerve, I thought."

"He was a very arrogant man. No one liked him, but people don't kill simply because a person is socially unacceptable."

"Don't be too sure. A man shot his neighbor last month in an argument over dog-doo."

"Yes, but that was Down Below. They don't behave that way up here . . . Excuse me." Her telephone rang, and she answered briskly. "This is Mrs. Duncan . . . Well, good morning!" she added in a softer tone, her face suddenly aglow with pleasure. She glanced at Qwilleran as she said, "I'm just fine, thank you . . . Absolutely! . . . Well, I'm in a conference at the moment . . . Yes, please do." She hung up the phone, smiling to herself.

Who was that? Qwilleran wanted to ask but decided against it. If Polly wanted him to know, she would tell. He said, "I'd better hie myself home. Bushy is taking pictures of the barn this morning."

"That's nice," she said, straightening papers on her desk. "He was the official photographer at the wedding." She seemed preoccupied, and Qwilleran left without making any further remarks.

In walking back to the barn he took the long way around in order to pass the office of the *Moose County Something*. It occurred to him that their police reporter might have information withheld from the public. The press always had an inside story or was privy to the latest rumor.

Junior Goodwinter hailed him from the managing editor's office. "Hey, Qwill! Did they let you out on bail?"

"If I'm charged, Junior, I'm going to implicate you. Maybe we can be cellmates. What's the latest?"

"No one has been charged yet. The police aren't talk-

ing, but we pumped the Dingleberry boys and found out
that the cremated remains are supposed to be sent to
Lockmaster at the request of VanBrook's attorney."

"No funeral here? That's his final insult to the public."
The citizens of Pickax dearly loved a celebrity funeral with
a marching band playing a dirge and a long procession to
the cemetery. It had been a cherished tradition since the
nineteenth century.

"That's right. No funeral," said the editor. "We called
Lyle Compton about the possibility of a memorial service,
and he said no one would attend. He said VanBrook's
assistant will be elevated to the job of principal, at least
protem. The board will have to vote on it, but the guy's
competent, and there's no reason why he shouldn't get the
job. . . . That's all the news to this moment, but Arch
wants to see you."

Arch Riker and Qwilleran had been lifelong friends
Down Below, and they had worked together at the *Daily
Fluxion*. During Riker's twenty-five years as an editor he
had never rated more than a desk, a telephone, and a
computer terminal. Now, as publisher of a backwoods
journal, he sat in a large carpeted office with a desk the
size of a Ping-Pong table. What's more—fellow staffers at
the *Fluxion* would never believe this—he had draperies on
the windows, installed by Amanda's Studio of Interior Design.

"Sit down," he said to Qwilleran. "Help yourself to coffee."

"Thanks, but I've just had three cups at Lois's."

"What's the scuttlebutt over there?"

"Everyone's on edge, fearing that some prominent
member of the community is guilty. They overlook the
fact that a brilliant man, who has done much for the education system, has been struck down in the prime of life.

True, he was an outsider and not well-liked, but a crime is a crime, even if the victim is a pariah or even if the murderer is the publisher of the *Something*."

"While you're on your soapbox, why don't you do a column on the subject, Qwill?"

"No, thanks. It happened in my backyard, and I'm keeping out of it, but I suggest you write an editorial." His hand went involuntarily to his moustache.

Riker recognized the gesture. "Are you getting the investigative itch? Do you think you might do some private sleuthing?"

"Not this time. I have confidence in Brodie. He grew up here, and he's a walking file on everyone in the county. It wouldn't surprise me if he knows who pulled the trigger and is setting a trap for him—or her." He started to leave the office.

"Aren't you getting any vibrations from Koko?" Riker asked mockingly.

"He keeps pulling engravings from my typecase, but so far the message is only FOOD. See you later, Arch."

On the way out of the building Qwilleran stuck his head in an office where Hixie Rice was selling a full-page ad to the owner of a food market, exuding charm and enthusiasm into the instrument.

"Any word about Dennis?" he asked after she had hung up triumphantly.

"His parking space is still empty. Why didn't he tell *someone*—you or me or Susan or Fran? It worries me."

"If you infer that he's a fugitive from justice, get it out of your head, Hixie. We all know he's a decent guy, and I maintain he's on his way home to see his wife and child—possibly because of some sort of family emergency down there, or because his wife found a buyer for their house. She probably called while he was at the theatre and left a message on his answering machine."

"I hope you're right, Qwill."

He declined her invitation to have a microwaved sub in the staff lounge and left to complete his errands. At the post office he picked up his mail and told them to hold future deliveries until the battered mailbox could be repaired.

"Kids out your way must be bashing mailboxes with ballbats again," the clerk guessed.

"Looks like it," Qwilleran said.

Other postal patrons were picking up their mail or buying stamps, and most were standing around in neighborly huddles, discussing the murder. They lowered their voices or changed the subject when they caught sight of Mr. Q.

By the time he arrived home the official cars were thinning out, but the photographer's van was still there. "How's it going?" he asked Bushy.

The photographer was packing up his gear. "Wait'll you hear what happened! Remember how the cats behaved when you brought them to my studio for portraits last year?"

"I remember. They wouldn't leave their carrying coop," Qwilleran recalled. "I drove one hundred twenty miles round trip, and we couldn't get them out of their carrier even with a can opener."

"Well, today it was different. They wanted to be in every picture! Every time I set up a shot, one of them was *right there!* I shot the kitchen, and they were both perched on the circular stairs. Whichever way I aimed the camera, there was a cat sitting on a railing or climbing a ladder."

"I should have locked them up," said Qwilleran. "Cats are perverse. They figure out what you want and then do the opposite."

"What's the difference? These photos are only for insurance purposes, aren't they? It'll look as if you've got twenty cats, that's all."

Qwilleran watched the photographer pack, marveling how much equipment can be fitted into a small case where there is a place for everything.

"Now I'm ready for that coffee," Bushy said.

"Would you like a drink of Scotch and a bowl of chili first?"

"Sure would, but I'd rather have wine if you've got it."

"Name it, and we have it. This is the best bar outside of the Shipwreck Tavern. I have thirsty friends."

"And you never touch a drop," the photographer marveled. "How come?"

"Let's just say that I paid my dues when I was young and reckless, and I dropped out of the club ten years ago."

The two men sank into leather chairs with wide arms, deep seats, and welcoming cushions—near the bookshelves and the printer's typecase.

"You've got a nice setup," Bushy said. "You've really got space. We have, too, but it's all cut up into rooms. I see you collect old printing stuff. I have a friend—the editor of the *Lockmaster Logger*—who collects typefaces and old advertising posters. He has a playbill from Ford's Theatre dated April 14, 1865—the night Lincoln was assassinated."

The Siamese, aware that chili was in the offing, made a sudden appearance and settled on the ottoman.

Bushy said, "I'd still like to photograph those two characters in my studio. There's a market for cat photos right now. Now that they know me, perhaps we could try it again. Would you like to bring them down to Lockmaster once more?"

"I'm willing to give it another shot," Qwilleran said.

"Have you ever been to our famous steeplechase?"

"No. Horse racing never appealed to me. I'm no gambler. If I put out a dollar I expect a dollar's worth in return."

"This is different. It's like a big picnic, with horses jumping over hedges, and hounds baying, and carriages on parade. Here's what I thought: The September steeplechase is next weekend. Bring the cats down and stay at our house. We have lots of room. The cats can prowl around and get used to the studio."

"I'll have to think about that," Qwilleran said, "but I appreciate the invitation."

"There's a party Saturday night after the races, and on Sunday a lot of us go to brunch at the Palomino Paddock."

"I've heard about the brunch. My friend Polly was there yesterday."

"I know. I saw her there, and she was really enjoying herself. She was at the wedding reception, too—living it up. They had a terrific buffet and an open bar. You should have been there, Qwill." Bushy was talkative by nature, and a glass of burgundy enhanced this propensity. His range of topics covered his new boat, fishing conditions at Purple Point, his wife's disappointment at being childless, and the problems of living in a century-old house. Qwilleran was a good listener; he never knew when he might glean a tidbit for his column.

Just as Bushy was telling about his wife's grandmother, who lived with them, a sudden impulse triggered the Siamese and catapulted them off the ottoman, round and round the fireplace cube, up the ramp, spiraling toward the roof, racing across the beams, leaping from catwalk to balcony, pounding down the ramp with thundering paws, then swooping to the main level, landing on the ottoman, where they came to a sudden stop and licked their fur. Time: thirty-five seconds.

"What was that all about?" asked the stunned photographer.

"I think they're telling me to go to the steeplechase. I accept your invitation."

After the bowls of chili (hot) and coffee (strong), Qwilleran helped carry the photographic equipment to the van, and Bushy asked, "What are you going to do with your orchard? It's pretty well shot."

"I'll clear out the dead trees and plant something else," said Qwilleran.

"You could make it a bird sanctuary. Keep those berry bushes and wild cherries and plant some cedars and maples and things like that. Our yard is a conference center for birdlife. Vicki's grandmother is a nut about birds."

Qwilleran returned indoors to ask the Siamese if they were in favor of a bird sanctuary and was greeted by Koko in his impertinent pose: legs splayed, head cocked, tail crooked.

"You scoundrel!" Qwilleran said as he picked up the printing blocks scattered around the floor. This time he found a squirrel, a rabbit, an eagle, and a seahorse, two of them hidden under rugs, a trick he attributed to Yum Yum. They're both bored, he thought. "Would anyone like to go for an outing?" he asked.

When he produced the harnesses and jingled them invitingly, Yum Yum promptly disappeared, but Koko was ready for action. Harnessed and leashed and perched on Qwilleran's shoulder, he was soon riding toward the mailbox on the highway. Qwilleran avoided the rutted trail and waded through the weeds in the orchard. Small birds landed on the tips of tall grasses and bounced them up and down, and he could feel Koko's body trembling.

Toward the end of the property the cat struggled to get down. Was this the spot where the killer parked his truck or van? More likely, Qwilleran concluded, there was an abandoned bird's nest in the grass. Some nest builders, Polly had told him, are groundlings.

Arriving at the highway, he allowed Koko to walk, and the cat investigated tire tracks on the pavement and pebbles on the shoulder. The crime lab had removed the mailbox for analysis, but Koko found a piece of glass they had overlooked. A fragment of a headlight? Or a shard from a whiskey bottle aimed at the mailbox by a Saturday-night carouser?

Whatever it is, Qwilleran said to himself, we're staying out of this case. Yet, Koko was tugging on the leash urgently. He was tugging toward the south—the direction in which the last vehicle had turned after the fateful party.

Five

The day after Qwilleran accepted Bushy's invitation to the steeplechase, the sun was shining; the weather prediction was favorable; the Siamese were well and happy. Yet, he greeted the day with a mild depression. The triangular windows in the upper walls of the apple barn were performing their usual magic, throwing geometric patches of sunlight about the interior. As the earth turned, those distorted triangles of warmth and brightness moved from place to place, confusing the Siamese, who were always attracted to cozy spots. Ordinarily, Qwilleran was fascinated by this slow-motion minuet of sunsplashes, but on this day he was nagged by a vague uneasiness.

The morning started well enough with a phone call from Lockmaster. "Qwill, this is Vicki Bushland. I'm so glad you and the cats will be spending the weekend with us."

"It will be my pleasure," he assured her.

"I hope the weather will be fine. It's beautiful today. Is the sun shining up there?"

"It's working overtime," he said, making note of the bright triangles on the floor and walls and the front of the *schrank*. "Is there anything I may contribute to the weekend?"

"Just bring your binoculars and your camera for the races. The Saturday night party at the Riding and Hunt Club is rather dressy. The women wear long dresses, but black tie is optional for the men. Otherwise, everything's casual. We have a tailgate picnic at the race course on Saturday."

"Sounds good," he said, more politely than truthfully. Meals alfresco had never appealed to him. The prospect entailed limp paper plates, plastic forks, stuffed eggs with fragments of eggshell mashed into the stuffing, tuna sandwiches gritty with sand, and ants in the chocolate cake. Nevertheless, the experience might produce worthwhile material for the "Qwill Pen," and he would have an excuse to absent himself from the apple barn during the public open house. On Saturday half of Moose County, at five dollars a head, would be tramping up and down the ramps, no doubt making disparaging remarks about the fireplace design and the contemporary furniture. But his underlying reason for accepting the Bushlands' invitation may have been his curiosity about the person who had brunched with Polly at the Palomino Paddock, sending her home late, tired, and starry-eyed. No doubt this was the caller with whom she had that brief and guarded conversation while Qwilleran squirmed in a hard oak chair.

"I'm looking forward to the whole weekend," he told Vicki.

"Could you arrive in time for dinner on Friday?" she asked. "We'd have cocktails at six. I'd like to give a little dinner party because my grandmother is dying to meet you. She adored your column when you were writing for the *Daily Fluxion,* and now we buy the Moose County paper every Tuesday and Friday so she can read 'Straight from the Qwill Pen.' Sometimes you switch days, and then the dear lady has a fit!"

"I'm sure I'll like your grandmother immensely," Qwilleran said.

"We'll invite a few others you might enjoy meeting. Everyone knows who you are, and all our friends have heard about the time you and Bushy were marooned on the island during a storm. So we'll all be looking forward to your visit."

"None more than I," he said in the graciously formal style he adopted on such occasions.

"Do you like pasta? We have to serve something my grandmother can swallow easily."

"I consider myself omnivorous—with the small exception of turnips and parsnips."

"How about the cats? What do they eat?"

"Don't worry about them. I'll take along some canned stuff."

Canned stuff to the Siamese meant red salmon, boned chicken, solid-pack white tuna, crabmeat, and lobster.

Although feeding the cats would be a simple matter, dressing for dinner at the Riding and Hunt Club would pose a problem. The navy blue suit that Qwilleran reserved for funerals had been lost in a fire. Furthermore, a dinner jacket would be preferable if only to dispel the Lockmaster notion that Moose County was populated with aborigines. He had never owned a dinner jacket. He had rented one for Arch Riker's wedding twenty-odd years before, and he assumed that the practice was still customary. He assumed that the young potato farmers and sheep ranchers whose wedding photos appeared in the *Something* were able to rent their dinner jackets and tailcoats from Scottie's Men's Shop.

Time was short. He headed downtown at a pace faster than usual, turning his head only to count the yellow posters in store windows—posters made brighter by the relentless September sun:

LIVING BARN TOUR
SAT., SEPT. 17, 10 A.M. to 5 P.M.
TICKETS $5

Scottie greeted him at the door. "Weel, laddie, you've done it again!" he said, putting on the brogue that pleased his Scottish and part-Scottish customers. (Qwilleran's mother, everyone knew, had been a Mackintosh.)

"Meaning what?" Qwilleran asked.

"You found another dead body! Canna remember any dead bodies before you moved to town."

Qwilleran huffed into his moustache as dismissal of the remark. "I want to rent a dinner jacket and everything that goes with it."

"Och! You want to *rent?* Is the Klingenschoen heir too hard up to buy one?"

"Look, Scottie, I've lived here for four years with no need for formal clothing, and I may never need it again. Waste not, want not."

"Spoken like a true Mackintosh! Or was your mother a Mackenzie?"

"Mackintosh," Qwilleran growled.

" 'Twill make a juicy bit of gossip when the word gets around that the richest man in Moose County is *rentin'* a dinner jacket. Every man in your position, laddie, should own a dinner jacket."

Reluctantly Qwilleran allowed himself to be sold, and as he was being fitted, the storekeeper brought up the subject of the murder again. "Let them say what they will about VanBrook, it were too bad. Aye, it were too bad."

"Was he a good customer of yours?" Qwilleran asked,

assuming that Scottie's reactions would be related to the cash register.

"Not good, but frequent. He come in here reg'lar to look for turtlenecks in colors they don't make . . . The police have a suspect, I hear."

"I was not aware of that, Scottie. Who is it?" Qwilleran asked innocently.

"There's a rumor that Dennis Hough is in hidin'." He pronounced it *Hoe*. "The mayor's wife were in Mooseville to a ladies' social, and she saw the laddie comin' out of the Shipwreck Tavern, lookin' furtive and in want of a shave."

"What kind of refreshments were they serving at that ladies' social? Dennis is driving to St. Louis to see his family for the first time in several months! The gossips want to suspect him because he's an outsider from Down Below. The people around here, if you ask me, are a bunch of xenophobes."

"If you mean they're slow in payin' their bills, you hit the nail on the head, laddie."

Leaving Scottie's store, Qwilleran met Carol Lanspeak going into the family's emporium. "Heard anything?" she asked.

"Not a word," he replied. "How about you?"

"Wait till you hear! We just received a letter that Hilary mailed last Friday, the day before he died, billing us for mileage for that woman from Lockmaster! Eight rehearsals and twelve performances at one hundred forty miles a round trip. Do you realize what that amounts to at twenty-five cents a mile? Seven hundred dollars! I know she used a lot of gas to come up here, but the point is: *We didn't need her!*"

"Can the club afford it?"

"Well, it'll put us in the red again. It's just another example of Hilary's arrogance. He never gave us a hint that we'd be liable for her travel expenses. Scott Gippel thinks we should just ignore it. We don't know the woman's address, and we don't know who's handling the estate."

"What does Larry say about it?"

"He hasn't seen the letter yet. He'll hit the ceiling!" Her eye caught the yellow poster in the store window. "Your Living Barn Tour is being well publicized, but isn't a five-dollar admission kind of steep for Pickax pocketbooks?"

"They'll pay five dollars just to see the scene of the crime," he said.

"That's ghoulish, Qwill."

"But true. You wait and see."

Carol went into the store, and Qwilleran went on his way, thinking about the letter posthumously received. Who was VanBrook's executor? What was the extent of his estate? Who would inherit? Only one person in Pickax, he thought, would know anything about the principal's connections. The superintendent of schools would have a file on the man. Qwilleran had a sudden urge to lunch with Lyle Compton, and he knew that Compton always liked an excuse to get out of the office.

Qwilleran phoned the board of education and made a date for noon, then called the Old Stone Mill for a reservation. Thriftily he used the phone in Amanda's Studio of Interior Design.

"Have you heard anything new?" Fran asked him when he hung up the phone. "I haven't been able to pry anything out of Dad. He isn't talking, not even to Mother, but there's an ugly rumor circulating about Dennis."

"How do these baseless rumors get started?" Qwilleran asked irritably.

"He left town suddenly."

"No doubt headed for St. Louis on family business."

"That's what I think, too, although he didn't mention it to anyone . . . How did the shoot turn out yesterday?"

"Pretty good, I guess. Bushy took a lot of pictures and promised to print a complete set for you. I'll see them this weekend when I go down to Lockmaster. Have you ever been to the steeplechase?"

"No, but I hear it's quite a blast."

Qwilleran looked at his watch. "I'm meeting Lyle at noon. See you later."

"Wait a minute, Qwill. Want to help me make that delivery to Hilary's house tomorrow?"

"What time?"

"Is nine o'clock too early? I know you're a slow starter."

"Not on Wednesday mornings! Mrs. Fulgrove comes to dust, and I like any excuse to get out."

"Okay, then. Park behind the studio, and you can help me load the screens in the van. They're in flat cartons, large but not heavy. And," Fran added slyly, "we won't charge you for the two phone calls."

Stroking his moustache with satisfaction, Qwilleran left for lunch with a singularly buoyant step. He was going to see what was behind those drawn draperies on Goodwinter Boulevard.

The Old Stone Mill was a picturesque restaurant converted from a nineteenth-century grist mill, and its outstanding features were a six-foot-seven busboy who talked a lot and an old millwheel that turned and creaked and groaned continuously. The two men were shown to Qwilleran's favorite table: it had the best view and the most privacy and was comfortably removed from the incessant racket of the ancient wheel.

As Derek Cuttlebrink sauntered over with water pitcher and bread basket, the superintendent said with his usual cynical scowl, "Here comes our most distinguished alumnus."

"Hi, Mr. Compton," said the gregarious busboy. "Did you see me in the play?"

"I certainly did, Derek, and you were head and shoulders above all the others."

"Gee!"

"When are you going to complete your education, my boy? Or is your goal to be the oldest busboy in the forty-eight contiguous states?"

"Well, I've got this new girl that kinda likes me, and she doesn't want me to go away to college," Derek explained plausibly. "I see her three times a week. Last night we went roller skating."

The hostess, hurrying past with an armful of menu folders, nudged him. "Setups on tables six and nine, Derek, and table four wants more water."

As the busboy drifted away with his water pitcher, Compton said, "The Cuttlebrinks were the founders of the town of Wildcat, but their pioneer spirit is wearing thin. Every generation gets taller but not brighter . . . What looks interesting on the menu? I don't want anything nutritious. I get all that at home." The superintendent was a painfully thin man who smoked too many cigars and scoffed at vegetables and salads.

Qwilleran said, "There's a cheese and broccoli soup that's so thick you could use it for mortar. The avocado-stuffed pita is a mess to eat, but delicious. The crab Louis salad is the genuine thing."

"I'll take chili and a hot dog," Compton told the waitress . . . "So they finally eliminated VanBrook," he said to Qwilleran. "I always knew he'd get it some day. Too bad it happened on our territory. It makes Moose County look bad."

"If you found him so objectionable, why did you keep renewing his contract?"

"He was so damned good that he had us over a barrel. There are devils you can live with, you know."

"What happens to his estate? Did he have any family elsewhere?"

"The only personal contact listed in his file is an attorney in Lockmaster. When the police notified me, I talked to this man and asked if there was anything we could do. He told me that Hilary had opted for cremation, with his ashes to be sent to Lockmaster. Then he asked for the name of an estate liquidator, and I referred him to Susan Exbridge."

"Hilary was a mystery man, wasn't he? I'm reading the biography of Sir Edmund Backhouse, the British sinologist, and I see a similarity: A brilliant, erudite man of astounding accomplishments but also an eccentric who doesn't fit the social norm."

"Hilary was that, all right," Compton agreed.

"Even his name rouses one's curiosity, if not suspicion."

"Hilary VanBrook was his professional name, assumed when he was acting on the New York stage. It's not the one used for social security, federal withholding, and so forth, but you have to admit it has a touch of class. His real name was William Smurple—not an auspicious name for a Broadway star."

"Or a high school principal," Qwilleran said. "I hear he claimed to speak Japanese fluently. Was that true?"

"To all appearances. We had a Japanese exchange student up here one year, and they seemed to converse glibly. So that checked out. I never had any qualms about his credibility, although I often questioned his judgment. We lost a helluva good custodian because of him, and a good janitor is a pearl beyond price. Pat O'Dell had been in the school system for forty years, and you couldn't find a more conscientious worker or more charismatic personality. He was the unofficial student counselor; the kids flocked to him for advice—a grandfather figure, you might say. Well, Hilary blew the whistle on *that* unorthodox arrangement! I think he was jealous of the man's popularity. At any rate, he made it so uncomfortable for old Pat O'Dell that he quit."

"What about the Toddwhistle incident?"

"Kids have been putting things on teachers' chairs and in principals' mailboxes for generations! Hilary overreacted. Now that he's gone, we'll probably give Wally a diploma, if he wants it. But I'll bet he earns more money stuffing animals than I do hiring teachers."

They ordered apple pie, and Qwilleran asked, "With all VanBrook's talents and background, why did he choose to live in remote places like Lockmaster and Pickax? Did he ever explain?"

"Yes, he did, when we first interviewed him. He said he had seen the world at its best and at its worst, and now he wanted a quiet place in which to study and meditate."

Qwilleran thought: He could be running from someone or something. He could be an upscale con man on the wanted list. His murderer could be an enemy from Down Below, settling an old score.

Compton was saying, "He claimed to have ninety thousand books in his library. He listed his major interests as architecture, horticulture, Shakespeare, and baroque music. He had three academic degrees."

"Did you verify them before hiring him?"

"Hell, no. We took him on faith, knowing what an outstanding job he'd done as principal of Lockmaster. As a matter of fact, he turned out to be so damned good for Pickax that we never crossed him. We were afraid we'd lose him."

"Well, you've lost him now," Qwilleran said.

"I hear the police are looking for your builder, and he's skipped town."

"Lyle, if I were a doctoral candidate in communications, I'd write my thesis on the Moose County rumor mill. Let me tell you something. Dennis Hough had no more motive than you or I have, and I happen to know he's on his way home to see his family Down Below."

"I hope you're right," said Compton. He lighted a cigar, and that was Qwilleran's cue to excuse himself, grabbing the check and saying he had another appointment. Actually, since giving up pipesmoking, he found tobacco fumes offensive. Yet, in the days when he puffed on a quarter-bend bulldog, he went about perfuming restaurants and offices and cocktail parties with Groat and Boddle Number Five, imported from Scotland, thinking he was doing surrounding noses a favor.

Qwilleran did indeed have another appointment—with Susan Exbridge—who was chairing the library committee in charge of the barn tour. As he headed for her antique shop, he was struck by a chilling thought. Suppose Dennis did not go to St. Louis! Suppose he drove to some out-of-county collision shop to have the damage repaired on his van! Suppose the mayor's wife really did see him coming out of the Shipwreck Tavern! He dismissed the thought with a mental shudder.

The Exbridge & Cobb antique shop on Main Street was a class act. The clean windows, the gold lettering on the glass, the polished mahogany and brass on display—all sparkled in the afternoon sun, thanks to the ministrations of Mr. O'Dell and Mrs. Fulgrove.

When Qwilleran walked in, Susan turned, expecting a customer, but the proprietorial smile turned to dismay when she saw him. "Oh, Qwill!" she agonized. "Have you heard the news? They're hunting for Dennis, and he's *gone!*"

"Don't be alarmed," he said with diminished confidence. "He's on his way Down Below to see his family. I saw you two leaving the party together. What happened after that, if you don't mind my asking?"

"He walked me to my car, which was at the far end of the lane, and then returned to his van. He didn't say a word about going to St. Louis."

"Will you take offense if I ask you something personal?"

"We-e-ell . . ." she hesitated.

"What were you and Dennis giggling about when you left the barn?"

"Giggling?"

"You were enjoying some private joke. I'm not prying into your affairs, but it might give a clue to his next move."

"Oh," she said, recollecting the episode. "It was nothing. It was about one of the Old Lady's lines to Anne Boleyn. She says, *And you, a very fresh fish, have your mouth filled before you open it.* On the last night, I said it with a certain significant emphasis. Someone in the audience guffawed, and Fran glared at me murderously. I'd give anything to know who laughed."

"Hmff," Qwilleran said. "I didn't come here to quiz you, Susan. I came to ask about the Barn Tour. Is everything under control?"

"There's one problem, Qwill. Dennis was going to give me some facts about the remodeling, to help the guides answer questions. What shall we do?"

"I'll type something out for you. Who are the guides?"

"Members of the library board and a few volunteers."

"How many visitors do you expect?"

"We've printed five hundred tickets, and they're selling well. The ad runs tomorrow, and we're taking a few radio spots."

"I'm leaving town Friday for the weekend. Why don't you come over Thursday morning before you open your shop? You can pick up the key to the barn and see that everything's in order. And don't worry about Dennis, Susan. I'm confident that it'll straighten out all right."

Qwilleran believed what he was saying, more or less, until he later met Hixie Rice coming out of the bank. "I've been trying to reach you, Qwill!" she cried. "I was in Mooseville this morning, calling on customers, and I saw Dennis's van! I was driving east on the lakeshore road. He was just ahead of me, and he turned into your property. Don't you have a letter *K* on a post at the entrance to your log cabin?"

Qwilleran nodded solemnly.

"When he made the left turn, I saw him clearly, hunched over the steering wheel. He looked ghastly! Does he have a key to your cabin?"

"No, he returned it. I let him use the cabin last month when he was rehearsing. He wanted to learn his lines while walking on the secluded beach."

"What should we do?"

"I'll drive out there to see what's happening."

"Be careful, Qwill," she warned. "If he's cracked up—and if he has a gun—and if he's killed once—"

"Dennis doesn't own a gun, Hixie. In fact, he's anti-gun. But something's happened to him. I'll get my car and drive out to Mooseville."

"I'll drive you. My car's right here. I hope you don't mind riding in a piece of junk; it's a loaner."

The route to Mooseville, thirty miles away, was fairly straight, and they far exceeded the speed limit. There was little traffic at this time of year—after the tourist season and before the hunting season. The highway passed through a desolate landscape ravaged by early lumbering and mining operations. Although the sun was shining, the scene was bleak, and so was the conversation.

Qwilleran said, "If he's in trouble, why didn't he confide in me? I thought we were good friends."

"Me too. I was thinking of quitting the *Something* and going into partnership with him. I could line up contracts and get publicity."

When they reached the lakeshore, the vacation cottages on the beach had an air of desertion. Qwilleran said, "It's around the next curve. Slow down."

"I'm getting nervous," said Hixie.

The letter *K* on a post marked the entrance to the Klingenschoen property, and the private drive led through patches of woods and over a succession of dunes until it emerged in a clearing.

"There's no one here!" Qwilleran said. "This is where he'd have to park."

They found tire tracks in the soft earth, however, and on the beach at the foot of the dune there were footprints. Sand and surf had not yet disguised the traces. The cabin itself, closed for the season, was undisturbed.

"If he's been on the run, he's been sleeping in his van," Qwilleran said. "How well do you know the manager at Indian Village?"

"We have a good rapport, and she's high on my Christmas list."

"Could you get the key to Dennis's apartment?"

"I could think of something . . . I could say that he's out of town and called me to send him papers from his desk."

"Good enough."

In Indian Village there were eight apartments in each two-story building, with a central hall serving them all. Hixie admitted Qwilleran into her own apartment and then went to see the manager. She returned with the key.

"It's my contention," Qwilleran told her, "that Dennis

returned from the party early Sunday morning and either found a message on his answering machine or found something in his Saturday mail that caused him to take off in a hurry. It would have to be serious business to make him hide out in his van—a threat perhaps."

Entering Dennis's apartment with caution and stealth, they went directly to the desk. It was cluttered with papers in connection with the barn remodeling. There was a pink or yellow order form for every can of paint and every pound of nails that went into the job. The only sign of recent mail delivery was an unopened telephone bill. Then Qwilleran pressed the button of the answering machine.

When he heard the first message, he reached for the pocket-size recorder that was always in his jacket along with his keys.

"We've got to tape this," he said. "I want to play it for Brodie. But don't say a word about this to *anyone,* Hixie. Let's get back to town."

Hixie drove to the theatre parking lot, and Qwilleran walked the rest of the way home—through the iron gate, through the woods. Approaching the barn, he could see a van parked at the back door—Dennis's van—and he quickened his step, torn between relief and apprehension.

The back door was unlocked, as he expected; Dennis knew where to find the key. Walking into the kitchen Qwilleran shouted a cheerful, "Hello! Anybody here?" The only response was a wild shrieking and gutteral howling from the top balcony. He had locked the Siamese in their loft that morning, troubled as he was by his gnawing sense of foreboding. The cacophony from the loft made his blood run cold, and an awareness of death made him catch his breath. He moved toward the center of the building and slowly, systematically, surveyed the cavernous interior.

The afternoon sun was slanting through the high windows on the west, making triangles on the rugs, walls, and white fireplace cube, and across one triangle of sunlight there was a vertical shadow—the shadow of a body hanging from a beam overhead.

Six

Dennis Hough—creator of the spectacular barn renovation and darling of the Theatre Club—had let himself into the apple barn Tuesday afternoon, using the hidden key. Then he climbed to the upper balcony, threw a rope over a beam, and jumped from the railing.

Brodie himself responded when Qwilleran made his grisly discovery and called the police. The chief strode into the barn saying, "What did I tell you? What did I tell you? This is the man who killed VanBrook. He couldn't live with himself!"

"You've got it wrong," Qwilleran said. "Let me play you a tape. Dennis arrived at his apartment early Sunday morning, following the party, and checked his answering machine for messages. This is what he heard."

There followed a woman's voice, bitter and vindictive. "Don't come home, Dennis! Not ever! I've filed for divorce. I've found someone who'll be a good daddy for Denny and a real husband for me. Denny doesn't even know you any more. There's nothing you can say or do, so don't call me. Just stay up north and have your jollies."

Qwilleran said, "Do you want to hear it again?"

"No," Brodie said. "How did you get this?"

"I had access to his apartment, just as he had access to this barn. I found the message this afternoon and taped it to disprove your theory. Dennis didn't know he was under suspicion—or even that VanBrook had been killed, probably. He was overwhelmed by his own private tragedy."

Brodie grunted and massaged his chin. "We'll have to notify that woman as next of kin."

"I'll be willing to do it," said Qwilleran, who prided himself on his comforting and understanding manner in notifying the bereaved. He punched a number supplied by directory assistance, and when a woman's voice answered he said in his practiced tone of sincerity and concern, "Is this Mrs. Hough?" The fact that he pronounced it correctly was in his favor.

"Yes?" she replied.

"This is Jim Qwilleran, a friend of your husband, calling from Pickax—"

"I don't want to talk to any friend of that skunk!" she screamed into the phone and banged down the receiver.

Qwilleran winced. "Did you hear that, Andy?"

"Gimme the phone." Brodie punched the same number, and when she answered he said in his official monotone, "This is the police calling. Your husband is dead, Mrs. Hough. Suicide. Request directions for disposition of the body . . . Thank you, ma'am."

He turned to Qwilleran. "I won't repeat what she said. The gist of it is—we can do what we please. She wants no part of her husband, dead or alive."

Qwilleran said, "His friends in the Theatre Club will handle everything. I'll call Larry Lanspeak."

"I'll take the tape," Brodie said. "Just keep it quiet. He was never declared a suspect, so there's no need to deny the rumor. Let the public think what they want; we'll continue the investigation."

While the emergency crew and medical examiner went about their work, Qwilleran notified one person about the suicide, and that was Hixie. "You'll hear it on the six o'clock news," he said. "Dennis has taken his life." He waited for her hysterical outburst to subside and then said, "Don't mention the message from his wife to *anyone*, Hixie. Those are Brodie's orders. When he finds the real killer, Dennis will be cleared."

At six o'clock a brief announcement on WPKX stated: "A building contractor—Dennis Hough, thirty, of St. Louis, Missouri—died suddenly today IN . . . a Pickax barn . . . he had recently . . . remodeled. No details . . . are . . . available." The name of the deceased was pronounced *Huck*. "Died suddenly" was a euphemism for suicide in the north country.

Qwilleran was loathe to imagine the anguish of his friend's private moments preceding his desperate act. He thought: If I had been here, I could have prevented it. Qwilleran's own life had once been in ruins. He knew the shock of a suddenly failed marriage, the pain of rejection, the guilt, the sense of failure, the hopelessness. He skipped dinner, finding the thought of food nauseating, and fed the Siamese in their loft apartment. Koko, who knew something extraordinary had been happening, was determined to escape and investigate, but Qwilleran brought him down with a lunging tackle.

Down on the main level he turned on the answering machine; he wished no idle gossip, no prying questions. Then he shut himself in his studio, away from the sight of those overhead beams, that fireplace cube, and those triangular windows. He tried to lose himself in the pages of a book. As he delved farther and farther into the Backhouse biography, it occurred to him that the life of the mysterious VanBrook would be equally fascinating. The mystery of the man's personality and background, whether resolved or not, would be intensified by his violent death. The search for the killer, sidetracked by false suspicions, would add another dimension of suspense.

There was a violent storm that night. Gale winds from Canada swept across the big lake and joined with heavy rain to lash the rotting apple trees. By morning, the orchard was a wreck, and Trevelyan Trail was a ribbon of mud. Qwilleran called the landscape service, requesting a clean-up crew and truckloads of crushed stone.

Then he showered and shaved in a hurry and fed the cats without ceremony. It was Wednesday, and he hoped to escape before the vigorous Mrs. Fulgrove arrived to dust, vacuum, polish, and deliver her weekly lecture. This week her topics would undoubtedly be murder and suicide, in addition to her usual tirade about the abundance of cat hair. He succeeded in avoiding her and even had time for coffee and a roll at Lois's Luncheonette before reporting to the back door of Amanda's Studio of Interior Design.

He was met by a distraught young woman. "Dad told me about it!" Fran cried. "He wouldn't discuss motive, but everyone says it means that Dennis killed VanBrook."

Irritably Qwilleran said, "What everyone in Pickax says, thinks, feels, knows, or believes is of no concern to me, Fran."

"I know how you must feel about it, Qwill. I'm distressed, too. Dennis and I worked so compatibly on the barn. I'll miss him."

"Larry is arranging the funeral. There'll be a private service in the Dingleberry chapel for a few friends, then burial next to his mother."

Fran asked, "How is Polly reacting?"

"We haven't discussed it," he said.

"Are you two getting along all right?" she asked with concern.

"Why do you want to know?" he asked sharply.

"Well, you know . . . she wasn't there at the barn Saturday night . . . and then someone saw you at Tipsy's on Sunday—with another woman, they said."

Qwilleran huffed into his moustache angrily. "Okay, where are the cartons? How many do you have to deliver? Let's get the van loaded!"

On the short drive to Goodwinter Boulevard the designer said, "Hilary's neighbors will have their telescopes out. They'll be sure I'm looting a dead man's house."

"I gather that snooping is a major pastime in Pickax."

"You don't know the half of it! There are two busybodies who make it their lifework to spy and pry and spread rumors. But if you meet them on the post office steps, they're *so sweet!*"

"Who are they?"

"I'll give you a couple of clues," Fran said teasingly. "One wears a plastic rainhat even when the sun is shining, and the other calls everyone Dear Heart."

"Thanks for warning me," Qwilleran said. "Was Hilary a good customer of yours?"

"He didn't buy much, but he liked to come in to the studio and look around and tell us things that we already knew. He considered himself an authority on everything. He bought a lamp once, and we upholstered a chair for him last year, but the screens are the first big order I wrote up. And then this had to happen!"

"I suppose your father got a search warrant and went into the house."

"I don't know," she said coolly.

"Does he know you're delivering merchandise?"

"No, but Dear Heart will see that he finds out. Actually, Qwill, Dad and I haven't been on good terms since I moved into my apartment."

"Too bad. Sorry to hear it."

Fran parked in the rear of the house, and they started to unload. The interior was similar to others on Goodwinter Boulevard: large, square rooms with high ceilings, connected by wide arches; heavy woodwork in a dark varnish; a ponderous staircase lavished with carving and turnings; tall, narrow windows. But instead of the usual heirloom furniture and elaborate wallcoverings, the main rooms were white-walled and sparsely furnished with tatami floor matting, low Oriental tables, and floor cushions. There were a few pieces of porcelain, two Japanese scrolls, and a folding screen decorated with galloping fatrumped horses. The only false note was the use of heavy draperies smothering the windows.

Fran explained, "Hilary was replacing the draperies with shoji screens so he could have light as well as privacy. He was quite secretive about his life-style."

"How could he live like this?" Qwilleran himself required large, comfortable chairs and a place to put his feet up.

"I believe he slept on a futon down here, but he said he had a study upstairs as well as rooms for books and hobbies."

Hobbies! Qwilleran found himself speculating wildly. "Okay if I look around?"

"Sure, go ahead," she said. "I'll be opening the cartons and putting each screen where it belongs. They were all custom-made, you know. We're talking about ten thousand dollars here, and God knows how long we'll have to wait to collect."

Qwilleran walked slowly up the impressive staircase, thinking about the ninety thousand books Compton had mentioned. He wondered if the collection included *City of Brotherly Crime*. He wondered if the books were cataloguen. When he started opening doors, however, his hopes wilted; the books had never been unpacked. He went from room to room and found hundreds of sealed cartons of books—or so they were labeled.

Only one room was organized enough to have bookshelves, and they covered four walls. This was evidently the principal's study, having a desk, lounge chair, reading lamp, and stereo system. As for the volumes on the shelves, they expressed VanBrook's eclectic tastes: Eastern philosophy, Elizabethan drama, architecture, Oriental art, eighteenth-century costume, Cantonese cookery, botany—but nothing on urban crime.

The desktop in this hideaway had an excessive tidiness reflecting the influence of the Japanese style downstairs. A brass paperknife in the shape of a Chinese dragon was placed precisely parallel to the onyx-base pen set. The telephone was squared off with the lefthand edge of the desk, and a brass-bound box (locked) was squared off with the righthand edge. In between, in dead center, was a clean desk blotter on which lay a neat pile of letters. Apparently they had been received and opened on Saturday, at which time they were read and returned to their envelopes.

There was a muffled quiet in the study. Fran's footsteps could be heard downstairs, and occasionally the ripping of a carton. Casually, with an ear alert to the activity below, Qwilleran examined the mail. There were bills from utility companies, magazine-subscription departments, and an auto-insurance agency. There were no death threats, he was sorry to discover. But one small envelope addressed by hand had a scribble in the upper lefthand corner that piqued his curiosity: F. Stucker, 231 Fourth

Street, Lockmaster. After determining that Fran was fully occupied with her screens, he gingerly drew the letter from its envelope and read the following:

> *Dear Mr. VanBrook—Thanks a lot for the $200. I didn't expect you to pay for my gas. It was nice of you to ask me to be in your play. But I can sure use the money. I had to buy new boots for Robbie. So thanks again.*
>
> > *Fiona*

"Two hundred bucks!" Qwilleran said softly to the surrounding bookshelves. "That faker was making five hundred on the deal!" Was petty cheating one of his "hobbies"? Qwilleran tried the desk drawers, but they were locked.

Then, as he carefully tucked the note back in its envelope, he heard a humming sound in the insulated silence. He had not heard it before. It seemed to come from the rear of the second floor, and he followed it down the hall. Ahead of him was a rosy light spilling from a doorway. He approached warily and peeked into the room. The humming came from a transformer; the ceiling was covered with a battery of rose-tinted lights, and a timer had just turned them on.

Under the lights were long tables holding trays of plants, greenhouse style, but they were beginning to wilt. Obviously no one had watered them since VanBrook's last day on earth. What were they? Qwilleran was no horticulturist, but he knew this was not *Cannabis sativa*. There were purple flowers among the greenery. He rubbed a leaf and smelled his fingers; there was no clue. He broke off a sprig and put it in his shirt pocket, thinking he would give Koko a sniff.

"Okay, Quill," Fran called from the foot of the stairs. "I've done all I can do. Let's go."

As they drove away from the house, with the empty cartons loaded in the van, she said, "Well, what did you think of the place?"

"Esoteric, to say the least. If the estate puts his books up for sale, I'd like to know about it. What are the plants he was growing upstairs?"

"I never saw any plants. I was never invited upstairs. When I came to measure for the screens, he gave me a cup of tea, and we sat cross-legged on the floor cushions. I sure hope Amanda can collect for those screens."

"Amanda won't let anyone cheat her, dead or alive."

"Can you stand some good news?" she asked. "Your tapestries have arrived, and we can install them tomorrow—in time for the open house!"

"How do they look?"

"I haven't opened the packages, and the suspense is killing me, but I'll wait till we deliver them."

"Need any help?"

"No, I'll bring Shawn, my installer—more brawn than brain—but what he does, he does well."

"How will you hang them?"

"With carpet tack-strips. Do you mind if we make it around five o'clock?"

Fran always made business calls to Qwilleran's residence in the late afternoon, obligating him to offer a cocktail, which led to a dinner invitation. How did VanBrook get away with a cup of tea? . . . Not that Qwilleran objected to dining with his interior designer. She was good company. But Polly disapproved.

Fran dropped him at Scottie's, where he was fitted for a dark blue suit. He was to be a pallbearer at Dennis's funeral, and it occurred to him—too late—that he should have opted for a dark blue suit instead of a dinner jacket for the steeplechase party. He wondered if Scottie would take it back. It irked him to buy two of anything if one would do. Still, he decided not to suggest it. During the fitting, Scottie wanted to talk about the suicide, but Qwilleran turned him off with frowns and curt responses.

His next stop was the *Moose County Something*, and when he walked into Arch Riker's office, the publisher jumped to his feet. "Qwill! Where've you been? I heard it on the air last night and tried to reach you. Why didn't you call back? Today we're running a 'Died Suddenly,' but no one at the police department would talk to us. What happened?"

"I don't know," Qwilleran said.

"Does this mean the VanBrook case is wrapped up?"

"No, it doesn't. That's definite."

"What makes you so sure? Are you getting vibrations from Koko?" Riker asked in an attempt at banter.

"The police have evidence to that effect. That's all I can say, and don't ask me how I know. But I'd like to make a suggestion, Arch."

"Let's hear it."

"I think you should run that editorial I suggested: A crime is a crime! Offer a reward of $50,000 for information regarding the shooting. It'll squelch the rumor that Dennis was a suspect, and it may help Brodie. The K Fund will cover it."

"Do we identify the benefactor?"

"No. Keep it anonymous. How soon can you run it?"

"Friday."

"Good. I won't be here. I'm going to Lockmaster for a steeplechase weekend."

"You lucky dog! I hear it's a gas!"

It was too early for Qwilleran to go home; Mrs. Fulgrove would still be there, furiously mopping and cleaning and polishing. He went instead to the library—to tell Polly about his plans for the weekend. He had neither seen her nor talked with her for two days, not since the unexplained phone call that made her cheeks redden and her eyes sparkle.

In the vestibule of the library the daily quotation was: *The evil that men do lives after them; the good is oft interred with their bones*. The greetings from the clerks were appropriately solemn. As he headed for the stairs to the mezzanine, one of them called out, "She's not in, Mr. Q."

"She's having her hair done," the other explained.

"I'm just going up to read the papers," he said.

On the table in the reading room was a copy of the *Lockmaster Logger,* a publication established during lumbering days, more than a century before. Circulation: 11,500. Editor: Kipling MacDiarmid.

The first page of the *Logger* was devoted to steeplechase news: Five races with a combined purse of $75,000, preceded by the Trial of Hounds, the parade of carriages, and a concert by the Lockmaster High School band. A few parking spaces overlooking the course were still available for $100, but that would admit as many persons as could fit into the vehicle. There were sidebars listing the horses, owners, trainers, and riders who would participate in the event, and there were instructive features on what to wear to the races and what to pack in the picnic basket.

When Qwilleran heard Polly's sensible library shoes on the stairs, he put down his newspaper, and their eyes met. She was looking well-groomed but not as girlishly radiant as she had been on the day following the long brunch at the Palomino Paddock.

She walked immediately to his table. "Qwill, I'm so

sorry about Dennis," she said softly. "You must be grieving."

"A lot of people are grieving, Polly."

"I suppose we can assume that Dennis . . . that the VanBrook case is closed now," she said, sitting down at the table.

"I don't assume anything, but I know that Moose County has lost a good builder and a talented actor."

"To some persons in Pickax the principal was such a villain that Dennis is now a candidate for a folk hero . . . Is that the *Lockmaster Logger* you're reading? What do you think of it?" Her face lighted up when she spoke the name of the town.

"It's more conservative than the *Something* in makeup, but it has a friendly slant. I hear Lockmaster is a friendly town. Did you find it *friendly?*" He gazed at her pointedly as he repeated the word.

Polly's eyes wavered for a fraction of a second. "I found everyone very cordial and hospitable." Then she added brightly, "Would you like to do something exciting this weekend? Would you like to go birdwatching in the wetlands near Purple Point?"

This was Qwilleran's moment. "I'd like to, but I'll be horse watching in Lockmaster. That's what I came to tell you. The Bushlands have invited me for the races. I'll be gone for three days."

"Oh, really?" she said with half-concealed disappointment. "You never told me you were interested in horses."

"Chiefly I'm interested in horse *people*. I may find some stuff for the 'Qwill Pen' column."

"Shall I feed Koko and Yum Yum while you're away?"

"Their royal highnesses are invited to go along—and have their portraits taken by a master photographer."

"How grand!" she said archly. "When do you leave?"

"Friday. After the funeral."

"Why don't you come over for dinner tomorrow night? I could prepare chicken divan."

"I wish I could, but Fran is hanging the new tapestries at five o'clock, and I don't know how long the operation will take or how many problems we'll encounter."

Polly straightened her shoulders and drew a deep breath as she always did when confronted by her personal demon: Jealousy. She stood up. "Then I'll see you when you return."

Qwilleran walked slowly back to the apple barn. The events of the morning had fired his determination to write a biography of the Mystery Man of Moose County. It would require prodigious research. First he would want to see Lyle Compton's file on the late principal. Teachers and parents in Pickax and Lockmaster would be glad to cooperate. VanBrook's attorney would no doubt grant an interview, and there would be Fiona Stucker, of course, whose connection with VanBrook might be a story in itself. The colleges that granted the man's degrees and the Equity records in New York would have to be researched. Qwilleran relished the challenge. He had a propensity for snooping and a talent for drawing information from shy or reluctant subjects.

He recalled the letter from Fiona Stucker. If VanBrook would chisel a few hundred dollars from the Theatre Club, he might have a history of other misdeeds, great or small: a fling at embezzlement, a witty financial fraud, some successful tax evasion. He had the nerve and the brains to carry off such schemes. The smuggling of Oriental treasures would appeal to him, both intellectually and esthetically. What was in those hundreds of cartons on the second floor of his strangely furnished house?

As Qwilleran approached the barn he could hear the

cats' yowling welcome, and that brought to mind another question: On the night of the party, when Koko stared so intently at VanBrook's head, was the cat sensing a questionable operator? A felonious mentality? Farfetched as the idea might seem, it was not beyond the capabilities of that remarkable animal.

On the other hand, Qwilleran had to admit, Koko might have been staring at hair that he recognized as false.

Seven

On Thursday morning Qwilleran emerged sleepily from his bedroom on the balcony and heard a familiar whistle: *who-it? who-it? who-it?* "Good question," he mumbled as he groped his way down the circular staircase to the computerized coffeemaker. "How about giving us a few answers?" He pressed a button and heard the grinding of the coffee beans, a reassuring sound. It was one of his constant fears that he might stumble down to the kitchen some bleak morning and find the machine out of order.

A feline imperative could be heard, drifting down from the upper reaches of the barn, and he went up the ramp to the top balcony to release the Siamese from their loft apartment. Yum Yum emerged sedately, like the princess that she knew herself to be, but Koko scampered down the ramp to the lower balcony, then flew through space, landing in the cushions of a lounge chair on the main floor. From there he rushed to the window-wall to greet his new-found friend. For a while he sat transfixed, fluttering the tip of his tail as the cardinal turned his head sideways to make eye contact. Shortly, the dump truck arrived to spread crushed stone on the trail, and the cardinal departed for more congenial surroundings.

Qwilleran thawed a Danish for his breakfast, fed the Siamese their roast beef from the deli with a garnish of Roquefort cheese, threw some clothing and towels into the washer, and finally showered and shaved in time to greet Susan Exbridge, who arrived in her long, sleek, top-of-the-line wagon.

"Oh, Qwill! I'm positively destroyed!" she said as she entered the barn and dropped into the nearest chair. "Dennis was such a darling! How could he throw it all away? What was his *motive?*"

Qwilleran said, "There's more to the story than meets the eye. Would you like a cup of coffee?"

"Could you add a touch of something *comforting?*"

"Like . . . rum?"

She nodded gratefully.

"Okay, Susan, tell me how you're going to handle the crowds on Saturday."

After taking a few sips she opened her briefcase and ticked off the arrangements. "The tickets instruct people to use the Main Street parking lots belonging to the theatre, courthouse, and church. We've cleared it with all of them."

"Suppose someone elects to drive up Trevelyan Trail to avoid the traffic jam?"

"The Trail is reserved for guides, and the entrance will be blockaded. Signs will direct visitors through the woods and to the front door of the barn. Indoors there will be plastic runners to protect the floors. Roped stanchions will keep visitors off the rugs. Only a certain number will be admitted at one time."

"Will they go up to the balconies? I wouldn't care to have them snooping in my bedroom."

"Definitely not. The ramps will be roped off. Visitors will simply circle the main floor and exit through the kitchen door. The guides will keep the line moving. No picture taking permitted."

"And for this they're paying five dollars?" he asked in amazement.

"The tickets are sold out, and we could have sold more. There was a sudden demand, you know, after . . . after Tuesday night. The library will realize twenty-five hundred dollars. Polly is simply *ecstatic!*"

Qwilleran knew that the chief librarian was never ecstatic. Pleased, or quietly happy, or even mildly overjoyed, but never ecstatic. Susan's mocking emphasis on *ecstatic* was a subtle reminder that the two women were library associates but not friends.

"You're very well organized, Susan," he complimented her. "Here are the keys for the front and back doors. Hang onto them after the tour, and I'll pick them up at your shop next week."

A handsome and interesting woman, he reflected as she drove away—more fashionable than Polly—but too aggressive and theatrical for his taste, and she never sat down and read a book.

Another woman visitor arrived in the afternoon while he was regaling the Siamese with the devious exploits of Sir Edmund Backhouse. Lulled by his mellifluous voice, they were lounging dreamily in relaxed postures when a sound inaudible to human ears suddenly alerted them. Ears perked, heads lifted, necks craned, bodies raised on forelegs, hindquarters prepared to spring, they raced to the front door as if to greet a shipment of fresh lobster. Moments later, Qwilleran heard what they heard: the rumble of a car that had not recently had a tune-up.

It was Lori Bamba's vintage vehicle—Lori, his part-time secretary and adviser on all matters pertaining to cats. She had long golden hair, which she braided and tied with ribbons, and these tempting appendages held a hypnotic fascination for the Siamese, who greeted her with enthusiastic prowling and ankle rubbing.

"A pleasant surprise, Lori," said Qwilleran as he admitted her to the barn. Her husband usually delivered her finished work and picked up the week's correspondence.

"Nick told me what miracles you've done with the barn, so I had to come and see for myself. I'll bet the cats love those ramps and balconies."

"May I show you around? The five-dollar tour on Saturday limits visitors to the main floor; as an intimate of Koko and Yum Yum you're entitled to go up on the catwalks and visit their loft."

"First let me give you your correspondence. There are forty-seven letters for you to sign. On the less personal ones, I forged your signature. The crank letters were chucked into the wastebasket."

Qwilleran and Lori walked up the ramps, followed by the Siamese with erect tails, then down again. As soon as she sat down, both cats piled into her lap.

Qwilleran said, "I wish I could get Yum Yum to walk on a leash. With Koko it's no problem; he walks me on a leash."

"Just let her wear her harness around the house until she gets used to the feel of it," she suggested. "And do you realize, Qwill, that you have a perfect setup here for blowing bubbles?"

"Bubbles?" he asked dubiously.

"Soap bubbles. Stand on the balcony and let them float down to the cats below. They'll have a wonderful time—jumping and trying to catch them."

"Hmmm," he said, stroking his moustache. He could imagine the town gossips peeking in the window and carrying the news back to the coffee shops: "Mr. Q has started blowing bubbles!"

"The best thing for blowing bubbles," Lori advised, "is

the old-fashioned clay pipe. They have them at the hardware store in Wildcat."

At that moment Koko leaped from her lap and bounded to the window, and they all heard the clear-toned *who-it? who-it? who-it?*

"That's a cardinal," Lori said.

"He's Koko's buddy."

"They're a couple of aristocrats," she said.

"Yes, they act like two potentates at a summit meeting. The orchard is full of other species, but somehow Koko is attracted to the cardinal. I don't know whether he appreciates the bird's regal demeanor or just likes red."

"I've read conflicting opinions about a cat's ability to see color. I'm inclined to believe they *feel color*. They get different sensations from different hues."

"I'll buy that," he said. "Koko is equipped with a lot more senses than the basic five. He's an especially gifted animal."

Lori said, "Let me tell you something interesting. I have an elderly aunt who lost her sight totally a few years ago, but she still recognizes red. She claims she can *feel it!* And she likes to wear red. She says it restores her energy."

"I'd like to meet her. It would make an interesting topic for my column . . . Would you like a glass of cider, Lori?"

"No, thanks, Qwill. Just give me the week's mail. I've got to dash. I've got a baby-sitter."

Later, he was signing the forty-seven letters when a black van with gold lettering on the panels pulled into the barnyard, and a young blond giant leaped out. He opened the rear doors and hoisted to his shoulders—with apparent ease—a large paper-wrapped cylinder, eight feet in length and about a yard in diameter. Fran Brodie was with him, and she directed him to the back door.

"This is Shawn, our world-class installer," she said to Qwilleran.

"Hi!" said the giant with an amiable smile.

She guided him through the kitchen to the great hall, four stories high, and told him to put the tapestry on the floor at the foot of the ramp. Going down on one knee, like Atlas with the world on his shoulders, Shawn dropped the cylinder on the floor with a thud. Then he stood up and gazed at the balconies, the triangular windows, and the fireplace cube with its three stacks.

"How much did this job cost?" he said in awe. "It's sure different! . . . Is this where the guy hung himself?"

"Shawn!" Fran said sharply. "Bring in the toolbox, the tack-strips, and the rope." To Qwilleran she said, "I want to unroll the tapestries down here for inspection. This is the moment of truth!"

The wrapping was carefully removed, and the eight-by-ten-foot wall hanging was spread out on the floor.

"Beautiful!" said Qwilleran.

"Gorgeous!" Fran said.

Shawn shook his head and said, "Crazy!"

The design was a stylized tree dotted with a dozen bright red apples the size of basketballs. Tufting gave them dimension.

"They look real enough for plucking," Qwilleran observed.

"Don't you think," Fran remarked, "that the artist actually captured their juiciness?"

"You guys must be nuts," said the installer. "All I know—it weighs a ton."

The Siamese, watching from the top of the fireplace cube, had no comment.

"Now, this tapestry," the designer explained, "will hang from the railing of the highest catwalk, Qwill, making an exciting focal point that draws the eye upward into that *delicious* galaxy of radiating beams and triangular windows. Also, it will add warmth and color to an interior with *lots* of wood and *lots* of open space. Don't you agree?"

"Yow!" said Koko.

"Okay, Shawn," she said, "roll it up again and carry it to the top level."

"No elevator?"

"You don't need an elevator."

The tack-strips were installed on the top surface of the catwalk railing; the top edge of the tapestry was pressed down securely on the tacks; and then it was slowly unrolled as the ropes were played out.

"Hope it doesn't drop and kill a cat," said the installer with a grin.

"If it does," Qwilleran said, "I'll be after you with a shotgun."

"The other tapestry will be easy," Fran assured Shawn. "We'll hang it on the blank wall of the fireplace cube, facing the foyer, and it's a little smaller."

"Why'n't ya put the heavy one down here?" he asked.

Again the wrappings were removed, and the tapestry was unrolled on the floor—a galaxy of birds and green foliage.

"Yow!" came a comment from the fireplace cube, and Koko jumped to the floor. Birds native to Moose County were flitting among weeds, grazing on the ground, sipping nectar from flowers, warbling from tree branches, and swaying on tall grasses. He walked purposefully across the tapestry and sniffed the red bird with black face patch and red crest.

"Amazing!" Qwilleran said.

The bird extravaganza was hung and admired, and then

Fran glanced at her watch. "I can't hang around," she said. "This is my mother's birthday, and Dad and I are taking her out to dinner. When are you leaving for Lockmaster, Qwill?"

"After the funeral."

"Have a good time at the races. Don't lose all your money."

Qwilleran was glad to avoid socializing. He wanted to stay home and plan his trip and learn how to pack his new luggage. It was the last word in nylon with leather bindings and straps and more pockets and compartments than he needed. It replaced his two old suitcases lost in a disaster Down Below. Imitation leather, scuffed and battered, they had traveled with him from city to city during his lean years. Polly said they were a disgrace. He said they were easy to pack. "Just throw everything in."

After dinner, when he opened his new luggage on the bed to consider its complexities, Koko moved into the two-suiter and Yum Yum took possession of the carry-on. He left them sleeping there and settled down with the Thursday edition of the *Lockmaster Logger*.

The race course, he learned, was a little over two miles—in a natural setting surrounded by gentle hills from which viewing was convenient. For first-time race goers there were instructions for reading the race chart: the name of the horse and the weight he was carrying; the names of owner, trainer, and rider; the color of the racing silks; the horse's color, sex, and age; the names of sire and dam. Such details were more than Qwilleran cared to know.

There was only one entry that aroused his interest: Robin Stucker would be riding in a race that permitted amateurs. He asked himself: Wasn't Stucker the name of the woman who played Queen Katharine? Didn't her note to VanBrook mention that she had to buy boots for Robbie? The horse, according to the chart, was owned by W. Chase Amberton. The trainer was S. W. O'Hare. The name of the horse—and this was what caused Qwilleran to smooth his moustache in speculation—was Son of Cardinal.

Eight

The funeral on Friday morning was a doubly somber affair attended by a few members of the Theatre Club—doubly somber because many of the mourners thought they were saying farewell to a murderer as well as a suicide. No one mentioned it, but glances were exchanged as the pastor of Larry Lanspeak's church spoke his ambiguous platitudes. Only the Lanspeaks and Fran Brodie believed stubbornly that the rumor was false. Only Qwilleran, Hixie Rice, and Chief Brodie knew the truth. Brodie was there—not in uniform but in kilt and tam-o'-shanter—playing a dirge on the bagpipe at Qwilleran's suggestion.

"It will allay suspicions without formally denying them," he told the chief.

Hixie drew Qwilleran aside and said in a low but emotional voice, "It's frustrating, isn't it? Why don't the police come up with a suspect? Why don't *you* do something about it, Qwill?"

He said, "It happened only a week ago, Hixie. The police have information not available to me. What's more, they have computers."

"But you solved the Fitch murders when the police were stymied. And you identified the killer at the museum before anyone knew there was a murder!"

Qwilleran massaged his moustache thoughtfully: He was reluctant to reveal that it was Koko's inquisitive sniffing and catly instincts that had turned up the clues. Only his closest friends and a few journalists Down Below knew about the cat's aptitudes, and it was better to leave it that way. "I'll think about it," he told Hixie.

He thought about it as he packed his binoculars and dinner jacket for the weekend at the races. Getting away from Pickax, he hoped, would restore his perspective. For the cats he packed some canned delicacies and vitamin drops, their favorite plate and water dish, the turkey roaster that served as their commode, and a supply of kitty gravel. This was to be their first experience as house guests. Qwilleran was nervous about the prospect, but Koko hopped into the travel coop eagerly—a good omen—and scolded Yum Yum until she followed suit.

When they pulled away from the barn, the route took them south past the potato farms and sheep ranches—and the usual dead skunk on the highway, which caused a flurry of complaints from the backseat. As they neared the county line, Qwilleran began to notice the name Cuttlebrink on rural mailboxes and then suddenly a roadside sign:

WELCOME TO WILDCAT
POP. 95

A few hundred feet beyond, another sign suggested that the Cuttlebrinks had a sense of humor:

YOU JUST PASSED WILDCAT

Qwilleran eased on the brakes and made a U turn slowly and carefully. Any sudden stop or start, or any turn in

THE CAT WHO KNEW A CARDINAL

excess of twelve degrees, upset Yum Yum's gastrointestinal apparatus and caused a shrill protest—or worse. Returning to the crossroads that constituted downtown Wildcat, he counted a total of four structures: a dilapidated bar, an abandoned gas station, the remains of an old barn, and a weathered wood building with a faded sign:

CUTTLEBRINK'S HDWE. & GENL. MDSE.
ESTAB. 1862

The windows, he guessed, had last been cleaned for the centenary of the store in 1962. The frame building itself had last been painted at the turn of the century. As for the items faintly visible through the dirty glass (dusty horse harness, fan belts, rusty cans of roof cement), they had evidently been dropped there at some point in history, and no one had ever happened to buy them.

The interior was dimly lighted by low-watt lightbulbs hanging from the stamped metal ceiling, and the floorboards—rough and gray with age—were worn down into shallow concavities in front of the cash register and the tobacco case. In the shadows a man could be seen sitting on a barrel—a man with a bush of yellowish-white whiskers and strands of matching hair protruding beneath his feed cap.

"Nice day," he said in a high-pitched, reedy voice.

"Indeed it is," said Qwilleran. "We're having beautiful weather for September, although the weatherman says we can expect rain in a couple of days." He had learned that discussion of the weather was one of the social niceties in Moose County.

"Won't rain," the old man declared.

While speaking, Qwilleran had been perusing the merchandise on shelves, counters, and floor: kerosene lanterns, farm buckets, fish scalers, flashlights, rolls of wire fencing, light bulbs, milk filters, corncob pipes . . . but no clay pipes.

"He'p ya?" asked the old man without moving.

"Just looking around, thank you."

"No law 'gainst that!"

"You have a remarkable assortment of merchandise."

"Yep."

There were nails by the pound, chains by the foot, rat traps, wooden matches, wire coat hangers, some things called hog rings, button hooks, work gloves, and alarm clocks. "I've seen some interesting stores, but this tops them all," said Qwilleran sociably. "How long has it been here?"

"Longer'n me!"

"Are you a Cuttlebrink?"

"All of us be Cuttlebrinks."

Qwilleran continued his search, trying to appear like a casual browser. He found rubber boots, steel springs, plungers, tarpaulins, more fan belts, fifty-pound salt blocks, gnaw bones for rabbits, dill pickles, ammunition . . . but still no bubble pipes. Examining a cellulose sponge—which, according to the label, would clean, sanitize, and remove manure—he asked, "Is this a good sponge?"

"You got a cow?" Cuttlebrink asked. "That be an udder sponge."

"It would be good for washing the car," Qwilleran said, although he intended it for cleaning and sanitizing the cats' turkey roaster.

The old man shrugged and wagged his head at the eccentricity of cityfolk. "You from Pickax?"

"I've lived there for a while."

"Thought so."

Paint thinner. Goat feed. Fuses. Axle grease. Razor blades. Red bandannas. Pitch forks. Swine dust. Another kind of work glove.

"You seem to have just about everything," Qwilleran remarked.

"Yep. What folks want. No fancy stuff."

"Do you happen to have any clay bubble pipes? I'd like to get some for my young ones."

The storekeeper hoisted himself off the barrel and hobbled to the rear of the store, where he climbed a shaky ladder, one unsure step at a time. On the top shelf he found a cardboard box in the last stages of decay and brought it down, one unsure step at a time.

"You amaze me," Qwilleran said with admiration. "How do you manage to find things?"

"They ain't lost."

The box held half a dozen clay pipes that had once been white but were now gray with dust.

"Good! I believe I'll take them all."

"Won't be none left to sell," Cuttlebrink objected.

"How about five?"

"Sell ya four."

Qwilleran paid for the four pipes, the sponge, and a dill pickle, and the sale was rung up on an old brass cash register on which was taped a crayoned sign: BROWNING GUNS WANTED. The storekeeper hobbled back to his barrel, and the three travelers went on their way.

At the county line the terrain changed from rocky pastureland to rolling green hills. This was Lockmaster's famous hunting country, where miles of fences dipped and curved across the landscape, and here and there an opulent farmhouse with barns and stables crowned a hill. Then came the restaurant known as the Palomino Paddock, with luxury cars in the parking lot, after which the highway became Main Street.

In the nineteenth century wealthy shipbuilders and lumber barons chose to build their residences fronting on the chief thoroughfare, to be admired and envied by all. With affluent families striving to outdo each other, houses as large as resort hotels were lavished with turrets, balconies, verandahs, bowed windows, bracketed roofs, decorative gables, and stained glass.

Zoning had changed with the times, however. Now they were upscale rooming houses, gourmet bed-and-breakfast establishments, law offices, insurance agencies. One imposing structure was a funeral home, another a museum, another the Bushlands' photographic studio. Having inherited it from Vicki's side of the family, they combined business with living quarters. It was a massive three-story frame building with a circular tower bulging from the southwest corner.

Qwilleran drove under the porte cochere that sheltered the side door, saying to his passengers, "We're here! I expect you to be on your best behavior for the next forty-eight hours. If you cooperate, you may wind up on the cover of a slick magazine." There was no reply. Were they asleep? He turned to see two pairs of blue eyes staring at him with inscrutable intensity as if they knew something that he did not know.

Leaving the Siamese and their gear in the car, Qwilleran lugged his own traveling bag to the carriage door and rang the bell. He was greeted by Vicki in a chef's apron.

"Excuse me for arriving early," he said. "I thought I might explore the town."

"Good idea!" exclaimed his hostess. "Come on in. Bushy's in his darkroom and can't be disturbed, and I'm wrestling with pie crust, but your room's ready and you can go straight up. We're giving you our really grand guestroom in the southwest corner. You can put the cats in the connecting room; I know they're used to having their own pad."

"Truthfully I'd prefer to have them with me," he said. "In a new environment I like to keep a fatherly eye on them."

"Whatever makes you comfortable, Qwill. Make yourself at home."

He walked slowly and wonderingly across the broad foyer and up the wide staircase, observing the carved woodwork, gaslight fixtures converted for electricity, velvety walls hung with ancestral portraits in oval frames, and the jewel-like stained glass in the windows. The choice guestroom was in the front of the house, a large, square space ballooning into a circular bay—actually the base of the tower. Furnished with canopy bed, writing desk, chaise, wingback chairs, dresser, highboy, blanket chest, and scattering of ruby-red Oriental rugs, it was homey enough for a week's stay. Nothing matched, but family heirlooms gave it a hospitable togetherness. In the circular bay, rimmed with window seats, there was a round table holding a bowl of polished apples, a dish of jelly beans, and magazines devoted to photography and equestrian arts. There was also a four-page newsletter titled *Stablechat*—a collection of steeplechase news and horsey gossip listing S. W. O'Hare as publisher and Lisa Amberton as editor.

Qwilleran sampled a red jelly bean, the only color he considered worth eating, and went downstairs for the cats' accoutrements. When at last he brought the carrier into the room, its occupants emerged cautiously and slithered under the bed, where they remained.

"For your future reference," he said, addressing the bed,

"your cushion's on the chaise; your water dish and commode are in the bathroom; and I'm going for a walk."

He went down to the kitchen in search of Vicki, who was cutting Z-shaped vents in the crusts of two apple pies. "May I ask you the significance of the Z?" he asked. "Or is it a horizontal N?"

"I don't know," she said. "My mother always did it that way, so I do it that way. How's everything upstairs?"

"Everything's fine. The room looks very comfortable. You have quite a collection of antiques."

"It's all been handed down in the family, with each generation adding its own touch, for better or worse. My great-great-grandfather Inglehart built the house. Grandmother Inglehart lives on the third floor. We call her Grummy. Are you going to drive around town?"

"I prefer to walk. Which way shall I go?"

"Well, you might go down the hill to the courthouse and turn right on Fourth Street. That's where all the stores are. It ends at the river. Originally both banks of the river were crammed with sawmills and shipyards. Now there's Inglehart Park on one side and condos on the other."

"Do you have a bookstore?"

"Two doors beyond the city hall. It's a cast-iron storefront where Bushy's grandfather used to have his watch-the-birdie photo studio before World War I."

Qwilleran enjoyed walking and sightseeing, and as he strode down the hill he was amazed at the huge houses, masterpieces of architectural gingerbread, their details accentuated with two or even three colors of paint. They looked festive compared to the stolid stone mansions of Pickax! He found the store with the cast-iron front and bought a book on horsemanship. In the basement there were used books, but *City of Brotherly Crime* was not among them. At an antique shop he found a collection of printshop mementos and bought a small engraving of a whale.

Many of the stores capitalized on the horseyness of Lockmaster. Equus was a men's store. The Tacky Tack Shop displayed gaudy sweatshirts, T-shirts, and posters with a steeplechase theme. In the Foxtrottery everything from paper napkins to fireplace andirons had a horse or fox motif, but nothing appealed to Qwilleran. And then he spotted the public library!

It was obviously built from the same set of Greek temple blueprints that produced the Pickax library—with the same classical columns, the same seven steps, the same pair of ornamental lampposts. He entered, expecting a Shakespeare quotation on a chalkboard in the vestibule, but there was only a bulletin board announcing new video releases. He asked for the chief librarian whom he knew only as Polly's friend, Shirley.

"Mrs. Corcoran is in her office on the mezzanine," said the clerk.

The stairway was the same design as in Pickax; the glass-enclosed office occupied the same location; and the woman sitting behind the desk could have been Polly's sister. She had the graying hair, pleasant face, conservative suit, and size sixteen figure.

He introduced himself. "Mrs. Corcoran, I'm Bootsie's godfather."

"Oh, you must be Jim Qwilleran," she cried. "Polly has talked about you so much. Do sit down. How is Bootsie?"

Qwilleran pulled up a chair, characteristically of varnished oak and hard-seated.

"He's a handsome cat with an insatiable appetite. In another few years, I estimate, he'll be the size of a small pony."

"His mother and siblings are the same way, and yet they

never put on weight. I wish I knew their secret. Are you down for the 'chase?"

"Yes, it's my first venture. I'm staying with the Bushlands."

"That should be pleasant. Bushy was the official photographer at my son's wedding. You should have come down with Polly. Everyone had a wonderful time. I've just received the album of wedding pictures. Would you like to see them?"

"Yes, I would," he said with convincing sincerity, although wedding pictures were second only to weddings on his list of things to avoid.

Mrs. Corcoran opened the album to a portrait of the happy couple at the altar, after the vows. "These are the kids, Donald and Heidi. Doesn't he look handsome? He's just out of law school and he has a position with Summers, Bent & Frickle. Heidi is a lovely girl, a dietician. Her father is a stockbroker and her mother is a psychiatrist. They go to our church. . . . And here they are with both sets of proud parents . . . And here are the attendants. The maid of honor caught the bouquet . . ."

Qwilleran murmured appropriate remarks as he politely viewed the candid shots of wedding guests. "Here's someone I know," he said, pointing to a man with ashen hair. "He's a reporter at the *Moose County Something.*"

"Yes. Dave Landrum. One of Donald's golfing friends," she said.

And then Qwilleran caught a glimpse of Polly. She was wearing an electric blue dress he had never seen before, and she was dancing with a man who wore a red beard. She was looking entirely too happy. She had probably been imbibing champagne instead of her usual thimbleful of sherry. As the pages of the album turned, he watched with more interest. There she was again! This time she was sitting at a table with the same bearded man and having an animated conversation. He was wearing a green plaid sports coat that seemed inappropriate at a wedding reception.

"Who is the fellow with the beard?" Qwilleran asked casually, adding untruthfully, "He looks familiar."

"Oh, he's one of Donald's horsey friends," the librarian said. "I can't remember them all. Perhaps you noticed the beautiful horse farms on your way down here."

"Did the wedding festivities continue at the Palomino Paddock Sunday noon?" Qwilleran asked innocently.

"Heavens, no! We were all exhausted. The kids left on their honeymoon at nine o'clock, and the rest of us carried on like blithering fools until the bar closed. I'm glad I have no more offspring to marry off!"

Qwilleran said, "As a quiet change of pace perhaps you and Mr. Corcoran would drive up to Pickax and have dinner with Polly and me—some weekend when the autumn color is at its height."

"We'd be delighted! Polly has told us about your apple barn, and I'd love to see how my little Bootsie has grown. Do you think he'll remember me?"

Qwilleran walked back up the hill without noticing the architectural splendors of Main Street. He was thinking about the man with the red beard and plaid coat. Had he also taken Polly to Sunday brunch at the Paddock? Was he the mysterious Monday morning caller who phoned her office and gave her a guilty thrill? It was not that Qwilleran felt any jealousy; he was merely curious. Polly had conservative tastes, and here was the type she would keep at arm's length: bearded, flashily dressed, and . . . *horsey!*

Arriving at the Bushland house he met the photographer coming out of his darkroom.

"What d'you think of our town?" Bushy asked.

"Looks like a thriving community."

"It's extra busy today—everybody getting ready for the 'chase."

"How much time do I have to clean up? I stopped at Cuttlebrink's on the way down, and I feel as if the dust of ages has settled on my person."

"I know what you mean. No hurry. People aren't coming till six, and you don't have to dress up. We've asked Kip and Moira MacDiarmid—he's editor of the *Logger*—and Vicki invited Fiona Stucker, the one who went up to Pickax to act in your play."

Qwilleran's moustache bristled with interest. "She did an excellent job," he said, "and I'll look forward to telling her so."

As he walked up the wide staircase to the second floor, he wondered what surprises the Siamese had devised for him. He was sure of one thing: They would have found their blue cushion on the chaise and would be taking their ease like visiting royalty.

That proved to be not quite true. They had come out of hiding, and their attitude was regal and aloof, but they were lounging in the middle of the canopy bed. It was remarkable how they always took possession of the best chair, the softest cushion, the warmest lap, and the exact center of a bed. Lori Bamba had told him that a person or object has an aura or field of energy, some more and some less. A cat, detecting the difference, moves in to take advantage of the vibrations. Lori had an explanation for everything.

As Qwilleran walked to the closet, stripping off his sweater, he stepped on something small and hard. Not completely hard. In fact, slightly squashy. He hesitated to look down, fearing what might be under his foot—a reaction based on past experience. Much to his relief it proved to be a jelly bean—a red one. There were fang marks in it. He should have known better than to leave the candy dish uncovered. Koko liked to sink his fangs in anything gummy or chewy. Checking the candy dish Qwilleran found that all the red jelly beans had been eliminated, and he found them scattered about the floor, camouflaged by the red Orientals. Something was at work in Koko's mind, although his intention was not clear. The Siamese watched from the bed as the man crawled about the room on his hands and knees. They watched the performance as if it were a freak show.

"You're the freaks in this family!" he scolded them. "I should have left you at home."

After hiding the candy in the top drawer of the highboy, he showered and dressed and spent some time with his new book on horsemanship. Always thirsty for knowledge on any subject, he learned for the first time in his life the location of a horse's withers. He discovered that a horse has no collarbone, and a "stud" is an establishment where horses are bred. He looked at pictures of the Arabian, the Morgan, the Andalusian, the Pinto, and his favorite, the Clydesdale. Finally, at six o'clock he opened a can of crabmeat for the Siamese and walked downstairs to the foyer that was ablaze with jewel-toned sunlight pouring through stained-glass windows.

The front parlor with its marble fireplace and sumptuous Victorian furnishings was stiffly formal. Bushy used it as a studio for posing brides and family groups in quaint settings. Now the photographer was in the back parlor preparing to mix drinks, and Vicki was in the adjoining dining room, putting finishing touches on the table.

"I'd like to ask one question," Qwilleran asked. "Why did the founding fathers build such large houses?"

"For one thing," Bushy said, "lumber was plentiful and labor was cheap."

"And they had lots of kids," Vicki added. "Usually there was at least one unmarried sister or widowed aunt or destitute cousin living with them. Also, when guests came for a visit, they stayed at least a month, because it took a week to get here by stagecoach and sailing ship. There were plenty of servants in those days."

"How are the cats doing?" Bushy asked.

"They've commandeered the bed, and I may have to spend the night on the window seat."

Vicki said, "Grummy is looking forward so much to meeting you, Qwill. She's a sweet old lady, just turned eighty-eight. When my parents retired to Arizona for Dad's health, Grummy deeded this house to Bushy and me, with no strings attached."

"How do you take care of such a big place?"

"I have part-time help. Once upon a time they had a housekeeper, cook, two maids, houseman, gardener, and a driver to take care of the horses and drive the family to church in the carriage."

"They didn't have any riding mowers or leaf-vacuums in those days," Bushy put in.

"And no microwaves or food processors," Vicki added. "Would you like to bring the cats down now, Qwill?"

"I think they should make their formal debut tomorrow morning," he said, "when there are no strangers around. You remember their behavior the last time we were here. I don't want to be embarrassed again."

"Whatever you think best. By the way, Grummy won't join us for cocktails. She'll come down for dinner at seven and won't stay long. She tires easily. We installed an elevator for her—velvet walls and a needlepoint bench—tiny, but she loves it."

Bushy interrupted. "Vicki, did I tell you that Fiona called?"

"No. What's happened *this time?*" she said with exasperation.

"She and Steve will be a little late. He got tied up at the track."

"Well, I'm serving exactly at seven, regardless. We can't keep Grummy waiting. It seems to me that Steve is always getting tied up. He's probably sleeping one off."

"Give him a break!" her husband said. "All kinds of emergencies come up before a race."

At that point the doorbell rang, and the editor and his wife arrived. They were introduced as Kip and Moira MacDiarmid.

"Spelled M-a-c-capital D-i-a-r-m-i-d," said Moira.

"I know how to spell a good Scottish name like that. My mother was a Mackintosh. The question is: Do you know how to spell Qwilleran?"

"With a *QW!*" they said in unison.

"We always read you in the *Something,*" the editor explained. "Don't tell your publisher I said so, but your column's the best thing in the whole paper! I wish you were writing for us."

"Make me an offer," Qwilleran said genially.

"I'm sure we couldn't afford you."

"Aren't you the collector of old typefaces? I picked up a few items at the Goodwinter sale this spring."

"So did I. Do you go in for book type or jobbing faces?"

"Mostly I'm interested in small mounted cuts of animals that will fit into a typecase, but I have a modest assortment of fat-face caps, like Ultra Bodoni. What's your specialty?"

"Book faces. I just acquired some 1923 Erasmus, the

most beautiful typeface ever designed. I'd like to show you my collection some day."

"Be happy to see it."

Moira said to Qwilleran, "Bushy tells us you've converted a barn."

"Yes, an octagonal apple barn, more than a hundred years old. The orchard is defunct, but the barn is in good shape."

"We ran a couple of pieces on the Orchard Incident," said Kip. "What's happening to the investigation? We have a morbid interest in the victim, you know. All the time VanBrook was principal here he was a thorn in everyone's side."

"That's a delicate way of putting it," said Moira with a smirk.

Kip explained, "My wife was president of the PTA during his reign of terror. Actually, though, he did great things for the school system. He was some kind of genius, but an odd duck."

Qwilleran agreed. "I'd like to write a biography of that guy, if I could unearth some of his secrets. The Mystery Man of Moose County, I'd call it."

"If you do, come down here and we'll tell you some tales that will make your blood boil."

At that moment the doorbell rang, and the couple who entered gave Qwilleran a mild shock. First to walk into the foyer was Fiona Stucker, who had played the role of Queen Katharine with such regal poise and forceful emotion. She was small; she was mousy; she extended a limp hand and smiled shyly. She had large eyes, but they were filled with anxiety. He remembered her eyes; with stage makeup they had been her most compelling feature.

Behind her was a man introduced as Steve O'Hare. Qwilleran took one look at him and thought, It's Redbeard! And he's still wearing the green plaid coat! So this was the "horsey friend" who had attached himself to Polly at the wedding festivities!

"Glad to meetcha," said the man with a hearty hand-grip.

It was too hearty, Qwilleran thought. He disliked him on sight. Nevertheless he said politely, "I hear you're involved in the 'chase tomorrow. What's your responsibility?"

"I'm just a stable bum," Redbeard replied with a grin.

"On the contrary," Bushy said, "Steve's a very good trainer."

Fiona piped up in her small voice, "He trained the horse Robbie's riding tomorrow. Robbie's my son."

"I understand he's riding Son of Cardinal," Qwilleran said, glad that he'd done his homework. "Does he have a chance to win?"

"Absolutely!" said the trainer, and he turned away to sneeze.

Someone said, "If you sneeze on it, it's true."

Turning to Fiona Qwilleran said, "Let me compliment you, Ms. Stucker, on your dynamic performance in *Henry VIII*."

"Ummm . . . thank you," she said, somewhat flustered. "I guess you saw the play."

"I saw it twice, and I was greatly impressed by your voice quality and the depth of your emotion, especially in your scene with Cardinal Wolsey . . . Did you see the play, Steve?"

"Naw, I'm not much for that kind of entertainment."

"Did your son see it?" Qwilleran asked Fiona.

"Ummm . . . No, he was working. He . . . uh . . . works with Steve. At the stables, you know. Amberton Farm."

"We have twenty horses," the trainer said. "We're up at five in the morning—feeding, watering, grooming, mucking, and exercising the nags. And that's seven days a week! Plus training sessions. No end to it! But I wouldn't want to do anything else." He sneezed again, and Fiona handed him a tissue.

Bushy announced, "Last call for a quickie from the bar. We're calling Grummy in a few minutes."

"Shall I go up and get her?" Moira volunteered.

"Better not. She likes to feel independent, and she likes to make a grand entrance."

"She descends in her electronic chariot like a goddess from Olympus," said the editor.

"That's right!" said Vicki as she moved toward the intercom. "Some old folks resent new technology, but not Grummy! . . . Fiona, would you help me a bit in the kitchen?" She spoke to the box on the wall. "Grummy, dear, dinner is served."

The party swallowed their drinks quickly and sauntered to the far end of the foyer where the elevator was located. A light on the touch plate indicated that the car was in operation. It descended slowly. The door opened sedately. Qwilleran found himself holding his breath in anticipation.

Nine

Qwilleran stood in the foyer of the grand old Inglehart house and waited—along with the other guests—for the elevator door to open. Never having known his own grandparents, he felt drawn to anyone over seventy-five years of age, and in this northern region, where many lived to be a hundred, he had met many memorable oldsters.

The elevator door opened sedately, and a distinguished-looking, white-haired woman in a floor-length hostess gown of wine red velvet stepped from the car, leaning on two ivory-headed canes yellow with age. She moved slowly, but her posture was erect. Seeing the waiting audience, she inclined her head graciously toward each one until she caught sight of Qwilleran in the background.

"And this is Mr. Qwilleran!" she exclaimed in a cultivated voice that had become tremulous with the years. She had a handsome face for a woman nearing ninety, like fine-lined porcelain, with kind, blue eyes and thin lips accustomed to smiling. No eyeglasses, Qwilleran noted. He guessed that Grummy would have the latest in contact lenses.

As he stepped forward she tucked one cane under the

other arm in order to extend a hand. "My pleasure, Mrs. Inglehart," he murmured, bowing gallantly over her trembling hand. It was a courtly gesture he reserved for women of a certain age.

"I'm thrilled to meet you at last," she said. "I used to read your column when you were writing for newspapers Down Below. But now you are living among us! How fortunate we are! I not only admire your writing talent, Mr. Qwilleran, and what you have to say, but . . ." she added with a coy smile, "I adore your moustache!"

Fleetingly he wondered if the Inglehart library might contain a copy of *City of Brotherly Crime.*

"Shall we go into dinner, Grummy?" asked Bushy, offering his arm. The others followed them into the dining room and waited until the elderly woman was seated on her granddaughter's left. Qwilleran was motioned to sit opposite, next to Moira, and the party waited for Grummy to raise her soup spoon.

Glancing brightly around the table she said, "For what we are about to receive, we give thanks."

Redbeard, sitting at the other end of the table, next to the host, sneezed loudly.

Fiona said apologetically, "He's allergic."

"To everything," said the man who was blowing his nose. "Including horses."

"Is that true?" Kip asked.

"Absolutely."

"You should give up horses and go in for newspapering. You're doing a good job with *Stablechat.*"

"Nothing to it," said Steve. "I've got a bunch of kids digging up the stuff, and Mrs. Amberton puts it together."

"What's your circulation now?"

"Almost a thousand."

"Another ten thousand," said the editor of the *Logger,* "and we'll start to worry."

Grummy leaned toward Qwilleran. "Victoria tells me you've brought your cats. I do hope they don't kill birds."

"Have no fear," he replied. "They're indoor cats, and their interest in birds is purely academic. Koko has a friend who's a cardinal, and they stare at each other through the window glass and communicate telepathically."

Steve said, "Take the glass away and it'd be a different story. Cats are cats."

Vicki said quickly, "Grummy has a feeding station outside her window in the tower, and she records the migration of different species in a notebook . . . Don't forget your soup, Grummy dear." With her spoon poised above the soup plate Mrs. Inglehart was gazing at Qwilleran like a starstruck young girl.

Moira said, "One year I decided to feed the birds, but all I attracted were starlings. They came from three counties to my backyard—millions of noisy, messy invaders. That was the end of birding for me!"

"My problem," Qwilleran said, "is blackbirds. When I bike on country roads, they rise up out of the ditch in a great cloud and dive-bomb me and my bike, screaming *chuck chuck chuck.*"

"That's in nesting season," said Grummy. "They're protecting their young."

"Whatever their motive, they're very unfriendly, and when I talk back to them, they're really burned up."

"What do you say to an unfriendly blackbird?" Moira asked.

"*Chuck chuck chuck.* But the biggest mystery is the behavior of seagulls when a farmer plows a field. Within five minutes after he starts, a hundred seagulls flock in from the lake, thirty miles away, and circle the field like vultures."

Kip said, "Seagulls have an intelligence network that puts the CIA to shame."

Vicki removed the soup plates, and Fiona helped serve the main course: pasta shells (easy for Grummy to fork with her trembling hand) with a sauce of finely chopped vegetables in meat juices, plus meatballs for the guests.

As the Parmesan cheese was being passed, Grummy returned to her favorite subject. "When I came to live in this house as a bride, I instructed the gardener to plant everything that would attract birds, and I've kept a birdbook for seventy years. Teddy Roosevelt had a birdbook, and he recorded the birds he saw on the White House lawn."

Occasionally there would be a sneeze from Redbeard; Bushy would ask if anyone wanted more wine; Fiona would cast surreptitious stares in Qwilleran's direction; Kip would mention the forthcoming millage vote. But always Grummy would bring the conversation back to birds.

The editor said, "One of the fillers that we ran recently stated that a hummingbird has a pulse rate of 615 beats a minute. I hope it wasn't a typo."

"Not at all," said the old lady. "The hummingbird is one of nature's small miracles."

Qwilleran confessed, "I can't tell one bird from another. They don't stand still long enough for me to look in the field guide."

"When I had my bird garden," Grummy said, "I could entice wild birds to eat out of my hand, and once I raised a family of baby robins after their mother was killed by a boy with a gun."

Steve sneezed again.

"Grummy dear," said Vicki quietly and gently, "don't forget to eat your pasta."

Mrs. Inglehart was having a wonderful time, but when the salad was served she seemed tired and asked to be excused. Bushy escorted her to the elevator.

After the apple pie and coffee, Steve said he had to get back to the farm and be up at five in the morning, and Fiona said she had to go home and make sure Robbie went to bed early on the eve of his first race. As she left she said to Qwilleran in her small voice, "I . . . uh . . . wanted to talk to you . . . about Mr. VanBrook, you know, but I didn't . . . uh . . . get a chance."

"Did you know him well?"

She nodded. "Maybe . . . tomorrow? Vicki invited me to the 'chase."

"We'll have a talk then," Qwilleran promised. "It's been a pleasure meeting you."

She left, giving him a backward glance. He was watching her go. Despite her self-effacing manner, there was something fascinating about the woman—her large and sorrowful eyes, perfect eyes for Queen Katharine.

Then the MacDiarmids said good night because they had hired a baby-sitter who wanted to be home by ten o'clock. "See you at the 'chase," they said, explaining to Qwilleran, "Our parking slot is next to Bushy's, so we do a little friendly betting."

The host and hostess kicked off their shoes and poured another drink. Qwilleran accepted his third cup of coffee. "Pleasant evening," he said. "Grummy is a treasure, and I liked Kip and Moira. Fiona came as a surprise; she was so different on stage. This fellow Steve . . . what's their relationship?"

The Bushlands exchanged glances, and Vicki spoke first. "Well, he's Robin's mentor in horsemanship, and Fiona's very ambitious for her son to succeed at *something*. He dropped out of high school, and his only interest is horses."

"He's not alone, I understand. What's our schedule tomorrow morning?"

"After breakfast," Vicki said, "you'll have time to take the cats up to visit Grummy. She'll be thrilled."

Her husband said, "We'll leave about eleven and pick up Fiona, and that will give us time to fight the traffic and get in place for a tailgate picnic before post time, which is two o'clock."

"Kip mentioned betting. How does that work?"

"It's more fun if you have a few bucks on a horse, so we usually have a five-dollar pool going with the MacDiarmid crowd."

"Breakfast at eight-thirty," Vicki said. "What do you like?"

"Coffee and whatever. And now I think I'll amble upstairs and see if the cats have adjusted."

"Would they like a meatball? We have some left over."

Qwilleran followed her into the kitchen. "How long have you known Fiona?" he asked.

"Ever since junior high. My family used to include her in our picnics and vacation trips because she had no decent homelife of her own. It was the old story: absent father, alcoholic mother. I liked her. She was so eager and appreciative, and she had those heart-breaking eyes!"

"That's what I remember most about her portrayal of Katharine. What kind of life has she had since schooldays?"

"Rough," Vicki said. "Her only dream was to have a home and family of her own, so she married right after high school. It was so ironic! Her husband deserted her right after Robin was born."

"How has she managed financially?"

"She does housekeeping. She helps me two days a week. With some kind of training she could do better, but she lacks confidence. If everything works out, I'd like to start a catering service with Fiona as assistant. We'd specialize in hunt breakfasts. They're all the rage in Lockmaster."

"What was her connection with VanBrook?"

Vicki shrugged mysteriously. "Better ask Fiona about that."

Qwilleran said good night to the Bushlands and started for the second floor. Halfway up the stairs he could hear exultant cries coming from the best guestroom. The Siamese knew he was approaching and bearing meatballs. They met him at the door, Koko prancing and Yum Yum snaking between his ankles. Putting the plate on the bathroom floor, he then gave the bedroom a quick inspection for evidence of mischief. Everything was in order except for shredded paper in the circular window bay, but it was only the copy of *Stablechat;* they frequently reacted to fresh ink.

After their treat, the two satisfied animals found their blue cushion on the chaise, where they washed up and settled down. Qwilleran read for a while before sinking into his own bed and reviewing his day. He had buried Dennis Hough, bought bubble pipes for the cats, discovered Polly's strange Lockmaster connection, and met a charming octagenarian. And tomorrow he might learn something about VanBrook from a woman who wanted to talk about him. He turned off the bedlamp, and in a few moments two warm bodies came stealing into the bed, nosing under the blanket, Yum Yum on his left and Koko on his right, snuggling closer and closer until he felt confined in a strait jacket.

"This is ridiculous!" he said aloud. Jumping out of bed he transferred their blue cushion to the bathroom floor, placed them on it with a firm hand, and closed the door. Immediately the yowling and shrieking began, until he feared they would disturb Grummy on the third floor and the Bushlands in the master bedroom below.

He opened the bathroom door, hopped back into bed and waited anxiously in the dark. For a while nothing happened. Then the first body landed lightly on the bed, followed by a second. He turned his back, and they snuggled down behind him. There they stayed for the night, peacefully sleeping, gradually pressing closer as he inched away. By morning he was clinging to the edge of the mattress, and the Siamese were sprawled crosswise over the whole bed.

"How did you guys sleep?" Bushy asked the next morning when the aroma of bacon lured the three of them to the kitchen.

"Fine," Qwilleran said. "Good bed! They didn't let me have much of it, but what I had was comfortable."

"How do you like your eggs?" Vicki asked.

"Over easy." He looked around the kitchen. "Do I smell coffee?"

"Help yourself, Qwill."

Nursing a cup of it he trailed after the Siamese as they explored the house, reveling in patches of tinted sunlight thrown on the carpet by the stained-glass windows. He himself checked the library, but there was no sign of *City of Brotherly Crime*.

By the time breakfast was ready, the two cats were chasing each other gleefully up and down the broad staircase. "They're making themselves right at home," he said to the photographer. "You shouldn't have any trouble getting pictures tomorrow."

"I have a couple of poses in mind," Bushy said, "but mostly I'll let them find their own way. When I took Grummy's tray upstairs this morning, she said to remind you she's expecting them after breakfast."

When the time came for the visit, Vicki called upstairs on the intercom, and Qwilleran collected the Siamese, climbing the stairs to the third floor with one under each arm. Grummy greeted them graciously, wearing a long flowered housecoat and leaning on her two elegant canes.

"Welcome to my eyrie," she said in a shaky voice. "And these are the two aristocrats I've heard about!"

They regarded her with blank stares and wriggled to escape Qwilleran's clutches. They were acting disappointingly catlike.

"I've made some blueberry leaf tea," she said to him, "and if you'll carry the tray we'll sit in the tower alcove."

The suite of rooms was furnished with heirlooms in profusion, and on every surface there were framed photographs, including one of Theodore Roosevelt, signed. Glass cabinets displayed a valuable collection of porcelain birds, causing Koko to sit up on his haunches and paw the air. One of them was a cardinal. Even Qwilleran knew a cardinal when he saw one.

As Mrs. Inglehart, veteran of thousands of formal teas, poured with graceful gestures, she said, "So this is your first steeplechase, Mr. Qwilleran! Do you know the origin of the name?"

"I'm afraid not."

She spoke in the precise, carefully worded style of one who has presided at thousands of club meetings. "In early days, horses and their riders raced through the countryside, taking fences and hedges and brooks, racing to the church steeple in the next village. In Lockmaster the sport of riding was unknown until my father-in-law introduced it. Until then there were only workhorses, pulling wagons, and tired old nags used for transportation. Then riding became fashionable. We all took lessons in equitation. I loved the hunt and the music of the hounds. I had my own hunter, of course. His name was Timothy."

"You have good posture, Mrs. Inglehart. I imagine you looked splendid in the saddle."

Yum Yum was now in Grummy's lap, being stroked. "Yes, everyone said I had a good seat and excellent balance and control. To control twelve hundred pounds of animal with one's hands, legs, voice, and body weight is a thrilling challenge . . . But I am doing all the talking. Forgive me."

"It's a pleasure to listen to someone so well-spoken. What provoked your interest in birds?"

"Well, now . . . let me think . . . After I married Mr. Inglehart, I avoided the needlework clubs and boring book clubs that young matrons were expected to join, and I started the Ladies' Tuesday Afternoon Bird Club. Oh, how the townfolk ridiculed us—for studying birds instead of shooting them! They wrote letters to the newspaper, referring to our idle minds and idle hands."

"Do you mean it was customary to shoot songbirds?"

"Yes, indeed! A young lad would come home with a string of tiny birds over his shoulder and sell them to the butcher. They were in demand for dinner parties! I'm sorry to say we still have a few sharpshooters who think of a bird as a target. Of course, it all started when the government put a bounty on birds because they were thought to destroy crops. Then scientists discovered that birds protect fields from rodents, insect pests, and even destructive weeds . . . Now, I'm afraid, the farmers rely on those spraying machines and all kinds of chemicals."

Koko could be heard chattering at the birds in the feeding station outside the east window as he stood on his hind legs with forepaws on the sill. Yum Yum was purring and kneading Grummy's lap with her paws.

"I believe she likes me," said the old lady.

"What kind of birds come to your feeder?" Qwilleran asked.

"Innumerable species! My favorites are the chickadees. They're so sociable and entertaining, and they stay all winter. Koko will have his friend all winter, too. Cardinals are non-migratory, and don't they look beautiful against the snow?"

"One wonders how birds survive in this climate."

"They wear their winter underwear—a nice coat of fat under their feathers," she explained. "Oh, I could talk forever about my bird friends, but you'll be leaving soon for the 'chase."

"I'm in no hurry," he said. "You must have a wealth of memories, Mrs. Inglehart, in addition to riding and bird watching."

"May I tell you a secret?" she asked with a conspiratorial smile. "You have honest eyes, and I know you won't tell on me. Promise you won't tell Victoria?"

"I promise," he said with the sincerity that had won confidences throughout his career in journalism.

"Well!" she began with great relish. "When everyone leaves the house, I go downstairs in my elevator—I call it my magic time capsule—and I walk from room to room, reliving my life! I sit at the head of the dining table where I used to pour tea for the Bird Club, and I imagine it laid with Madeira linen and flowers in a cut-glass bowl and silver trays of dainties—and all the ladies wearing hats! . . . Does that sound as if I've lost my senses?"

"Not at all. It sounds charming."

"Then I go into the front parlor and sit at the rosewood piano and play a few chords, and I can almost hear my husband's beautiful tenor voice singing, 'When you come to the end of a perfect day.' I can almost see the sheet music with pink roses on the cover. How happy we were! . . . I go into other rooms, too, and give the housekeeper her orders for the day and take a basket of cut flowers from the gardener . . . Sometimes—but not always—I walk into the reception hall and remember reading the telegram about my son in Korea." She turned to gaze out the window. "After that, nothing was quite the same."

"Where are you?" called a voice from the head of the stairs. "Oh, there you are!" Vicki walked toward the alcove with a covered tray.

"Not a word to Victoria," Grummy cautioned Qwilleran in a whisper.

"Grummy dear, it's time for us to leave for the 'chase, and I'm putting your lunch in the refrigerator. Just warm up the soup, and there's a muffin and a nice little cup custard."

"Thank you, Victoria," said the old lady. "Have a lovely time. I'll be with you in memory."

Vicki gave her grandmother a hug. "We'll see you after the fifth race."

"Thank you for your hospitality, Mrs. Inglehart," said Qwilleran, bowing over her trembling hand and returning her confidential wink.

"Please leave the little ones with me," she said. "I'll enjoy their company."

Vicki said to Qwilleran as they walked downstairs, "She refuses to have a sitter when we go out, but she has a hot line to the hospital. In case of emergency, she only has to press the red button."

Bushy had removed the photographic gear from the van, and they packed it with food baskets and coolers, folding chairs, and snack tables. Vicki, wearing a flamboyant creation from the Tacky Tack Shop, said, "How do you like my sweatshirt? Fiona gave it to me for my birthday."

When they picked up Fiona at her apartment over a drug store, she too was wearing a shirt stenciled in the rah-rah spirit of the steeplechase—quite unlike her drab attire of the night before. En route, she sat quietly, biting her thumbnail.

"I suppose you've attended many of these events," Qwilleran remarked.

"Ummm . . . yes . . . but I'm kind of nervous. It's Robbie's first race."

The stream of traffic heading for the race course included cars and vans packed to the roof with passengers, the younger ones boisterous with anticipation. South of town the route lay through hunting country, finally turning into a gravel road where race officials in Hunt Club blazers checked tickets and sold souvenir programs of the seventy-fifth annual Lockmaster Steeplechase Race Meeting. After one more hill and a small bridge and a clump of woods, the steeplechase course burst into view—a vast, grassy bowl, a natural stadium, its slopes overlooking the race course, which was defined by portable fencing.

Bushy backed into the parking slot designated G-12, with the tail of the van down-slope. Chairs and snack tables were set up on the downside, and he went about mixing drinks. "Bloody Mary okay for everybody?" he asked.

"You know how I want mine," Qwilleran said.

"Right. Extra hot, two stalks of celery, and no vodka."

Already the hillsides were dotted with hundreds of vehicles and swarming with thousands of fans. Race officials in pink riding coats, mounted on thoroughbreds, patrolled the grassy course, controlling the crowd that crossed over to the refreshment tents in the infield. Near G-12, there was a judges' tower overlooking the finish line. Across the field a stand of evergreens concealed the backstretch. Three ambulances and a veterinary wagon were lined up in conspicuous readiness.

An amplified voice from the judges' tower announced the Trial of Hounds, and soon the baying and trumpeting of the pack could be heard as they came down the slope from the backstretch.

Bushy said, "That sound is music if you're a fox hunter."

Or blood curdling, Qwilleran thought, if you're a fox.

Then the MacDiarmid camper pulled into G-11. The door opened, and a stream of young people poured out. Qwilleran counted three, six, eight, eleven—emerging with exuberance and rushing off to the refreshment tents. Kip and Moira and four other adults stepped out of the camper in their wake.

Qwilleran asked the editor, "How many of these kids are yours?"

"Only four, thank God. Did we miss the hounds? We got lost. They sent us to the wrong gate." He introduced his guests, all connected with the newspaper, and the women busied themselves with the food. Joining with the Bushlands they set up a tailgate spread of ham, potato salad, baked beans, coleslaw, olives, dill pickles, pumpkin tarts, and chocolate cake.

Again the voice from the tower reverberated around the hillsides, announcing the parade of carriages, and a dozen turn-outs came around the bend: plain and fancy carriages drawn by high-steppers, the drivers and passengers in period costumes.

There was still a half hour before post time. The high school band was blasting away, with drums and trumpets almost drowned out by the hubbub of the race crowd, all of whom were wildly excited. They were circulating, greeting friends, showing off their festive garb, sharing food and drink, shouting, laughing, screaming. Qwilleran observed them in amazement; they were getting a high-voltage charge from the occasion that totally escaped him.

"Would you like to stroll around?" he asked Fiona, who had been quiet and introspective.

She responded eagerly, and as they circled the rim of the bowl she ventured to say, "It's quite a sight!" Long folding tables were laid with fringed cloths, floral center-pieces, champagne buckets, and whole turkeys on silver platters.

"I'm sorry I didn't meet you during the run of the play," he said, "but you always disappeared right after the cur-tain."

"I had a long drive home," she explained, "and then . . . ummm . . . I have to keep an eye on Robbie."

"Altogether, with rehearsals and performances, you had to do a lot of driving. I hope VanBrook appreciated that."

"Oh, yes," she said. "He sent me money out of his own pocket to pay for my gas."

Qwilleran huffed silently into his moustache. "Very thoughtful of him. How did you two meet? In the the-atre?"

"Oh, no! I was . . . uh . . . working in a restaurant . . . and this man used to come in to eat all the time. He was . . . well, not very good-looking, and the other waitresses made fun of him. I liked him, though. He was, you know, *different*. Then one day he asked me—right out of no-where—if I'd like a job. He needed a live-in housekeeper. Robbie was eight then, and we both went to live with him. It was, well, like a gift from heaven!" As Fiona talked, the wonder of it overcame her shyness.

"Was he hard to get along with?" Qwilleran asked. "People in Pickax found him rather crotchety."

"Well, he was strange in some ways, but I got used to it. He kept saying I should *educate* myself, and he gave me books to read. They weren't . . . uh . . . very inter-esting."

"How did you get involved in *Henry VIII?*"

"Well, he was going to do the play—here in Lockmaster, you know—and he said he wanted me to be in it. I almost fell over! I'd never been in a play. He said he'd coach me. I was good at memorizing, and I just did everything the way he told me to."

"Would you like to be in another play?"

"Ummm . . . it would be nice, but I couldn't do it without him."

"How did he and Robin get along?" Qwilleran asked.

"He treated Robbie like a son—always getting after him to study and get better grades. After he moved to Pickax, he came down to see us once a month. He was always offering to put Robbie through college if he'd study *Japanese!* He said the future belongs to people who know Japanese." Fiona uttered a whimsical little laugh. "Robbie thought he was crazy. So did I."

The high school band stopped playing, and Qwilleran's watch told him it was almost post time. "We'll talk some more at the party tonight," he promised. They hurried back to G-12 and arrived just as Kip MacDiarmid was passing a hat.

"Five dollars, please, if you want to get in the pool," he said.

Qwilleran drew Number Five, a four-year-old chestnut gelding named Quantum Leap, according to the program. Following an announcement from the tower, the band played the national anthem. There was a fanfare of trumpets, and a mounted colorguard came around the bend in the course, followed by Hunt Club officials on horseback. The field for the first race was in the paddock, with the riders in their colorful silks. Number Five wore blue and white. Then the officials led the racers to the starting line, and before Qwilleran could focus his binoculars, they were off and taking the first hurdle.

They disappeared around the bend and behind the trees.

In a moment, they came around again. The crowd was cheering. Qwilleran couldn't even find Quantum Leap. Horses and riders disappeared again and reappeared at the far end of the course, and in a few moments it was all over. Number Five had finished sixth, and one of Kip's guests won the fifty-dollar kitty. Qwilleran felt cheated—not because of losing but because it had all happened so fast.

Vicki said, "You're supposed to cheer your horse on, Qwill. No wonder he came in sixth!"

By nature Qwilleran was not demonstrative, and the fleeting glimpses of his horse in the next three races failed to arouse him to any vocal enthusiasm. He could wax more excited about a ballgame, and even in the ballpark he seldom shouted.

Fiona won the pool in the second race, and everyone was pleased. In the third race, Qwilleran's horse went down on the fourth hurdle, according to an announcement from the tower, and immediately the veterinary wagon and one of the ambulances started for the back-stretch.

One of the MacDiarmid youngsters soon came racing back to the camper. "Hey, Dad, they had to shoot the horse!" he shouted.

"How about the rider?"

"I dunno. They took him in the ambulance. Can you let me have five bucks against my allowance?"

"You'll have to clear it with your mother."

There were only five entries in the last race, in which amateur riders were acceptable, and Kip as official book-maker suggested going partners on the bets.

Fiona said, "I can't bet. I'm rooting for Robbie."

"So am I," said Qwilleran.

"We will, too," said the Bushlands.

The pool was called off, and the Bushland and Mac-Diarmid crowd swarmed down the hill to the infield fence, the better to cheer for Son of Cardinal. As the horses were led from the paddock, Robin Stucker looked pathetically young and thin in his red and gold silks.

"Oh, God! Oh, God! Let him win!" Fiona was saying softly.

They were off! And for the first time Qwilleran felt moved to cheer. They took the first hurdle and thundered up the slope, disappearing behind the distant trees. Before they came into view again, there was a shout of alarm from the spectators on the backstretch.

"Oh, no!" Fiona whimpered. "Oh, no! Somebody's down!"

The emergency vehicles rushed to the scene, and a crackling announcement came from the tower: "Number Four down on the third hurdle!"

Qwilleran's group groaned with relief. Robin was Number Three.

As the four horses finished the first lap, Robin's rooters were in full voice, cheering him over the next hurdle and up the slope to the hidden backstretch. When the field came into view again, Son of Cardinal was running a close second.

Other fans were yelling, "Go, Spunky!" or, "Go Midnight!" But the crew from G-12 and G-11 was howling, "Go, Robbie! . . . Ride 'im, Rob! . . . Keep it up! You're gaining!" Son of Cardinal took the hurdle smoothly and pelted up the slope. "Attaboy, Rob! Three to go!" There were moments of suspense as the horses covered the backstretch. "Here they come! He's ahead! . . . Go, Robbie! . . . He's in! He's in! . . . A winner!"

Fiona burst into tears. Vicki hugged her, and the others clustered around with congratulations.

"Let's have a drink to celebrate!" Bushy announced. "And it'll give the traffic time to thin out."

"If you don't mind," Fiona said, "I'll just walk over to the stables to see Robbie. Steve can drive me back to town."

"Okay," Vicki said, "but be all dressed and ready to go at seven-thirty. We'll pick you up."

The MacDiarmids collected their horde of youngsters and said goodbye. "When are you coming down again, Qwill?" asked Kip. "I'd like to show you my type collection."

On the way home in the van Qwilleran asked, "Does Robin's win have any importance other than the $5,000 purse?"

"It should increase the value of the horse and give Robin a boost up the ladder," Bushy said. "Also it should sweeten the deal for the Ambertons when they sell the farm."

"Are they selling? Why are they selling?"

"The way I hear it, Amberton wants to move to a warmer climate. He's pushing sixty and has arthritis pretty bad. His wife doesn't want to sell. She's the one who edits the *Stablechat* newsletter."

"Lisa is quite a bit younger than her husband," Vicki put in, "and she's interested in Steve O'Hare as well as the newsletter."

"That's unfounded gossip, Vicki," her husband reproved her.

"Steve is a womanizer," she explained to Qwilleran. "I hate that word, but that's what he is."

When they reached the turreted mansion on Main Street, Qwilleran could hear Koko howling.

Bushy said, "I hear the welcoming committee."

Qwilleran pounded his moustache with a fist. "That's not Koko's usual cry! Something's wrong!"

The three of them jumped out of the van, Bushy and Qwilleran dashing up the steps and into the foyer, with Vicki close behind. Koko was in the foyer, howling in that frenzied tone that ended in a falsetto shriek. Yum Yum was not in sight.

Bushy started up the stairs three at a time. Vicki ran to the intercom. "Grummy!" she shouted. "Are you all right? We're coming up!" Then she, too, bolted up the stairs.

Koko bounded to the elevator at the rear of the foyer, and Qwilleran followed. Touching the signal panel, he could hear a mechanical door closing. Then the car started to descend, activating a red light on the panel. Koko was quiet now, watching the elevator door.

The Bushlands had reached the third floor, and their voices echoed down the open stairwell. "She's not here!" Vicki screamed in panic.

Slowly the car descended, and slowly the door opened on the main floor. There they were—both of them: Grummy slumped on the needlepoint bench, and Yum Yum crouched at her feet, looking worried.

Ten

Vicki was hysterical. Bushy was yelling into two phones at once. Qwilleran quietly picked up both cats and carried them upstairs. From the window he could see the paramedics arriving, then the doctor's car, and finally the black wagon from the funeral home. When all was quiet, he went downstairs.

"Is there anything I can do?" he asked.

Vicki was walking back and forth and moaning. "Poor Grummy! The excitement was too much for her."

"She lived a long life, enjoying it to the very end," Qwilleran said, "and she went quickly. That's a blessing."

"Why was she on the elevator? Upstairs she could have pressed the emergency button. They might have saved her. She had no need to come downstairs."

Qwilleran knew the answer, but he kept her secret. He suspected she had already been downstairs, reliving her life, and was on her way up again. The memory of the telegram from the war department may have triggered the attack.

Bushy said, "You'll have to go to the club without us, Qwill. You can take the tickets and pick up Fiona."

"No . . . no!" Qwilleran protested. "Not under the circumstances. I'd better pack up and drive back to Pickax. You'll be busy for the next few days."

"The funeral will probably be Tuesday."

Vicki said to her husband, "Would you call Fiona and break the news? I can't talk to anyone about it—yet. Ask her if she wants to use the tickets."

Qwilleran went upstairs and packed the dinner jacket he had never worn and the blue cushion the cats had not used. Then he said a somber farewell to his stunned and saddened hosts. "We'll talk about this another time," he said, "after the shock has worn off. She was a grand and glorious Grummy."

Bushy said forlornly, "Bring the cats again some weekend, Qwill. We'll give it another try."

Qwilleran drove away—up the avenue of giant gingerbread houses—thinking about the last twenty-four hours. The Siamese, knowing they were on the way home, snoozed peacefully in their carrier, leaving him free to think about many things. He had explored a new city, experienced his first steeplechase, met a fellow journalist, witnessed the swansong of a gallant old lady, and discovered the bearded man who had evidently captivated Polly. He stroked his moustache in wonderment as he drove. She had always disliked beards and avoided anyone from the sporting world. It also puzzled him how she had managed to buy that bright blue dress without his knowledge; she usually consulted him on the rare occasions when she went shopping for something to wear.

Yet, the most amazing discovery of the weekend was the diffident little woman who had been transformed into the regal Katharine on stage. VanBrook had endowed her with a completely new persona for the duration of the play. She moved like a queen; she projected her voice; she actually looked taller. Offstage she reverted to nervous mannerisms, anxious glances, and shy conversation, but for a few hours she had been VanBrook's creation. His failure to fashion Robin in his own image must have been a vexing disappointment.

There were other questions Qwilleran wanted to ask Fiona: Did VanBrook ever talk about his past Down Below or in Asia? Was his Lockmaster house furnished in the Japanese style? Did he cultivate an indoor garden, and if so, what did he grow? Why did he wear turtlenecks all the time? Was he hiding something? A scar perhaps. Did he ever unpack all his books? After four years in Pickax the majority were still in cartons. And there were other questions of a more personal nature that might be asked.

When Qwilleran reached the Moose County line, his watch said seven o'clock. The Living Barn Tour would be over. He hoped the interior would not look like a bus terminal on Sunday morning. Undoubtedly his answering machine would be jammed with messages, which he would ignore until Monday; there was no reason to explain his premature return to the world at large. His only call would be to Polly. He would tell her about the death in the family, and then he would say, "I stopped in the library and met your friend Shirley. She inquired about Bootsie and showed me the wedding pictures. There were a couple of candids of you in a blue dress that I've never seen." And then he would say, "I met some interesting individuals down there. One was a horse trainer—an amiable fellow with a red beard. His name was Steve something or other." After a moment's pause her reaction would be a nonchalant, "Oh, really?"

This entertaining scenario occupied his attention until he arrived at Trevelyan Trail. Mr. O'Dell had installed a new mailbox. The driveway was graded and graveled. In the orchard the debris left from the storm had been removed. Inside the barn there was no indication that half of Pickax had tramped through the place, but the Siamese knew that five hundred strangers had been there. With inquisitive noses they inspected every inch of the main floor.

Meanwhile, Qwilleran phoned Polly and received no answer. She might be having dinner with her widowed sister-in-law. He called back at nine o'clock and again at eleven. No answer. Most unusual! Polly never stayed out late when she was driving alone. Weary after his eventful visit to Lockmaster, he retired early but was slow in falling asleep. Polly's absence worried him.

On Sunday morning he called her number again. It was the hour when she would be feeding Bootsie and preparing poached eggs for her own breakfast. The phone rang twelve times before he hung up. This was disturbing. He began to fear she had arranged a date with Redbeard. The trainer could have left Lockmaster after the fifth race and reached Pickax in an hour. Qwilleran put on a jacket and went for a brisk walk on the pretext of picking up the Sunday papers. Detouring down Goodwinter Boulevard, he noted that Polly's car was not parked in its accustomed place; she might have driven to meet the man at some out-of-the-way rendezvous.

Polly and Qwilleran had been close friends for two years, sharing confidences, giving each other priority, consulting on every question that arose. And now she had bought a dress of strikingly different style and color without mentioning it. There was a possibility that her good friend Shirley had arranged to pair her with Redbeard at the wedding reception. There was no knowing what those two women talked about when they were together! It seemed significant that Shirley, when asked about the fellow photographed with Polly, *had forgotten his name!*

Systematically, Qwilleran reviewed the evidence: Polly canceled a dinner date at Tipsy's the day after the wedding, claiming to be tired. She was secretive about the mysterious phone call that came to her office. She had been to the hairdresser twice in less than a week—after a lifetime of washing and setting her own hair. Everything pointed to a rift in their intimate relationship. True, the last two years had seen ups and downs, tiffs and misunderstandings, but only because Polly was inclined to be jealous of the women he met in the course of everyday life.

Feeling frustrated and perhaps a trifle lonely, Qwilleran called Susan Exbridge to inquire about the barn tour.

"Darling, it was magnificent!" she cried. "Everyone loved everything!"

"I called to compliment you on leaving the place in perfect condition, but can you explain why I smelled apple pie when I walked in?"

"Did you like it? We simmered apples and cinnamon on the range all day. The Mayfus Orchard donated seven bushels of apples, and every guest was invited to take one. How was your weekend?"

"Pretty good. Were there any momentous local happenings while I was away?"

"Only an editorial in the *Something,* offering a huge reward for information on the VanBrook murder. I hope something develops to exonerate Dennis soon. You know, Qwill, I spent a lot of time and pulled a lot of strings in order to introduce that boy to Moose County's finest families—hoping to get him some jobs—and it will reflect on me if he turns out to be a murderer."

His next call was to Arch Riker at the publisher's apartment in Indian Village. "I hear you ran the editorial and offered the reward, Arch. Get any response?"

"Two, only. The city desk got a call from a crackpot who's always calling the paper. They know her voice. They call her Dear Heart. First she accused Lyle Compton. Her second choice was Larry Lanspeak. Take your pick . . . Then there was a tip that involved a member of our own staff."

"Who?" Qwilleran's mind raced through the roster of employees.

"Dave Landrum."

"Dave! He was in Lockmaster at a wedding Saturday night, I happen to know. That's why Roger took the night shift. How did they try to connect Dave with the case?"

"Well, this is a roundabout explanation. Are you ready? A year ago there was a fatal accident at the humpback bridge. Remember?"

The humpback bridge over Black Creek was notorious as an accident site. By speeding across it, young drivers could get a roller-coaster thrill, and if they traveled fast enough they were airborne for a second or two.

Qwilleran said, "As I recall, two kids were killed at the bridge, but it turned out to be a double suicide. Right?"

"That's the one—a lovers' pact. It happened September tenth—exactly one year before VanBrook got his. The person who called us seemed to think that was noteworthy."

"Do you know who called?"

"He declined to identify himself, but we gave him a code name so he can collect his fifty grand if the tip checks out."

"How was Dave supposed to be involved?"

"He's the father of one of the kids."

"I don't get it," Qwilleran said.

"Neither did I, until we checked our files. Dave's daughter was valedictorian of the June class at Pickax High, and her boyfriend was a football player. We ran a 'Died Sud-

denly' obit when it happened, and then the usual letters
came in from irate readers demanding that the humpback
bridge should be flattened out. Nothing was ever done
about the bridge, of course, but Roger, who gets around
to the coffeeshops a lot, came up with the scuttlebutt. The
young couple had hoped to attend a state college where
they could live in a coed dorm. Unfortunately, the boy's
grades were borderline, and VanBrook refused to gradu-
ate him."

"Nothing wrong with that, is there?"

"Except that it was considered an act of vengeance on
the principal's part. His regime had been opposed by Concerned Parents of Pickax for a couple of years, and the
football player's father was the most outspoken of the
whole pack. After the suicides, he went to VanBrook's
office and staged a violent scene in front of witnesses. He
may have made threats."

"What's his name? Do I know him?"

"Possibly. He has a soft-drink distributorship—Marv
Spencer."

"Are we supposed to assume that the two fathers collaborated on revenge—on the anniversary of the suicides?"

"That was the general idea. We turned the information
over to the police."

"They'll listen, but they won't buy it," Qwilleran said,
although he later recalled that Dave Landrum had been
rehearsing for the Duke of Suffolk in *Henry VIII* until
insulting treatment from the director caused him to walk
off the set in anger.

Riker asked, "How was the steeplechase?"

"I'm writing a column on it for Tuesday. You'll have it
at noon tomorrow. Frankly, it would be a better show
with more horses and fewer people."

At six o'clock Qwilleran tried once more to reach

Polly—and again at eight o'clock. Worried, he phoned her sister-in-law and expressed his fears.

"She went away for the weekend," said the woman. "She didn't say where, Mr. Q, but the invitation came up suddenly, and she asked me to feed Bootsie. She'll be home later this evening."

"Thank you," he said. "Now I can stop worrying." Truthfully, the news only exacerbated his unease.

He wrote his Tuesday column, presenting Lockmaster and the steeplechase from a Moose County point of view: factual, descriptive, politely complimentary, and not overly enthusiastic. He hand-delivered it to the city desk Monday morning and then headed for the public library.

Passing the Toodle Market (Toodle was an old family name in Moose County) he stopped in to buy powdered soap for bubble blowing—a brand recommended by Lori Bamba. He also purchased some deli turkey breast for the Siamese. That was when he noticed a sign behind the butcher counter: YES, WE HAVE RABBITS.

"How do you sell the rabbits?" he asked the butcher.

"Frozen," said the man, with the expressionless face of one who has spent too much time at ten degrees Fahrenheit.

"I'll take one," Qwilleran said, thinking he could keep it in his freezer while scouting for someone to cook it for the Siamese.

The butcher disappeared into the walk-in cold vault and returned clutching something that was almost the size and shape of a baseball bat, but red and raw.

"Is that a rabbit?" Qwilleran asked with a queazy gulp.

"That's what you asked for."

"Will it stay frozen till I get it home?"

"If you don't live south of the equator." For emphasis he raised the rabbit and slammed it down on the butcher block, neither of which suffered from the blow.

"Wrap it well, please," said Qwilleran. "I'm walking."

The package he received resembled a concealed shotgun, and he shouldered it for the walk to the library, covering the four blocks more briskly than usual. In the foyer the Shakespeare quotation on the chalkboard was *Silence is the perfect herald of joy.* He huffed into his moustache. What was that supposed to mean? Dodging the friendly clerks he headed for the stairs to the mezzanine.

There she was, in her glass-enclosed office, like a sea captain in the pilot house, wearing her usual gray suit but with a blouse that was brighter and silkier than usual.

"Good-looking shirt," he said, dropping into a chair with a loud thump; he had forgotten the hard oak seats.

"Thank you," she said. He waited for her to say where she had bought it—and why—but she merely smiled pleasantly. And cryptically, he thought. Had it been a gift from Redbeard? he wondered.

"I tried to reach you this weekend," he said. "You should train Bootsie to answer the phone."

"Perhaps I should invest in an answering machine," she said.

Polly had always resisted the idea, and he found her sudden change of attitude suspect. "Did you have a good weekend?" he asked.

"Very enjoyable. Irma Hasselrich invited me to her family's cottage near Purple Point. We went birding in the wetlands and saw hundreds of Canada geese getting ready to migrate."

Qwilleran drew a deep breath of relief. "I didn't know Irma was a birder."

"One of the best! Her lifelist puts mine to shame. Last year she sighted a Kirtland's warbler while she was traveling in Michigan. How did you enjoy the steeplechase?"

"I ate too much and lost twenty bucks, and somehow the sight of ten thousand people screaming and jumping up and down like puppets fails to stir my blood, but I explored Lockmaster, and when I found the library I went in and met your friend."

"How did you like Shirley?"

"She's as friendly as an old shoe. In fact, I suggested that she and her husband come up here and have dinner with us some weekend. She showed me the wedding pictures, including a couple of shots of you. You seemed to be having an unusually good time. I hardly recognized you in that bright blue dress."

"Do you like it? Now that my hair is turning gray, I think I should start wearing brighter colors. Did you have brunch at the Palomino Paddock?"

"No, but the Bushlands gave a dinner party, and I met the editor of the *Lockmaster Logger*—also a fellow who trains horses and publishes a newsletter called *Stablechat.*" Qwilleran was observing her reactions closely. "He said he'd met you at the wedding. Perhaps you remember a stocky man with a reddish beard and receding hair."

"I don't recall," said Polly, although he thought her cheeks became suddenly hollow. "There were so many guests—about three hundred at the reception. Would you like some tea?"

"No, thanks."

"Coffee?"

"No, thanks. In the snapshots you were dancing with this fellow. His name is Steve, as I recall."

"I think perhaps I do remember him," she admitted uncertainly.

"I also met the woman who played Katharine in *Henry VIII*. We should invite her and Steve up here some weekend. We could have drinks at the barn and then dinner at the Mill."

Polly turned pale, and he relented. He had taunted her

long enough; it pained him to see her squirm. Charitably, he asked if she might be free for dinner.

"I have a dinner meeting with the library board," she said with obvious regret. "Tomorrow night . . . perhaps?"

"There's a funeral in Lockmaster tomorrow, so I'd better not count on dinner. The editor down there has a type collection he wants me to see."

"How about Wednesday?"

"That's the judging of the Tipsy contest. But we'll get together soon." He stood up. "I've got to get this thing home before it starts leaking."

"What is it?"

"A frozen rabbit from Toodle's. For the Siamese."

"Really? Are they eating wild game now?"

"Well, they like venison and pheasant, and when they started knocking the rabbit out of my typecase, I assumed they were trying to tell me something."

"Perhaps they want you to read *Watership Down,*" she said, and it was not clear whether she was teasing or being helpful.

After two years of intimacy, during which Qwilleran had confided in Polly about Koko's uncanny modes of communication, he was still unsure whether she really believed. He sometimes suspected she humored him—going along with the gag, so to speak. Nevertheless, he took her suggestion and checked out *Watership Down* from the library's fiction room. He had read it before, and it merited being read aloud.

At the apple barn he was greeted vociferously by his housemates, who showed no interest in the package from the butcher but plenty of interest in the library book. Either they knew it was all about rabbits, or they knew it had been previously borrowed by subscribers who lived with pets. He tossed the frozen rabbit into the freezer and invited the Siamese to join him for a read in the library area. Here were deep-cushioned lounge chairs in pale taupe leather, arranged around one wall of the fireplace cube. White lacquered shelves were loaded with old books. Over the white lacquered desk hung the printer's typecase, its eighty-nine compartments half-filled with old type-blocks.

"Is everyone comfortable?" Qwilleran asked as he opened the book. His feet were on the ottoman, Yum Yum was on his lap, and Koko made a comfortable bundle at his elbow. No sooner had he read the first sentence, which consisted of only four words, than the telephone rang. Grumbling mildly, he disturbed his listeners and went to the desk to take the call.

"Hello . . . Is this . . . uh, Mr. Qwilleran?" asked a wavering voice.

"Yes."

"This is Fiona in Lockmaster—Fiona Stucker."

"Of course. I recognized your voice," he said. "I'm sorry about Saturday night, but we were all upset about Mrs. Inglehart, and it was hardly an occasion for celebration."

"Ummm . . . yes, it's too bad. She was a nice old lady."

"Are you going to the funeral tomorrow?"

"I don't think so. I have to work."

There was an awkward pause during which Qwilleran heard voices in the background. He said, "How does Robin feel about being a winner?"

"He's all excited. He's only seventeen, you know."

There was another pause, and Qwilleran filled in with the usual pleasantry. "How's the weather down there? It's a beautiful day in Pickax."

"It's nice here, too."

Employing his professional escape clause he said, "I'm sorry our conversation will have to be brief, but I have a newspaper deadline."

"Oh. I'm sorry," she said. "Steve wanted me to call you about something."

"In connection with what?"

"Ummm . . . would you like to . . . buy a horse farm?"

"A horse farm!"

"There's one for sale. He says it's a good bet."

"I'm afraid that's not my kind of venture, Fiona."

"It's the Amberton farm. Steve is stablemaster, you know, and Robbie works there."

"I know, but—"

"He gave me a list of things to tell you. Want me to read them?"

"Go ahead."

Koko was on the desk, standing on his hind legs and reaching for the typecase. Qwilleran pushed him away, at the same time listening attentively as Fiona read:

"Sixty-eight acres, one-third wooded. All pastures fenced. Eight horses, including Son of Cardinal. Stables for twenty. Twelve horses now being boarded. Restored seventy-year-old farmhouse with all improvements, worth four hundred thousand. Swimming pool. Guest house. Historic barn on property."

Somewhat awed by this recital, Qwilleran failed to notice Koko's stealthy return to the desk until a typeblock was spirited out of its niche, landing on the telephone book and bouncing to the floor. Mention of the historic barn prompted him to ask, "Is the farm a going business or just a hobby for the owners?"

"Steve says it makes money. They breed horses and train them, and board horses for people, and give riding lessons."

Wild fantasies were racing through Qwilleran's head. "Is it on the market yet? Is it listed with a broker?"

"Not yet. Mr. Amberton wants to try selling it first. Steve says he has a couple of leads."

"I'd like to speak with Amberton."

"He's in Arizona. Steve drove him to the airport yesterday, but he has all the information—Steve, I mean—if you want to talk to him."

"Is he there? Let me speak with him."

"He's . . . no, he's at the farm, but—uh—he'd be glad to come up and see you. Wednesday is his day off."

"Okay. Wednesday afternoon," Qwilleran said. "Tell him to come equipped with facts and figures."

"Ummm . . . could I come with him and bring Robbie? I'd like you to meet Robbie."

"All right. Make it about one-thirty."

Qwilleran hung up the phone slowly and thoughtfully, telling himself, This is insane! And yet . . . he had lived in Pickax for four years, and he was becoming restless. As a journalist Down Below he had lived the life of a gypsy, switching newspapers, moving from city to city, seeking challenges, accepting new assignments. His present circumstances required him to live in Moose County for five years or forfeit the Klingenschoen inheritance. He had one more year to go . . .

"What do you think about this, Koko?" he asked the cat, who was sitting nearby with his ears cocked and his tail flat out on the floor.

"Yow!" said Koko.

Absentmindedly, automatically, Qwilleran picked up the scattered typeblocks. There were now three on the floor. One was the rabbit. One was a skunk. The other was a horse's head.

Eleven

Driving south to Lockmaster for Grummy's funeral on Tuesday morning, Qwilleran crossed the county line into horse country with its hilly pastureland, picturesque fences, and well-kept stables. Horses were being exercised. Riders were practicing jumps. A large recreation vehicle was pulling away from a posh farmhouse, drawing a horse trailer. One could adapt to that kind of life, he thought: horse shows, equitation events, steeplechasing, show jumping, carriage driving.

The funeral services were held in an impressive brick church overlooking Inglehart Park on the riverbank, after which Qwilleran drove to the cemetery with the MacDiarmids.

"Grummy was the last Inglehart around here," said Kip. "The others are scattered all over the country. We seem to have a big population turnover—old families moving out, new ones moving in. The equestrian environment attracts them."

"Do you consider Lockmaster a good place to live?" Qwilleran asked.

"Are you thinking of moving down here?" the editor countered. "If so, we've got a place for you at the paper. We'll put your column on page one."

The cemetery was an old one located on a wooded hill, and Grummy was laid to rest in a large family plot dominated by an Inglehart monument befitting a founder of the town. At the instant of interment her Bird Club associates released flights of doves, and the mourners raised their heads and watched them disappear into the sky.

"I'm sorry I knew her such a short time," Qwilleran said. "She might have converted me to birding. No one else has succeeded."

On the way back to town, Kip pointed out big-name horse farms, the Riding and Hunt Club, kennels of the Lockmaster Hounds, the Foxhunters' Club, and other points of interest related to the local passion. Moira sat quietly alongside him in a pensive mood.

From the backseat Qwilleran asked, "Is a horse farm a good investment?"

"I doubt it. The average one around here is a status symbol or a private obsession, to my way of thinking," Kip said. "Do you like horses? Do you ride?"

"The horse is an animal I admire greatly. They're beautiful beasts, but I've never had any particular desire to sit on one. I might enjoy living among them, though, if I didn't have to do any of the work."

"The Ambertons are selling their farm, and they have good stock and the best of everything in facilities."

"Horse breeding is a high-risk venture, you know," Moira put in quietly.

"What do you know about their stablemaster?"

"Steve? He hasn't been here long," Kip replied, "but people say he's an excellent trainer. You saw how Son of Cardinal came through on Saturday. From what I hear, he knows the business inside out."

"Where did he come from?"

"Various places—New York State, Kentucky, Tennessee, I believe."

"Why is he working in Lockmaster?" Qwilleran asked.

The driver changed his grip on the wheel and looked out the side window before answering. "I suppose he liked the environment . . . and the opportunity to move around. The Ambertons travel around the country, eventing."

Moira spoke up sharply. "Why don't you tell the truth, Kip?" She turned to face Qwilleran. "He got into trouble Down Below, doping racehorses."

Her husband said, "I'm sure he's clean now."

The car was slowing, and she was unbuckling her seatbelt. "Maybe so," she said, "but most owners are afraid of him." She hopped out in front of the insurance agency where she worked. "Next time we see you, Qwill," she said with a wave of the hand, "let's hope it's a happier occasion."

They drove on, and Kip said, "Why don't you stick around and have dinner with us tonight?"

Suddenly Qwilleran wanted to return to Pickax. "Thanks, but I'm due home at five o'clock."

"Okay. Next time. By the way, that's a very generous reward Pickax is offering in the VanBrook case. We picked it up and ran a short piece in yesterday's paper."

"I hope it gets results," Qwilleran said absently. He was pondering Moira's statements.

"Where do you want to be dropped off?"

"My car's parked at the church . . . Moira seems to have reservations about Steve, doesn't she?"

"Well, he's not a bad guy . . . but we were all at a party at the Hunt Club on New Year's Eve—a boozy affair, you know—and Steve got out of line, rather crudely. Moira took umbrage, to put it mildly. She's still miffed. It wasn't anything serious. He was drunk. He likes his liquor, and he likes women."

Qwilleran picked up his car and stopped at a phone booth to call Polly at the Pickax library. "Correction," he said. "I can be home in time for dinner. If you're free, we could go to the Mill." She accepted, and he found himself driving back to Pickax faster than usual.

At the barn Koko greeted him with the excited chasing that meant a message on the answering machine. He checked it out and immediately put in a call to Susan Exbridge, suspecting an auspicious development in the Dennis Hough situation that had been bothering her.

"Darling! I have exciting news!" she exclaimed. "Hilary's attorney in Lockmaster called me about liquidating the estate, and he came up here today to discuss it. He's Torry Bent of Summers, Bent & Frickle, and he's the personal representative for the estate."

"Did you go through Hilary's house?"

"Yes, he had a key, which he turned over to me after he decided I had credentials and an honest face. It's a strange place, and I do mean *strange!* The upstairs rooms are filled to the ceiling with boxes of books, and one room is full of dead plants!"

"What will you do with all those books?"

"God knows! Secondhand books are an absolute *glut* on the market, but we'll open all the boxes—what a job!— and hope to find something rare and valuable. Edd Smith will be able to advise us on that."

"I'll be glad to help you open boxes," Qwilleran said with alacrity. "I'm very good at sorting books, and after tomorrow night I have nothing scheduled."

"Qwill, you're a darling! How about Thursday morning? I'll take you to lunch. I took Torry to lunch at the Mill, and he was *quite* impressed!"

"By the restaurant or the liquidator?"

"Both, if I'm tuned in to the right channel, and I might add that he's a charmer! Also, he's *divorced*—tra la!"

On this salubrious note the conversation ended, and

Qwilleran marked Thursday for Susan in his datebook—something he would avoid mentioning to the chief librarian.

When he called for Polly at her carriage house, she was wearing a vibrant pink blouse with her gray suit—her *other* gray suit, reserved for social occasions.

"That color is becoming to you," he said. "What do you call it?"

"Fuchsia. You don't think it's too intense?"

"Not at all."

It was a short drive to the Old Stone Mill on the outskirts of town, and they filled the time with comments on the weather: the highs and lows, humidity and visibility, yesterday and today. At the restaurant they were shown to Qwilleran's favorite table, and he ordered the usual dry sherry for Polly and the usual Squunk water for himself. When the drinks arrived, they both raised their glasses and said "Cheers!"

There was a lull before Polly ventured, "Whose funeral did you attend?"

"Vicki Bushland's grandmother. A splendid woman, eighty-eight years old and an enthusiastic birder. You would have liked her."

"You seem to be gravitating toward Lockmaster lately."

"It's very pleasant country down there," he said, "and there's a horse farm coming up for sale that might be an investment for the K Fund. I believe I could get interested in horses without trying too hard."

"You wouldn't live down there, would you?"

"Not right away, but it's a beautiful setup." He then gave a glowing description of the Amberton farm. "A delegation is coming up tomorrow for a conference."

"It sounds as if you're serious."

"It's tempting! I have one reservation, however. The

stablemaster is highly competent, but he has an unsavory past. Besides having a reputation as a heavy drinker and a womanizer, he was chased out of jobs Down Below for illegal use of drugs in connection with racehorses. Too bad. I believe I mentioned him before. His name is Steve O'Hare."

Polly put down her glass abruptly and turned pale.

"Do you feel all right?" he asked.

"A little dizzy, that's all. I skipped lunch—trying to lose a few pounds," she said with a pathetic smile. "The sherry—"

"We'll have the soup served right away." He signaled the waitress. "Eat a roll. I'll butter it for you. And don't worry about losing weight, Polly. I like you best just the way you are." When the chicken gumbo was served and she had revived, he went on. "Do you realize this is our first dinner together in ten days? And we've missed two weekends! That's no kind of track record for you and me."

"I know," she said ruefully. "We belong together. The last two years have been the best years of my life, dearest."

"I could say the same . . . What are we going to do about it?"

"What do you want to do about it?"

The halibut steaks arrived, with broccoli spears and squash soufflé, and the answer was deferred.

Polly said, while dealing with a small bone in the fish, "Is there . . . anything new . . . at the barn?"

"You won't recognize the orchard. It was damaged by last week's storm, but the debris has been cleared up and some of the worst trees removed. The number of prowlers has increased since the barn tour. Those who objected to paying five dollars are now trying to get a free peek. I've ordered mini-blinds, but it takes three weeks."

"Have the tapestries arrived?"

"Yes, and they've been hung. I think you'll like them. The largest hangs from the railing of the topmost cat-walk, and I only hope it's secure. It's hooked onto tack-strips, and in our household we're subject to Yum Yum's law: *If anything can be unhooked, untied, unbuckled, or unlatched, DO IT!* She started with shoelaces and advanced to desk drawers. Tapestries may be next on her list, so I'm monitoring the situation closely. Her voice is changing, too. After all, she's about five years old—a mature female. Frequently she delivers a very assertive contralto yowl that sounds suspiciously like NOW!"

"What does Koko think about all of this?" Polly asked.

"He has his own pursuits. Lately he's been chummy with a cardinal in the orchard. They commune through the window glass, and here's the astonishing thing: Last Saturday a horse named Son of Cardinal won the fifth race at the stee-plechase. Is that a coincidence or not? Suppose Koko could pick winners! He'd be a very valuable animal . . . Did I tell you I met the woman who played in *Henry VIII*? She's a retiring, insecure little creature that VanBrook reshaped in the image of Queen Katharine—a Pygmalion act that must have bolstered his ego."

Qwilleran was unusually talkative, rambling from one subject to another—evidence that he had missed Polly's company more than he realized. She, on the other hand, was unusually quiet, simply asking questions.

At one point she asked, "Did you read the letter that an eleven-year-old girl wrote to the editor of the *Something* last week?"

"I never read anything written by eleven-year-old girls," he stated in his mock-curmudgeon style.

"There were several replies in Friday's paper. I knew you were out of town, so I photocopied them for you. It's about the Tipsy problem."

"Problem? What kind of problem?"

"Read the original letter, and you'll see what I mean."

The communication from one Debbie Watts of Kennebeck had been printed with all the juvenile errors that made Qwilleran wince.

> *I am 11 years old in 5th grade. My gramma told me to rite. We have a famly ablum. It has a pitcher of my gramma when she was a girl. She worked at Tipsy's. They took a pitcher of her and Tipsy out in front. She says Tipsy had white feet. Her feet are white in the pitcher.*

"Hmmm," Qwilleran said, considering the significance of this revelation. "The portrait in the restaurant has black feet."

"Exactly! If the prize goes to a Tipsy look-alike, does that mean black feet or white feet? Now read the replies."

The first was signed by a Mrs. G. Wilson Goodwinter of West Middle Hummock. That was an old family name of distinction, and the suburb was an affluent one.

> *Little Debbie Watts is correct. My housekeeper's daughter works in a nursing home Down Below, and one of her patients is an old sailor who knew Tipsy when she lived at Gus's Timberline Bar on the waterfront. Gus was from Moose County, and during the Depression he came back here and opened a restaurant, bringing Tipsy with him and naming the establishment in her honor. The patient describes Tipsy as having white feet. He is quite definite about it.*

Qwilleran said, "This looks bad for Hixie Rice and her bright idea."

"Read on," Polly instructed him.

Next was a letter from Margaret DeRoche of Sawdust City:

> My husband's cousin was the artist who painted the portrait of Tipsy in the 1930s. He was an artist of great integrity and would never paint black feet on a subject if that were not the case. I write because he is not here to defend himself, having passed away three years ago. His name was Boyd Smithers, and he signed the canvas with his initials.

"The plot thickens," Qwilleran said. "Here's one from the Kennebeck Chamber of Commerce. I'll bet they're in favor of black feet. This is getting to be a political issue."

> For fifty years or more Tipsy with black boots has been the image we connect with the restaurant and the town of Kennebeck. Two generations of Moose County residents have raised cats with black boots and named them after Tipsy. Why rock the boat now?

Polly said, "Read the one from Samantha Campbell. She's the registrar of the Historical Society."

> In reference to the Tipsy debate I wish to note that the Historical Society archives contain a Tipsy file of clippings from the late lamented Pickax Picayune. In 1939 a brief article referred to Tipsy as being "all white with a black hat." An item in the same paper in 1948 refers to Tipsy's "black boots." I mention this to emphasize the necessity of accuracy in the public press, since newspaper accounts go into historical records. Thank you.

"And thank *you*, Ms. Campbell," Qwilleran said. "I should take Koko to the restaurant and let him give the portrait the Siamese Sniff Test. He knows right from wrong."

Polly said, "You're not taking this seriously, Qwill. Read the last one." It was written by Betty Bee Warr of Purple Point.

> My grandmother, who is in the Senior Care Facility with arthritis real bad in her hands, remembers that a man named Gus brought Tipsy to Kennebeck in the Depression and had an artist paint her picture. When Gus sold his place in the 1940s the new owners paid my grandmother, who did a little painting as a hobby, to touch up the feet with black. They said it would give the picture "more oomph." Now she realizes she did wrong to paint over it, but she needed the money.

Qwilleran said, "This is the stickiest mess since the flypaper controversy in the city council meeting, but Hixie and the chamber of commerce will have to cope with it. I'm only a judge, and I have other things on my mind."

"Is the mystery of VanBrook's murder bothering you?" Polly asked, knowing he could be tormented by unanswered questions.

"No. The mystery of his identity. Was he what he claimed to be or was he a phony? I suspect the latter. Koko knew there was something not quite genuine about him from the beginning. That cat knows a fake when he sniffs it, whether it's a hairpiece or imitation turkey."

Polly sighed. "Do you think Bootsie will ever be as smart as Koko?"

"Not with a moniker like that! It lacks dignity. Koko's name is Kao K'o Kung, as you know . . . Will you have dessert?"

"No, thank you. I'd better not."

"Coffee?"

Polly hesitated, then said sweetly, "Shall we go to my place for coffee?"

Later that evening, when they were saying good night at her carriage house, Polly mentioned casually, "This weekend may be the last chance to go birding in the wet lands. Shall we?"

"Sure," said Qwilleran, after concealing a gulp. "Or we could fly down to Chicago with the Lanspeaks for a ball game."

"That would be nice," she said.

He arrived home elated and charged with energy, but it was midnight, and his housemates wanted only their bedtime snack and lights-out. Qwilleran retired to his studio to continue reading the biography of Sir Edmund Backhouse. What a difference: The British sinologist had a winning personality and a deferential manner; Van Brook was all contempt and ego.

The next day being Wednesday, he rose early to avoid the garrulous and censorious Mrs. Fulgrove. He avoided her by writing his Friday column at the newspaper office, visiting the bookstore to chat with Edd Smith, and buying a pair of cashmere gloves for Polly at the Lanspeak store— gray to go with her gray winter coat.

While cashing a check, he met Hixie at the bank. He said, "Are you concerned about the controversy over Tipsy's feet?"

She tossed her pageboy defiantly. "No problem, Qwill. It's simply creating more publicity. We'll award two prizes—one for the popular Tipsy with black boots and one for the authentic look-alike. Don't forget, we're expecting you as our dinner guest before the judging . . . Want to have lunch?"

"Can't," he said. "I'm expecting company at the barn."

Promptly at one-thirty a van made its way up Trevelyan Trail, and the delegation from the Amberton Farm emerged: Fiona carrying a tissue box and wearing nondescript garments that flapped about her thin frame, then the red-bearded stablemaster, walking with a broad-shouldered swagger, and finally the boy, short and thin like his mother, ambling with the loose gait of his generation, his thumbs hooked in his back pockets. The two men wore dark jeans and navy blue nylon jackets with the Amberton insigne—a red cardinal—embroidered on the breast pocket.

Qwilleran greeted them at the door and invited them into the foyer. They entered slowly, swinging their heads from side to side and up and down in astonishment.

"Oh! I've never seen anything like it!" Fiona cried.

"Hey," said Steve, nudging Robbie, "how about this, kid?"

Robbie nodded, and a half-smile passed between them, which Qwilleran interpreted as: *We've got our pigeon; he's loaded; this setup cost a coupla million, easy.* Three or four years ago the thought would have annoyed him, but now he was accustomed to the imaginary dollar sign tattooed on his forehead.

Fiona said, "Mr. Qwilleran, this is—uh—my son Robbie."

"Congratulations, young man. I saw you ride on Saturday. Good show!"

The boy nodded, looking pleased.

Qwilleran ushered them into the lounge area with its luxurious oatmeal-colored seating pieces. "Won't you sit down?"

Robbie looked at the pale upholstery and then at his mother.

"It's all right," she said. "Your pants are clean. I just washed them."

Qwilleran thought, Her son's a mute! No one had ever mentioned that he couldn't speak. "Would anyone like a glass of cider?" he asked.

"Do you happen to have a beer?" Steve replied.

"Robbie and I will have cider," said Fiona. Mother and son were sitting close together on one sofa; Steve sprawled comfortably on the other and had thrown his jacket on the rug.

The Siamese were observing the strangers from the railing of the first balcony, and Steve caught sight of them. "Are those *cats*?"

"Siamese," Qwilleran said.

"Why are they staring at me?"

"They're not staring; they're just nearsighted."

The trainer jerked his thumb toward the remains of the orchard. "What happened to your trees?"

"They suffered a blight some years ago," Qwilleran explained, "and the storm last week raised havoc, so I thought the time had come to get rid of the dead wood."

"It'd make a good pasture if you wanted to board a couple of horses."

"Unfortunately there's a city ordinance: No horses, cattle, pigs, chickens, or goats within the city limits."

While they drank their refreshments, the visitors ogled the fireplace cube, the loft ladders, the catwalks and massive beams. Steve said, "I read in the *Logger* that some guy hung himself up there."

"What's the ladder for?" Robbie asked.

He can speak! Qwilleran thought. "Sort of a fire escape," he replied. "Did you bring the information about the farm, Steve?"

"Absolutely!" He fished an envelope from his jacket pocket and handed it over. "I got these figures from Amberton. He'd like to meet you and show you around when he gets back from Arizona."

"Where does the operation derive its income?"

"Breeding horses. Selling horses. Winning races. Boarding and training horses. Giving riding lessons. There's a lot of wealthy families in Lockmaster, wanting their kids to take lessons and win ribbons."

"Would you manage the operation?"

"Absolutely! That's what I do."

"Do you have a résumé?" When the stablemaster hesitated, Qwilleran added, "I must explain that I have no money of my own to invest. All business ventures are handled by the Klingenschoen Memorial Fund, and I'll have to discuss the proposition with the trustees. They'll want to know your background, where and for whom you've worked, and for how long. Also why you left each employ, and so forth."

Steve sneezed, and Fiona got up and handed him the tissue box, saying, "I could write it out for you, Steve."

He mopped his brow. "Whew! It's hot in here."

"It's his allergy," Fiona explained. "He gets hot and cold flashes."

Qwilleran turned to Robbie. "And what is your job on the farm?"

"I help Steve," said the youth, with a glance at his mother.

"He's very good with horses," she said with maternal pride. "He's going to ride some big winners when he gets older, isn't he, Steve?"

The trainer sneezed again.

"You should get shots for that allergy," Qwilleran suggested.

"That's what I told him," said Fiona.

At that moment there was a slight commotion on the balcony—some rumbling and a little yipping, after which both cats took off as if shot from a cannon: up the ramps and across the catwalks, circling up to the roof and then racing down again until they reached the first balcony. From there they swooped down like dive-bombers, Koko landing on the back of the sofa behind Steve and Yum Yum landing virtually in his lap. He flinched and Fiona squealed.

"Jeez! What's happening here?" he demanded.

"Sorry. You've just attended the seventeenth Weekly Pickax Steeplechase Race Meeting," Qwilleran said.

Koko was still on the sofa back exactly as he had come to rest: legs stiff, back arched, tail crooked like a horse-shoe. Then he sneezed: *chfff*. As sneezes go, it was only a whisper, but a fine spray of vapor was discernible in the sunlight slanting in from the triangular windows.

The trainer mopped his neck with a tissue. "Guess we'd better be getting back to the farm."

"Thanks for bringing this information," said Qwilleran, waving the sheet of paper. "If you'll send us that résumé, we'll go to work on it and hope that the trustees are interested."

"Come on, Robbie," said his mother. "Say thank you for the cider."

The three visitors stood up, and as Steve put on his jacket he noticed something on the floor. He picked it up. "What's this?" It was a small metal engraving of a horse's head, mounted on a wooden block.

"That's an old printing block," said Qwilleran. "The cats have been batting it around."

"I could use that on the front page of *Stablechat*."

"Take it. You're welcome to it."

"Oh! That's very nice of you," said Fiona.

"Don't forget your tissue box."

"Here's the latest issue of *Stablechat*," Steve said, tossing it on the coffee table. "It has all the race results from the 'chase."

Qwilleran accompanied the delegation out to their van,

making the requisite remarks about the temperature and the possibility of rain. When he returned, Yum Yum was wriggling flatly out from under the sofa, and Koko was busy tearing up the last issue of *Stablechat*. Holding it down with his forepaws, he grabbed a corner with his fangs and jerked his head. Qwilleran watched the systematic destruction, admiring the cat's efficiency. Was there something about the smell of the ink or the quality of the paper that gave him a thrill? This was the second time he had shredded the horsey newsletter.

Abruptly, Koko dropped his task. His head rose on a stretched neck and swiveled like a periscope in the direction of the entrance. The tableau lasted for only a second before he dashed to the window adjoining the door.

At the same moment, Qwilleran heard a gunshot, followed by a triumphant laugh. He made a dash for the door. The van was starting down the lane, and on the ground near the berry bushes lay a small red body.

"My God!" he gasped. "That stupid kid shot the cardinal!"

Twelve

Qwilleran dug a hole near the berry bushes and buried the lordly cardinal in a coffee can to keep marauding animals from desecrating the remains. Raccoons and roving dogs sometimes appeared from nowhere in violation of city ordinance. From a window Koko watched the interment with his ears askew, and when Qwilleran returned indoors he was yowling and pacing the floor.

"Okay, we'll go out and pay our respects to the deceased," Qwilleran said calmly, although his teeth were clenched in anger.

He harnessed both cats. Yum Yum rolled over in a leaden lump of uncooperative fur, but Koko was eager to go. As soon as he was outside the door, he walked directly to the spot on the earth where the cardinal had fallen, then sniffed the burial place. Eventually he was persuaded to explore the perimeter of the barn, and after ten minutes—when the telephone summoned them indoors—he had had enough. He toppled over and lay on his side to lick his paws.

The call was from Mildred Hanstable, one of the judges in the Tipsy contest. "You sound angry," she said after Qwilleran had barked into the mouthpiece.

"Someone shot a cardinal in my barnyard! I'm not angry; I'm mad as hell!"

"Do you know who did it?"

"Yes, and he's going to get a tongue lashing that he won't forget! What's on your mind? Is the contest called off?"

"No, you'll be sorry to hear. We're due at Tipsy's for dinner around six o'clock. I have a hair appointment this afternoon, and then I'll have some time to kill, in case you want to invite me over. I could use a fortifying drink before having dinner with my boss. Lyle is such a sourpuss!"

"It's all an act," Qwilleran reassured her. "Lyle Compton is a pussycat masquerading as an English bull."

"Anyway, I'm dying to see the barn without five hundred paying guests bumping into me. I was one of the guides, you know."

"You're invited," he said with curt hospitality.

Koko was still licking his paws, and Yum Yum was still in a simulated coma, although she revived promptly as soon as the harness was removed. Qwilleran glanced at his watch. The delegation would have had time to return to Lockmaster, unless Steve stopped on the way for a drink.

He phoned the Bushland house. "This is Qwill. How do I reach Fiona?"

"You sound upset. Is anything wrong?" Vicki asked in alarm. "She was due at your place with Steve and Robbie a couple of hours ago."

"They were here and they left, and that brat shot a bird in my barnyard—a cardinal! I want to have a few words with his mother before I light into him."

"I'm so sorry, Qwill. I'll have her call you," Vicki said. "She's due here to help me with a hunt breakfast for tomorrow."

"Do that. Not later than five o'clock."

The arrival of Mildred Hanstable was therapy for Qwilleran's bruised sensibilities. A healthy, happy, outgoing, buxom woman of his own age, she had an aura of generosity that attracted man and beast. The Siamese greeted her with exuberance, sensing there was a packet of homemade crunchies for them in her voluminous handbag.

Seating herself on a sofa, Mildred arranged the folds of the ample garment that camouflaged her avoirdupois. She had given up the battle to lose weight and now concentrated on disguising the excess. "I'm happier," she confessed to Qwilleran, "now that I've decided Nature intended me to be rotund. I'm the prototypical Earth Mother. Why fight it? . . . And, to answer the question you haven't asked: Yes, I'd like a Scotch. . . . Tell me, Qwill, how does it feel to be wallowing in space?" She waved an arm to indicate the vast interior of the barn.

"Wide open spaces are fine," he said, "but I'm used to four walls and a door. Instead of rooms I have areas: a foyer area, a library area, a dining area. You're sitting in the main lounge area. I'm going to do the honors in the bar area adjoining the snack area. It's all too vague." He served drinks and a bowl of nuts on a small pewter tray, a barn-warming gift from his designer.

"Your kitchen area is scrumptious," she said. "Are you going to learn to cook? Or are you thinking of getting married?" she asked mischievously. Mildred taught home economics in the Pickax schools and had offered to give him lessons in egg boiling.

"Neither could be further from my mind," he said as he picked up a few dark blocks scattered on the pale Moroccan rug.

"What are those things, Qwill?"

"I've started collecting antique typeblocks, and the cats

keep stealing them out of the typecase that hangs in the library area."

"Why don't you move it to an area they can't reach?"

"There's no such thing as a place Siamese can't reach. They'll swing from a chandelier if necessary." He showed her a small metal plate mounted on wood. "This is their favorite block, which I take to mean that they'd like an occasional dish of hasenpfeffer. Do you know how to cook rabbit?"

"Of course! It's just like chicken. When we were first married, Stan did a lot of rabbit hunting, and I made Belgian stew every weekend."

"Would you be good enough to cook a batch for the cats? I bought a frozen rabbit from Toodle's."

"You know I'd be happy to. And may I ask a favor? Now that you've moved out of your garage, Qwill, would you allow the hospital auxiliary to use it for a gift shop? We need a central location."

"I'll put you on the list," he said, "but the Arts Council wants it for a gallery, and the Historical Society wants it for an antique shop. Actually, I hesitate to let it go until I've spent one winter in this barn. The cost of heating and snow removal may be prohibitive."

"If you can afford to feed the Siamese lobster tail, you can afford a big heating bill," she said. As if they understood "lobster tail," Koko and Yum Yum immediately presented themselves, and Mildred went on: "The father of one of my students runs the animal shelter, and he told me that one mating pair of cats can produce twelve cats in a year and sixty-three in two years. In ten years there will be *eighty million* direct descendents!"

"Tipsy lived fifty years ago," Qwilleran said. "No wonder there are so many black-and-white cats around."

"The animal shelter is swamped with unwanted cats and

kittens. Also, hundreds of homeless cats roam the countryside—having litters, starving, freezing, and getting run over."

"What are you trying to tell me, Mildred?" He knew she was a zealous crusader for causes.

"I think the Klingenschoen Fund should underwrite a campaign for free spaying and neutering. I'll be glad to present a proposal to the trustees. Hixie Rice could organize it. We'll need publicity, programs in schools, rescue teams—" She was interrupted by the telephone.

"Excuse me," Qwilleran said. He took the call in the library area.

"Oh, Mr. Qwilleran!" cried a shaken voice on the line. "I feel terrible about the bird! Robbie didn't do it. He wanted to use Steve's gun, but I wouldn't let him. Steve likes to—uh—take pot shots at—uh—targets, you know."

"I appreciate your calling," he said stiffly. "Sorry I accused your son. I'll have plenty to say to Steve about this thoughtless act!"

When he returned to the lounge area, Mildred was struggling to get out of the deep-cushioned sofa. "I guess it's time we got on the road," she said.

"Before we leave, Mildred, I'd like your opinion on a domestic problem—in the laundry area." He led her to a partitioned alcove where racks were hung with yellow towels, yellow shirts, and yellow undershorts.

"My favorite color!" she said.

"But not mine."

"Did you leave something in a pocket when you put it in the washer? What was it? Do you know?"

"It was a sprig of green leaves with a purple flower."

"Where did you get it? And why was it in your pocket? Or am I being too nosey?"

"It's a long story," he said evasively.

She buried her nose in a towel. "It could be saffron. I used to put it in boiled rice, and it turned it a lovely color. Do you know what saffron costs today? Twelve dollars for a measly *pinch!* The stores up here don't even carry it any more."

"Why so expensive?"

"Well, it comes from the inside of a tiny flower. That's all I know. Have you tried bleach?"

They drove to Kennebeck in Qwilleran's car, and while Mildred chattered about roadside litter and the high cost of art supplies, he was pondering VanBrook's indoor garden. If the man had been raising saffron, he had a $20,000 crop in one small room. He would have to export it, of course—to gourmet centers around the country. By using lights he might grow five crops a year—a lucrative hobby for a rural principal . . . And then Qwilleran thought, Did VanBrook know of another use for saffron? Did he learn something in the Orient? Perhaps it could be smoked! In that case, the crop was worth millions! And then he wondered, as he had done earlier, What was in those hundreds of boxes—besides books?

Before he could formulate a satisfying guess, they arrived at Tipsy's restaurant. Hixie Rice greeted them and conducted them to a table, the one beneath the fraudulent black-booted Tipsy. Lyle Compton was already there, sipping a martini.

Hixie said, "I'll brief you and then leave you while I marshal the contestants in the lodge hall across the street." She produced two stacks of snapshots. "These are the finalists in both categories, a total of fifty. Run through them while you're having your drinks and choose the likeliest candidates, based on markings. Later, when you judge them live, your final selection will be based on the sweetest and funniest . . . See you shortly. The crowd is already lining up on the sidewalk, and the doors don't open for another hour." She bounced out of the dining room with the supreme confidence that was her trademark.

"I'm having another drink," Compton announced, bestowing his grouchy grimace on the other two judges.

Mildred said, "I'm not sure I approve of a duplicate prize based on a forgery. What kind of values are we presenting to our young people?"

Qwilleran said, "No one ever told me what the prize is going to be."

"Don't you read your own newspaper?" she scolded. "It's a case of catfood, fifty pounds of kitty gravel, and an all-expense weekend for two in Minneapolis."

"Let's go through this bunch of fakes first," said the superintendent, picking up the black-booted entries. He was accustomed to taking charge of a meeting. "The definitive marking, as we all know, is the so-called hat—the black patch over one ear and eye. That'll eliminate most of them."

Qwilleran said, "I see black collars, black earmuffs, black moustaches, black sunglasses, black epaulets, and black cummerbunds, but no hats."

Mildred spotted a hat with a chin-strap.

"Hang onto it. You may have a winner," said Compton.

"Are all these finalists going to be present in person?" Qwilleran asked.

"That's the idea. With fifty live cats in one room, there won't be much sweetness of expression," the superintendent predicted.

The white-footed entries were in the minority, and there

were only three with hats, as opposed to seven hatted contestants in the other category.

"Having any luck?" asked Hixie when she breezed back into the dining room.

"Here's the best we can do." Mildred spread the ten snapshots on the table.

"Good! Turn them over, and you'll see a code number on the back: W-2, B-6, B-12, and so forth. Okay? When the cats parade in front of you, each will be accompanied by a chaperon wearing the assigned code number. When you spot the ten preselected numbers, direct them to the runner-up platform. Then put your heads together and make the final decision. Take your time. Delay will add to the suspense . . . Now, is everything clear? I'll be back to get you in an hour. Enjoy your dinner. Be sure to have the bread pudding for dessert; it's super! . . . And wait till you see the enthusiastic crowd! This is the greatest thing that ever happened to Kennebeck! By the way, we have sweeter-and-funnier T-shirts for you if you care to wear them."

"Are you kidding?" Mildred asked.

The judges watched Hixie stride from the dining room. Every time the restaurant door opened, the hubbub across the street could be heard, and Compton said, "Sounds more like a riot to me!" They ordered steaks, and he turned to Qwilleran. "My wife says your barn tour was a big success."

"So I hear. I was glad to be out of town."

"It's true," said Mildred. "The visitors loved it, and they were simply *floored* by the apple tree tapestry. They objected to the zoological prints, though. Why do people have such an antipathy to bats? They're such cute little things, and they eat tons of mosquitoes."

"They're disgusting," Compton said.

"Not so!" Mildred was always ready to defend the underdog. "When I was in the second grade at Black Creek Elementary, our teacher had a bat in a cage, and we fed him bits of our lunch on the point of a pencil."

"They're filthy little monsters."

She flashed an indignant rebuttal at her boss. "We called him Boppo. He was very clean—always washing himself like a cat. I remember his bright eyes and perky ears, and he had a little pink mouth with sharp little teeth—"

"—which can start a rabies epidemic."

Mildred ignored the remark. "He'd hang upside down from his little hooks, and then he'd walk on his elbows. Such a clown! And I'm sure that both of you educated gentlemen know that a bat's wing structure is a lesson in aerodynamic design."

"I only know," Compton said with a scowl, "that there are other topics I'd rather discuss with my steak."

They talked about the steeplechase, the questionable merits of tourism, the success of *Henry VIII*, and the VanBrook case. After coffee, when Mildred excused herself briefly, the superintendent hunched his shoulders and leaned across the table toward Qwilleran.

"While she's out of hearing," he said, "I have something confidential to report. You questioned Hilary's credentials the other day, so I did a little checking on the three colleges that supposedly granted his degrees. One institution doesn't exist and never did, and the other two have no record of the guy—by either of his names."

Qwilleran said in a low voice, "There's evidence that he was deceitful in petty ways, so I'm not surprised."

"This is off the record, of course. I see no need of announcing it, now that he's gone. He did a helluva good job for us, even though he was a miserable tyrant."

"The amazing thing is that he had such a fund of erudition, or so it seemed. Did you check Equity?"

"Yes, and I drew another blank—no evidence that he'd

ever been a professional actor. But he wasn't all bad."
Compton glanced around. "Here she comes. There's more
to the story. I'll tell you later."

Mildred announced, "The crowd is fighting to get into
the lodge hall. I hope they can control them during the
judging."

At that moment Hixie arrived, flushed and breathless.
"We have more people than we expected," she said. "A
troop of Cub Scouts came just to see the show, and the
first three rows are filled with seniors from the retirement
village. Every cat has from five to a dozen supporters. We
didn't count on that. The fire department may stop people
from entering the building. All the chairs are taken, and
yet most of those outside are contestants. We can't start
until they're all in the hall, and we can't throw the first-
comers out."

"Turn on the fire hose," Compton grumbled.

"Is there anything we can do?" Mildred asked.

"Just put on your judges' badges and take your places
on the platform. I'll take you in the back door."

"Do I have to wear a badge?" Qwilleran asked. "I'd
rather be anonymous when the shooting starts."

Hixie smuggled them into the lodge hall, and their appearance on the platform was greeted by cheers and whis-
tles. They seated themselves at a long table covered with
black felt, on which was a bushel basket of catnip toys
thoughtfully provided by the promoters—one toy for each
contestant whether a winner or not.

The rows of folding chairs were already filled, and an
overflow crowd was standing in the aisles. At the rear of
the hall, members of the chamber of commerce, wearing
sweeter-and-funnier T-shirts, were trying to reason with
the horde that demanded admittance. Those carrying feline finalists were loudly vocal in their indignation. Over-
powering the official attendants, they pressed into the hall,

and soon the room was filled with squabbling families and caterwauling cats. Some were in arms and some were in carrying coops, but all were black-and-white and all were unhappy.

"Something tells me," Compton said drily, "that this whole thing is not going to work."

In an effort to restore order and explain the unexpected situation, the president of the chamber of commerce appeared on the platform. He was greeted by a round of booing and catcalls. Raising his hand and shouting into the microphone, he tried to get the attention of the noisy audience, but the public address system was useless. Nothing could be heard above the din, and the feedback added ear-shattering electronic screeches to the pandemonium. Cat chaperons were shaking their fists at the stage. Mothers shrieked that their children were being trampled. Two black-and-white cats-in-arms flew at each other and engaged in a bloody battle. At the height of the confusion, a giant black-and-white tomcat broke away from his chaperon and bounded to the platform and the basket of catnip toys. Instantly, every cat who could break loose followed the leader, leaping across the white heads of screaming seniors in the front rows, until the judges' table was alive with fighting animals and the air was thick with flying fur. The judges ducked under the table just as the police appeared on the platform with bullhorns and, mysteriously, the sprinkler system went into operation.

Under the table Compton yelled, "For God's sake, let's get out of here!" The three of them crawled backstage on hands and knees and escaped out the back door. For a moment they stood and looked at each other as they caught their breath.

Mildred was the first to speak. "I move that we go back to Tipsy's for a drink."

"I second the motion," said her boss.

"Too bad there's no TV coverage in Moose County," Qwilleran observed. "The crews would have a field day with this one. It has everything: kids, cats, old folks, even blood!"

Main Street was choked with police cars and emergency vehicles, their red and blue lights flashing, as sheriff's deputies and state police tried to control the mob. Ambulances were standing by, and fire trucks were primed for action. The only prudent way for the judges to reach the restaurant was to circle the block and enter through the kitchen door.

In the relative quiet of Tipsy's bar they collapsed into chairs. They saw no more of Hixie that evening, and as soon as it was deemed safe, they were glad to leave.

Qwilleran pulled Lyle Compton aside. "What else were you going to tell me about VanBrook? You said there was more to the story."

"It hasn't been officially announced," the superintendent said in confidential tones, "and I haven't even told the school board yet, but his attorney notified me today that VanBrook left his entire estate to the Pickax school system. I believe we've earned it, to be perfectly frank."

Qwilleran heard the news with skepticism. "What's the catch? Do you have to rename it VanBrook High School?"

"Nothing like that, although we might name the library after him. His book collection is supposed to number ninety thousand volumes."

Later that evening Qwilleran made a call to Susan Exbridge. "What time tomorrow are we unpacking books?"

"How about nine o'clock? It's a big job—and probably a dirty job. Wear old clothes," she advised.

"Would you object if I brought Koko along? He has a nose like a bloodhound when it comes to sniffing out rare books."

"Darling . . . do *whatever* makes you happy."

Qwilleran was exhilarated, the VanBrook revelation having canceled out the Tipsy fiasco. He said to the Siamese, "How would you guys like a little sport? Something new!" He produced a bubble pipe and whipped up a bowl of suds in the kitchen, watched by two bemused cats who were baffled by a bowl of anything that was inedible and unpotable.

"You stay down here," he said as he carried the equipment to the first balcony. They followed him up the ramp.

He dipped the pipe in the suds and put it to his lips, making one mistake. His pipe-smoking days had accustomed him to drawing on a pipe; bubble blowing was different. He spat it out and tried again. This time he produced one beautiful bubble—iridescent in the barn's galaxy of uplights and downlights—until it burst in his face. He tried again, gradually mastering the technique.

"Okay. Go downstairs," he commanded the cats, adding a tap on the rump. "Down! Down!" They wanted to go up! It was past their bedtime. They stayed on the balcony.

To tantalize them he blew a series of bubbles and bubble clusters and bubbles within bubbles, wafting them into space, watching them float lazily in the air currents until they spontaneously disappeared. The Siamese were unimpressed. They watched this absurd specimen of homo sapiens blowing a pipe, waving his arm, and peering over the railing. Bored, they ambled up the ramp to their loft.

"*Cats-s-s!*" Qwilleran hissed.

Thirteen

Thursday, September 22, would be one of the most memorable days in Qwilleran's four-year residency in Pickax. It started routinely enough. He fed the cats, thawed a roll for his own breakfast, and harnessed Koko for the trip to Goodwinter Boulevard. He also buckled up Yum Yum for the sake of practice, hoping she might eventually accept the idea. This time, instead of falling over, she stood in the awkward crazy-leg posture that resulted from the buckling process. Koko, on the other hand, strutted on his slender brown legs, dragging his leash, eager for action. For two minutes and seven seconds, according to Qwilleran's watch, Yum Yum remained in her unlovely pose as if cast in stone, with an air of martyrdom, until he removed the harness. Then she walked away with the exasperatingly graceful step of a female Siamese who has succeeded in making her point.

Moments later, Susan Exbridge arrived in her wagon, and Qwilleran placed Koko's carrier on the backseat. As they set out for VanBrook's house he asked, "Have you had a chance to spend any time at Hilary's place?"

"A couple of mornings," she said. "I have to keep my shop open in the afternoon, you know. But I'm getting an overview of his collection, and in the evening I check my art books. It's really fascinating!"

"Have you found anything valuable?"

"Definitely! There's a Japanese screen with horses in color and gold that the horsey set in Lockmaster will *swoon* over! And there's a magnificent cloisonné vase, two feet high, that I'd love to have myself. Then—hidden away in lacquered cabinets—are small objects like inro and net-suke and fans. It's all very exciting! Hilary had a *staggering* collection of fans."

"Fans?" Qwilleran echoed, doubting that he'd heard correctly.

"Folding fans, you know, with ivory sticks and hand-painted leaves, most of them *signed!* To research these I may have to fly to Chicago . . . Want to come along?" she added playfully.

"How about the stuff on the second floor?"

"Oh, *that junk!* I threw out a roomful of dead plants, but there were a lot of growing lights that will be salable."

It occurred to Qwilleran that she might have thrown out a $20,000 crop of whatever VanBrook was cultivating in the back room.

"I haven't touched the books," she was saying. "Most of the cartons are sealed, so I brought a craft knife for you to use and a legal pad in case you want to make notes, or lists, or whatever. I don't know how to tell you to sort them. You can decide that when you see what's there."

"I wonder if Hilary catalogued his books. There should be a catalogue."

"If there is, you'll probably find it in his study upstairs. It's really good of you, Qwill, to do this for me."

"Glad to help," he murmured.

"Yow!" came a comment from the backseat.

Koko entered the spacious high-ceilinged house in grand

style, seated regally in his carrier as if in a palanquin. He was conducted around the main floor on a leash to avoid accidental collision with a two-foot cloisonné vase. He was tugging, however, toward the staircase, a fact that Qwilleran considered significant. The cat liked books, no doubt about it. He enjoyed sniffing the spines of fine bindings, probably detecting glue made from animal hides, and occasionally he found cause to knock a pertinent title off the bookshelf. (To discourage this uncivilized practice, Qwilleran had installed a shelf in the cats' apartment, stocked with nickel-and-dime books that Koko could knock about to his heart's content, although it was characteristic of feline perversity that he ignored them.)

"Where shall we start?" Qwilleran asked as the cat pulled him up the stairs.

For answer, Koko tugged toward VanBrook's study with its four walls of bookshelves. There he prowled and sniffed and jumped effortlessly onto shelves eight feet above the floor, while Qwilleran made a superficial search for a catalogue of the 90,000 books. Ninety thousand? He found it difficult to believe. Unfortunately the desk drawers were locked and the Oriental box had been removed from the desktop, no doubt by the attorney. Either place would be the logical spot for a catalogue.

"No luck," Qwilleran said to his assistant. "Let's go next door and start unpacking." There were several large rooms on the second floor, originally bedrooms but now storerooms for book cartons. He chose to begin with the room nearest the staircase. Like the others, it contained nothing but casual stacks of corrugated cartons, formerly used for shipping canned soup, chili sauce, whiskey, and other commodities. Now, according to the adhesive labels, they contained Toynbee, Emerson, Goethe, Gide and the like, as well as classifications such as Russian Drama,

Restoration Comedy, and Cyprian History. Each sticker carried a number in addition to identification of the contents.

"There's got to be a catalogue," Qwilleran muttered, for the benefit of any listening ear.

There was no reply from Koko. The cat was surveying the irregular stacks of boxes like a mountain goat contemplating Mount Rushmore, and soon he bounded up from ledge to ledge until he reached the summit and posed haughtily on a carton of Western Thought. Meanwhile, Qwilleran closed the door and went to work with his craft knife, slitting open a box of Dickens, labeled A-74.

It was no idle choice, Dickens being a writer he admired greatly. It was no treasure trove either; the volumes were inexpensive editions. He took time, however, to look up his favorite passages: the opening paragraph of A Tale of Two Cities; the description of the coachman's coat in The Pickwick Papers; and a scene from A Christmas Carol that he knew virtually by heart. Every Christmas Eve, he remembered, his mother had read aloud the account of the Cratchits' modest Christmas dinner, beginning with that mouth-filling line: "Then up rose Mrs. Cratchit, Cratchit's wife, dressed out but poorly in a twice-turned gown, but brave in ribbons, which are cheap and make a goodly show for sixpence." A wave of nostalgia tingled his spine. The room was quiet except for an occasional murmur or grunt from Koko as he explored his private mountain, and Qwilleran read greedily from The Pickwick Papers until alerted by the unmistakable sound of claws on corrugated cardboard. The thinking man's cat was diligently scratching a box on the fifth tier, labeled "Macaulay A-106." Qwilleran immediately pulled it down, slit the flaps, and found the famous three-volume History of England, plus essays, biographies, and the questionably titled collection of poems, *Lays of Ancient Rome*. He huffed into his moustache as he realized that the Macaulay box had originally contained a shipment of canned salmon. Koko was no fool.

Nevertheless, Qwilleran had always wanted to check out a statement made by a typesetter of the old school—a claim that Macaulay used more consonants in his writing, while Dickens used more vowels. Sitting cross-legged on the floor with a pad of paper, he started counting consonants and vowels, selecting random excerpts from each author. It was a brain-numbing, eye-torturing task, and he was disappointed with the result. While racking up 390 consonants, Dickens used 250 vowels and Macaulay actually used more—a total of 258. The typesetter was either misinformed or a practical joker, but there was nothing he could do about it; the man had died two years before.

There was a tap on the door, and Susan called out to him, "Coffee's ready downstairs."

Qwilleran confined Koko to the room with the Dickens and Macaulay and joined her in the kitchen.

"Making good progress?" she inquired.

"I haven't found anything of value as yet," he replied, truthfully.

"I've found a green dragon dish documented as fourteenth century!"

He wondered: *Yes, but are the documents forged?*

"I have a feeling," she said, "that a lot of these things should go to New York for auction. They'll bring a *fortune* on the east coast."

If they're genuine, Qwilleran thought.

After coffee he returned upstairs, and as he opened the door Koko shot out of the room and made a skidding U-turn into the study where the books were on shelves instead of in boxes. Qwilleran followed, but the cat was already on one of the top shelves, looking down impudently at his pursuer.

"Get down here!" Qwilleran demanded at his sternest.

Koko rubbed his jaw against a large volume—teasing, knowing he was just beyond reach.

Qwilleran climbed on a chair and made a grab for him. With infuriating impertinence Koko slinked behind a row of books with only the tip of his brown tail giving a clue to his whereabouts.

"I'll get you, young man, if I have to strip this whole bookcase!" Shifting the chair a few feet, he started removing books from the top shelf, piling them in his left arm, until the cat was revealed, crouched mischievously in his hiding place.

"You devil!" Qwilleran clutched him with his free hand, stepped off the chair, dumped his armful of books on the desk, and deposited the cat in the other room, slamming the door as a rebuke. Then he returned to the study to replace the dislodged books, which appeared to be a collection of eighteenth-century erotica. Squelching his curiosity he lined the books up on the high shelf. That was when he noticed a volume that had been concealed behind the others, either purposely or accidentally. *Memoirs of a Merry Milkmaid* was the title tooled in gold on good cowhide. He put it under his arm and stepped off the chair. As he did so, the book rattled in a muffled way. He shook it, and it rattled again. Enjoying the excitement of discovery he returned to the Dickens-Macaulay room, closed the door, and opened the book. It was all cover and no pages!

There in the hollow volume—a secret filing place—was a small notebook, alphabetized. He turned to the letter *D* and found "Dickens A-74." Under *M* there was listed "Macaulay A-106" as well as Mencken, Melodrama, Milton, Morality Plays and others. This was the catalogue he knew must exist. Though inadequate for finding titles, it was apparently useful for VanBrook's purposes, whatever they might be. If he had anything to hide, this was not a bad system.

There were other documents and scraps of paper in the hollow book, but for the moment the catalogue was all that mattered. Entries were grouped from *A* to *F*, evidently referring to the six rooms in which boxes were stored. It was while leafing through its pages that he spotted a small red dot alongside certain items: "Latin A-92," for instance.

Koko was sitting quietly on A-106 in his sphinx pose, guarding the salmon carton. "We've got to find A-92," Qwilleran said impatiently as he began slinging boxes around. They were stacked in no particular order, and the noise of heavy boxes being shifted soon brought a tap on the door.

"Come in," he yelled without stopping his frenzied search.

"Are you onto something?" Susan asked.

"I think so . . . I found the catalogue . . . Boxes, not titles," he said between heavy breathing. "Some have a special mark . . . A red dot . . . I'm looking for A-92."

He found it at the bottom of a stack, behind two other stacks—a vodka carton filled with textbooks, grammars, ponies, a Latin-English dictionary, and the works of Cicero and Virgil.

"They're Latin books, all right," he announced with disappointment. "Nothing but books."

"Well, let's work another half hour and then go to lunch," Susan suggested.

"If you don't mind," he said, "I'll take a raincheck, since I have Koko with me and I'm not dressed for lunch at the

Mill. But if you want to pick us up again, I'll be glad to help any day you say."

He repacked A-92, shoving Koko away as the cat tried to climb into the vodka carton. Then, working fast during the next half hour, he opened other boxes that warranted a red dot. He found only books in an eclectic assortment of subjects: Nordic Mythology, Indian Authors, Chaucer, Japanese Architecture. One box contained Famous Frauds—accounts of imposters, swindlers, and other white-collar crooks. In the stacking of boxes a slight pattern emerged; the red dots were all found to the left of the door as one entered the room, concealed behind other book-boxes. Qwilleran counted the red dots in the catalogue, and there were fifty-two, distributed equally among rooms A to F.

When they pulled away from the house in Susan's wagon, Qwilleran had three books tucked under his arm. He said, "I hope no one objects if I borrow something to read. I found a couple of good titles."

"Keep them," she said. "No one will ever know or care."

Sandwiched between novels of Sir Walter Scott, which came from a red-dot carton, was *Memoirs of a Merry Milkmaid*.

When Susan dropped her passengers off at the apple barn, Koko was greeted by his mate as if he had returned from an alien planet, contaminated by radioactive gasses. Belly to the floor, Yum Yum crept toward him cautiously, caught a whiff of something evil, and skulked away with lowered head and bushy tail. Unconcerned, he walked to the kitchen area and stared pointedly at an empty plate on the floor until a piece of turkey appeared on it miraculously.

Qwilleran had dropped his three books on a table in the foyer area. After his exertions at the VanBrook house he was tremendously hungry. He thawed a carton of chili, a small pizza, and two corn muffins, and while sitting down to this lunch in the snack area he heard a loud *plop!* It was followed by another loud *plop!* He recognized the sound, that of a book falling on an uncarpeted floor. Leaving his lunch, he investigated the main floor and found two volumes of Sir Walter Scott on the earthen tiles of the foyer. Koko was pushing *Ivanhoe* around with his nose, but it was not the spine he was sniffing; he was nosing the fore-edges.

Qwilleran retrieved it—a book in flexible leather binding with gold tooling and gilt edges—published in 1909 with end papers and frontispiece in Art Nouveau style. It was a better edition than the set of Dickens but damaged by dryness. He riffled the pages—and gasped! They were interleaved with money! With ten-dollar bills! The other book, he soon discovered, was the same. The "bookmarks" in *The Bride of Lammermoor* were twenties! Both books had come from a red-dot carton. He tried a little computation: fifty-two red-dot boxes . . . approximately twenty books per carton . . . twenty or thirty bills in each box . . . And yet, considering the rate of inflation and opportunities for investment, who would hide this amount of money in the house? Unless . . .

Hurrying to the telephone he called Exbridge & Cobb Antiques. "Susan," he said, "I've discovered something remarkable about the red dots, and I think you should get the attorney up here in a hurry before we open any more cartons . . . No, I can't tell you on the phone . . . Yes, I'm willing to meet with him—any time."

Qwilleran had forgotten his chili, and he knew the pizza would be cold, but they could be reheated. There was little left to reheat, however. The cheese and pepperoni had disappeared, and the chili was reduced to beans, while two cats washed up assiduously. No matter; food was no longer on Qwilleran's mind. He carried the two volumes of Scott and *Memoirs of a Merry Milkmaid* to his studio, followed by two well-fed Siamese.

There were other personal papers in the hollow book, in addition to the catalogue: unidentified phone numbers on scraps of paper, legal documents in Summers, Bent & Frickle envelopes, columns of figures in five digits or more, cryptic memos that the late principal had written to himself, onion-skin copies of old business agreements signed "William Brooks." Little of it seeped into Qwilleran's comprehension, but Koko, who was sitting on the desk watching every move, occasionally extended a tentative paw. Yum Yum was on her hindlegs searching the wastebasket for crumpled paper, which had an irresistible attraction for her. She searched, however, in vain. Qwilleran had learned never to crumple discarded paper if he expected it to stay in the round file for more than three minutes.

Among the items that tempted Koko's paw was an envelope labeled "Copies." The originals, according to the notation, were in the files of Summers, Bent & Frickle. One of them, titled "Last Will and Testament of William Smurple," was dated recently, September 8, and it bequeathed the principal's entire estate to the Pickax School District, exactly as Lyle Compton had confided to Qwilleran.

The other document caused a tingling in Qwilleran's upper lip that made him reach for the phone. He asked directory assistance for a number in Lockmaster, and when he called it, a woman's musical voice said, "Amberton Farm."

"This is Jim Qwilleran, calling from Pickax," he said. Soothed by her pleasant voice he spoke less brusquely than he had intended. "Is this the right number for Steve O'Hare?"

"No, Mr. Qwilleran, this is the farmhouse. His office in the stables has its own phone—"

"I'm sorry."

"That's perfectly all right. I'm Lisa Amberton, and I understand you're interested in our farm. I'd like to show you around if you'd care to drive down."

"I'll take you up on that later, but right now I need to talk to Mr. O'Hare."

She gave him the number, and he called the trainer. "Okay, Steve, I'm ready to talk," he announced. "How soon can you come up to Pickax?"

"Jeez, that's sooner than I expected, but I can come any time. I'd like to bring Mrs. Amberton, okay? She says she wants to meet you."

"Not this time. I want you to come alone for some private discussion—just a deal between you and me."

"Sure. I understand," Steve said genially. "How about at five o'clock? I get through at three, and I'll have to clean up. I didn't line up that information you wanted, though." He sneezed loudly.

"The résumé? Forget it for now. See you at five."

Qwilleran massaged his moustache with satisfaction and tripped jauntily down the spiral staircase to the kitchen, where he pressed the button on the coffeemaker.

While he was waiting for the beverage to brew, the telephone rang, and he took the call in the library area. It was Vicki Bushland's anxious voice. "Qwill, there's been an accident down here!" she said. "Fiona's son is in the hospital. We're very much upset. I thought you'd want to know."

"What kind of accident?"

"He was taking jumps, and the horse went down. Robbie's hurt seriously. He wasn't wearing his hard hat. I don't mind telling you, Fiona's almost out of her mind."

"When did this happen?"

"A couple of hours ago. Isn't it tragic? So soon after winning his first race! Fiona's afraid he'll never walk again—let alone ride. I think it's his spine."

"Terrible news," Qwilleran murmured. Then he added, "I was talking to Steve just a moment ago. To Mrs. Amberton, also. They never said a word about an accident."

"They're very cool—that Amberton crew," Vicki said with a sign of bitterness. "The way they think, stableboys are a dime a dozen. Twenty more are begging to take Robbie's place! It would have been a different story if the horse had been Son of Cardinal. They had to destroy it."

Qwilleran was silent.

"Fiona says you're interested in buying the farm, Qwill."

"Let's put it this way: They're interested in selling it . . . What's Fiona's number? I'll call her."

"Try to give her some hope. She's terribly down. If she isn't home, try the hospital." Vicki gave him two numbers.

Phoning the hospital he learned only that the patient was in surgery; no report on his condition had been issued.

"Could you locate Fiona Stucker, his mother?"

"I'll connect you with the ICU lounge," the operator said.

The volunteer who presided over the lounge said Ms. Stucker had just stepped out. "Will you leave a message?"

"No, thanks. I'll call back."

As he hung up he heard Yum Yum mumbling to herself in the adjacent lounge area, intent on some personal project. Here was a situation he always investigated; she had a hobby of stealing wrist watches and gold pens and stashing them away under the furniture. As he suspected, she was lying on her side near one of the sofas, reaching underneath it to fish out a hidden treasure. It was a piece of crumpled paper. To her consternation he confiscated it, knowing she would swallow pieces of it—the predatory instinct.

"N-n-NOW!" she demanded.

"No!" Qwilleran insisted.

It was a yellow slip of paper he had not seen before, and when he smoothed it out, it proved to be a salescheck from the Tacky Tack Shop, Lockmaster, for the purchase of two sweatshirts. The date of the transaction was September 9. The customer's name was not recorded, but it appeared that Fiona had dropped it when she visited on the day before. Penciled scribbling on the back looked like directions for reaching the Qwilleran barn. Yum Yum had found it, hiding it under the sofa for future reference.

A sudden movement from the cats alerted him, and he caught a glimpse of activity in the woods. Someone was approaching from the direction of Main Street—on foot. That alone was unusual. Although the gate was left open during daylight hours, most visitors arrived on wheels. Very few persons in Pickax chose to use their legs. This caller was walking timidly, and he was carrying a book.

Putting the salescheck in his pocket, Qwilleran went out to meet Eddington Smith.

"I found something for you," said the elderly bookseller.

"Why didn't you phone me? I could have picked it up."

"Dr. Hal told me to start taking walks. It wasn't far. Only a few blocks." He was breathing hard. "It's a nice day. I think this will be the last warm weekend we have."

Qwilleran reached for the book. Like most of the stock

in Eddington's shop it had lost its dust jacket, and the
cover suggested years of storage in a damp basement.
Then he looked at the spine. *"City of Brotherly Crime!*
It's my book!" he yelped. "You found it! This is worth a
lot to me, Edd."

"You don't owe me anything, Mr. Q. I want you to
have it. You're a good customer."

Qwilleran clapped the frail man on the back. "Come in
and have a drink of cider. Let me show you around the
barn. Say hello to the cats."

"I was here the night Mr. VanBrook was shot, but I
didn't see much of the barn. Too many people."

Qwilleran served cider with a magnanimous flourish and
explained the design of the building: the fireplace cube,
the triangular windows, the ramps and catwalks, and the
use of tapestries.

"That's quite an apple tree," said Eddington, looking
up at the textile hanging overhead. He was chiefly impressed, however, by the presence of books on every
level. Even in the loft apartment the cats had their own
library: *Beginning Algebra, Learning to Drive,* Xeno-
phon's *Anabasis,* and other titles from the ten-cent table
at his shop.

After climbing the ramps—slowly, for the old man's
sake—they reached the topmost catwalk and could look
down on the dramatic view of the main floor.

"I've never been this high up, where I could look down,"
the bookseller said in wonder.

Yum Yum, who had followed them on the tour, jumped
to the catwalk railing, now conveniently cushioned by the
top edge of the tapestry, and arranged herself in fiddle
position: haunches up, body elongated, and forelegs
stretched forward like the neck of a violin.

"Siamese like a high altitude," Qwilleran explained. "It's

their ancient heritage. They used to be watch-cats on the walls of temples and palaces."

"That's interesting," said Eddington. "I never knew that before."

"Yes, so they say, at any rate. But Yum Yum's developed a bad habit of pulling everything apart with her paw . . . NO!" he scolded, tapping the corner of the tapestry back on the tack-strip.

She gazed into space, afflicted by sudden deafness, a common disorder in felines.

"Someone's coming," said the bookseller. "I'd better get back to the store." A van winding up the Trevelyan Trail was visible through the high triangular windows.

"That's my five o'clock appointment," Qwilleran mumbled. He combed his moustache with his fingertips. "I'd appreciate it, Edd, if you'd stay a little longer."

"It's getting late."

"I'll drive you home."

"I shouldn't put you to the trouble, Mr. Q."

"No trouble."

"Won't I be in the way?"

"You'll be doing me a favor, Edd. Just stay up here— and listen." Qwilleran started down the ramp. "And keep out of sight," he called over his shoulder.

The bookseller opened his mouth to speak, but no words came. What could he say? It was a strange request from a good customer.

In the barnyard Qwilleran greeted Redbeard as he jumped out of his van. "Nice day," he said.

"Yeah, this is the last warm weekend coming up. It's gonna rain, though, sometime. I can always tell by the way the horses act."

"I envy someone like you who's an expert on horseflesh," Qwilleran said, indulging in gross flattery. He himself was an expert in uttering complimentary untruths.

"Spent my whole life with the buggers," said Steve. "Ought to know something by this time."

"Come on in and have a drink . . . How long does it take you to drive up here?" Qwilleran asked as they entered the barn.

"Fifty minutes. Sometimes less. I like to drive fast."

"One thing you don't have to worry about is red lights."

"Yeah. Only problem is the old geezers driving trucks and tractors down the middle of the road like they owned it." Steve was eyeing the pale tweed sofas with uncertainty.

"Let's sit over there," Qwilleran suggested, motioning toward the library area. "It's closer to the bar."

"Man, I'm all for that! It's been a hard day. I could use a drink." He dropped his jacket on the floor and sank into a big leather chair with a sigh that was almost a groan. "Shot and a beer, if you've got it."

Koko had taken up a position on the fireplace cube where he could keep the visitor under surveillance, his haunches coiled, his tail lying flat in a horseshoe curve.

Without ceremony Qwilleran put a shot glass and a can of beer on a table at Steve's elbow. His own drink of Squunk water was in a martini glass, straight up, with a twist. "I hear you had an accident at the farm today," he said casually.

The trainer tossed off the whiskey. "Where'd you hear that?"

"On the radio." Not true, of course.

"Yeah. Too bad. He was a good horse—great promise—but we hadda put him down."

"What about the rider? Did he get up and walk away?"

"Damn that Robbie! It was his own fault—pushing too

hard, taking chances! You know how kids are today—no discipline! Serves him right if he has to quit riding. There'll be other riders and other horses, I always say. You can't let yourself get upset about things like that."

"You're remarkably philosophical."

"You hafta be in this business. But we got some good news. Wanna hear some good news?"

"By all means."

"Mrs. Amberton is staying on at the farm after it's sold. She's a helluva good instructor, and it'd be a crime to lose her. Plus, she has an idea for a tack shop—setting it up right on the farmgrounds. Only top-grade gear—everything from boots and saddles to hats and stock-ties. It'll be a big investment, but it'll pay off. The kids around here have a lotta dough to spend, and Lisa—Mrs. Amberton, that is—insists they've gotta have the best turnout if they ride under her colors. A good tack shop will be a money-maker!"

"Who are these kids you talk about?"

"Local kids, crazy about riding—some talented, some not—but they're all hell-bent on winning ribbons and working their way up to Madison Square Garden! Lisa—Mrs. Amberton—has as many as fifty in some of her classes. If you like young chicks, we've got 'em in all shapes and sizes."

"How often do they compete?"

"Coupla times a month. Lessons three times a week. Costs them plenty, but they've got it to spend. There's all kinds of money in Lockmaster."

Qwilleran stood up and headed for the bar. "Do it again?"

"Sounds good," said Steve.

"Same way?"

The trainer made an okay sign with his fingers.

Koko was still staring at the visitor. Qwilleran kept the

man talking and drinking, and eventually he began to fidget in his chair. "Well, whaddaya think about the farm? How does it sound, price and all?"

"Sounds tempting," Qwilleran said, "but first I wanted to ask you a question."

"Shoot."

"Why did you land in Lockmaster?"

"Tried everywhere else. Nice country up here. Good working conditions. Healthy climate. Everybody'll tell ya that."

"Is it true you got into trouble Down Below?" Qwilleran asked the question in an easy conversational tone.

"Whaddaya mean?"

"I heard some scuttlebutt about . . . illegal drugs at the racetrack."

Steve shrugged. "Everybody was doin' it. I just got caught."

"I have a bone to pick with you," Qwilleran said in a casual way.

"Yeah? What is it?"

"When you were here yesterday, you shot a bird on the way out."

"So? Something wrong with that?"

"We don't shoot birds around here."

"Hell! You got millions more. One'll never be missed. I can't say no to a redbird."

"You seem pretty handy with a gun."

"Yeah, I'm a good shot, drunk or sober." He looked up at Koko on the fireplace cube. "Sittin' right here I could get that cat between the eyes." He cocked a finger at Koko, who jumped to the floor with a grunt and went up the vertical loft ladder in a blur of fur—straight up to the top catwalk, ending on the railing forty feet above Steve's head. "What's with him?" the trainer asked.

Qwilleran could envision an aerial attack, and he launched an attack of his own. He said calmly, "Were you drunk or sober when you killed VanBrook?"

"What! Are you nuts?"

"Just kidding," Qwilleran said. "The police can't come up with a suspect, and I thought you were here that night."

"Hell, no! I was at a wedding in Lockmaster."

"The party was over at midnight. You can drive up here in fifty minutes. VanBrook was killed at 3 a.m."

"I don't know what the hell you're talkin' about."

"How about another drink?" Qwilleran said amiably, standing up and ambling to the bar area. He made bartending noises with bottles and glasses as he went on talking. "You knew VanBrook was going to be here, didn't you? You found out somehow."

"Me? I never knew the guy!" Now Steve was standing up and facing the bar.

"You also knew there'd be a lot of other people here to provide a cover-up." Qwilleran pulled a yellow slip of paper from his pocket. "Does this look familiar? It came out of your pocket, and it has directions for finding this place."

"You lie! I was never here before yesterday! I didn't know the guy you're talkin' about."

"You don't need a formal introduction when you've got a good motive for murder. And I happen to know your motive. I've also got a dead bird in a coffee can, waiting for the crime lab."

Hearing that, Steve pulled a gun, and Qwilleran ducked behind the bar.

"Don't shoot! I've got three witnesses upstairs!"

There was a motionless moment as a befuddled brain wrestled with the options.

Then came a muffled *whoosh* overhead. The man looked up—too late. The apple tree was dropping on him.

Steve pulled the trigger, but the bullet went wild as he went down under the weighty tapestry.

Groans came from beneath the eight-by-ten-foot textile, and a hunched body squirmed to get free. Qwilleran, rushing to the kitchen, grabbed a long, blunt object from the freezer. He gave it a mighty swing above his head and brought it down on the struggling mass. It stopped struggling.

"Call the police!" he shouted to Eddington on the catwalk. "Call the police! Use the phone in my studio!"

As Qwilleran guarded the silent mound under the tapestry, the bookseller trotted feebly down the ramps to the second balcony and leaned over the railing to ask in a barely audible voice, "What shall I tell them?"

Qwilleran enjoyed excellent police protection in Pickax. If anything were to happen to the Klingenschoen heir, his fortune would go to alternate heirs on the east coast and be lost forever to Moose County. In a matter of three minutes, therefore, two Pickax police cars and the state troopers were on the scene, and Chief Brodie himself was the first to arrive.

Brodie said to Qwilleran, "Funny thing! Just half an hour ago an informant called us and fingered this guy. We didn't expect to have him delivered to us . . . at least, not so soon."

"Who tipped you off?"

"Anonymous caller. We gave them a code name so they can collect the reward. What was he doing here, anyway?"

"Trying to sell me a horse farm. I might have killed him with my club if one of those apples hadn't cushioned the blow."

"Club? Where is it?"

"I put it back in the freezer."

Brodie grunted and gave Qwilleran the same incredulous look he bestowed on fireplaces with white smokestacks.

"Excuse me," said Eddington Smith. "Is it all right if I go now?"

Qwilleran said, "Stick around for a while, Edd, and if Andy doesn't drive you home, I will. What made you think of releasing the tapestry?"

"The cats were pulling the corners up off the tacks, so I helped them a bit," said the bookseller. "Did I do right?"

"I would say you created a successful diversion."

Koko was back on top of the fireplace cube, hunched in his hungry pose, gazing down disapprovingly at the strangers in uniform, and probably wondering, *Where's the red salmon?* Yum Yum was absent from the scene, although the two of them usually presented a united front at mealtime. In fact, it was the female—with her new assertiveness—who had recently assumed the role of breadwinner, ordering dinner with a loud "n-n-NOW!"

As the police scoured the barn for the bullet that went wild, a chill swept over Qwilleran. *Where was Yum Yum?*

"My other cat's missing!" he yelled. "You guys look around down here! I'll try the balconies!"

Fourteen

After searching the upper reaches of the barn, calling Yum Yum's name and hearing no answer, Qwilleran finally spotted her on one of the radiating beams just below the roof. The gunshot had frightened her, and she was hiding in one of the angles where all eight beams met, her ears flattened like the wings of an aircraft. No amount of coaxing or endearments would convince her to come forth.

"What can we do?" Qwilleran asked Koko, who was trotting back and forth on the beam between the cat and the man. They had to leave her huddled in her secluded corner.

After a while the bullet was discovered in the typecase, lodged between a mouse and an owl. Only when Qwilleran boiled a frozen lobster tail did the prima donna make an appearance, ambling down the ramp with a relaxed gait as if she had spent a week at a spa.

"Cats!" he muttered.

He was watching them devour the lobster when the phone rang and he heard an exultant voice. "Qwill, Robbie's going to be all right! With therapy he'll be able to walk!"

"That's extremely good news, Vicki. Fiona must be greatly relieved. I was unable to reach her at the hospital."

"She's here now, and she wants to talk to you."

"Good! Put her on."

"Mr. Qwilleran," came a faltering voice, "you don't know what I've just been through. I still can't believe the doctors could save him."

"We were all pulling for him, Fiona."

"I don't care if he'll ever . . . ride in competition any more, but he's promised to go back to school."

"That's a plus," Qwilleran said, adding lightly, "He may switch his interest from horses to Japanese."

"Mr. Qwilleran," she said hesitantly, and it was clear she had not noticed his quip, "I have something terrible to tell you, and I . . . uh . . . don't know how to begin."

"Start at the beginning."

"Well, it's something Robbie told me before he went into surgery. The poor boy thought . . . he thought he was going to die . . ." She stopped to stifle a few whimpering sobs. "He told me he knew about . . . Mr. Van-Brook's murder . . ." Her voice trailed off.

"Go on, Fiona. I think I know what you're going to say."

"I can't . . . I can't . . ."

"Then let me say it for you. VanBrook had written a will making Robin his heir. Is that right?"

"Yes."

"And when Robin dropped out of school, VanBrook threatened to cut him off entirely."

"How did you know that?"

Qwilleran passed over her question. This part of the scenario he had only deduced, but he had been right. He went on. "Robin had the bright idea of killing VanBrook before he had a chance to rewrite his will."

"No! No! It wasn't Robbie's idea!" she cried. "But they talked about it—him and Steve. They thought they could use the money and buy the farm . . . O-h-h-h!" she wailed. "They didn't tell me! I could have stopped it!"

"When did you find out?"

"Not till Robbie was . . . Not till they were wheeling him into the operating room. 'Mommy, am I gonna die?' he kept saying."

"Was Steve the shooter?"

"Yes."

"Did Robin ride along in the van?"

"Oh, no! He was in bed when I got back from the theatre that night. I told him I wouldn't go to the party. I got home about one o'clock."

"Are you sure Robin didn't sneak out after you returned home?"

There was a gasp followed by a breathless silence.

"The police have Steve in custody, Fiona."

She groaned. "I turned him in. Robbie begged me to. He said there was a big reward. He thought he was going to die . . ." Her voice dissolved in a torrent of sobs.

Vicki returned to the line. "What will happen now?"

"Robin is an accessory, but he can turn state's evidence," Qwilleran told her.

Soon afterward, Arch Riker called the apple barn in high spirit. "It worked! It worked!" he said. "The reward brought in a tip to the police, and they've arrested the suspect. He'll be charged with murder. And Dennis is off the hook. Tell Koko he can stop working on the case."

"Good," was Qwilleran's quiet reply.

"It was someone from Lockmaster, just as you said from the beginning. It'll be in the paper tomorrow. For once, something big happened on our deadline . . . You seem remarkably cool. What's the matter?"

"I know the story behind the story, Arch, but it's not for publication."

"You rat!"

Fran Brodie was the next to call. "Dennis is cleared!" she exclaimed. "Isn't that wonderful? . . . But I hear the apple tree came down! Shawn will rehang it tomorrow."

As far as Qwilleran was concerned, the VanBrook case was closed, but the Mystery Man of Moose County would remain a puzzle forever. He spent Friday with Susan and the attorney at the house on Goodwinter Boulevard, slitting red-dot boxes and shaking out the leaves of almost a thousand books.

On Saturday he wanted Polly to fly to Chicago for a ballgame; she wanted to go birding in the wetlands. They compromised on a picnic lunch—with binoculars—on the banks of the Ittibittiwassee River. When he called for her at her carriage house shortly before noon, he was in a less than amiable mood—after an abortive bubble-blowing session with two unresponsive and ungrateful Siamese, followed by a hair-raising incident involving Yum Yum and her harness.

On arrival, he handed Polly four clay pipes and a family-size box of soap flakes. "Now you can blow bubbles for Bootsie," he said grumpily. "Lori Bamba says cats like to chase bubbles."

"Well . . . thank you," she said dubiously. "Do yours chase bubbles?"

"No. They don't think they're cats . . . What do we have to pack in the car?"

"You take the folding table and chairs, and I'll carry the picnic basket. Did you remember to bring your binoculars?"

There was a maudlin scene as Polly said goodbye to Bootsie, causing Qwilleran to grumble into his moustache. Then they headed for the Ittibittiwassee—past the spot where he had fallen from his bicycle three years before, and past the ditch where his car had landed upside down the previous year.

As they unfolded the table and chairs on a flat, grassy bank at a picturesque bend in the river, Polly said, "Look! There's a cedar waxwing!"

"Where?" he asked, picking up the binoculars.

"Across the river."

"I don't see it. I don't see anything."

"Take the lens covers off, dear. It's in that big bush."

"There are lots of big bushes."

"Too late. It flew away." She was unpacking a paper tablecover and napkins. "It's breezier than I anticipated. We may have trouble anchoring these . . . Do you like deviled eggs?"

"With or without mashed eggshells?"

"*Really,* Qwill! You're slightly impossible today. By the way," she added with raised eyebrows, "I hear you spent the day at the VanBrook house with Susan Exbridge yesterday."

"Has Dear Heart been prowling with her telescope?"

"Quick! There's a male goldfinch!"

"Where?" He reached for the glasses again.

"On that wild cherry branch. He has a lovely song, almost like a canary."

"I don't hear it."

"He's stopped singing." Polly poured tomato juice into paper cups. "What were you doing at VanBrook's house?" she persisted. "Or shouldn't I ask?"

"I was helping Susan *and the attorney from Lockmaster* to open sealed boxes said to contain books. She's been commissioned to liquidate the estate."

"And what did you find in the boxes?"

"Books . . . but there's also some valuable Oriental art."

"We were all delighted to read in the paper that he

bequeathed everything to the Pickax schools . . . Help yourself to sandwiches, Qwill."

He loaded a limp paper plate with moist tuna sandwiches and hard-cooked eggs with moist stuffing, neither of which was compatible with an oversized moustache. "VanBrook was a complex character," he said. "I'd like to delve into his past and write a book."

"I hear his credentials were falsified."

"Where did you hear that?"

Polly shrugged. "The story is going around."

"I suspect he was a self-educated genius," said Qwilleran. "He had a couple of aliases, and that's probably why he avoided personal publicity in my column. He was in hiding—or in trouble . . . Hey!" A sudden gust of wind caught his paper plate and conveyed it across the river like a flying carpet, carrying part of a stuffed egg. "VanBrook spoke Japanese and was familiar with Asia. He might have tricked Americans into investing in fictitious enterprises in Japan."

"Isn't that rather a bizarre venture for a school principal?"

"Not for VanBrook." Qwilleran was thinking of some flimsy business agreements he had found in *Memoirs of a Merry Milkmaid*. He was thinking of the secret of the red dot. He had no intention, however, of telling Polly that books in fifty-two cartons were leaved with paper money—*counterfeit* paper money.

"Listen to that blue jay," she said.

"Now there's a bird with decent visibility and audibility!" he said. "I'm for blue jays and cardinals. Face it, Polly. I can identify a split infinitive or dangling participle or hyphenated neologism, but I'm not equipped to spot a tufted titmouse or yellow-bellied sapsucker."

"Are you ready for coffee?" she asked, uncorking a Thermos bottle. "And I made chocolate brownies."

After several brownies Qwilleran was feeling more agreeable. In a mellow mood he murmured, "This is supposed to be our last warm weekend."

"I've enjoyed our picnic," she said. "I've enjoyed every minute of it."

"So have I. We belong together, Polly."

"I'm happiest when I'm with you, Qwill."

"Say something from Shakespeare."

"My bounty is as boundless as the sea, my love as deep. The more I give to thee, the more I have, for both are infinite."

Qwilleran reached across the table and grasped her hand—the one with the birthstone ring he had given her. With brooding eyes intent on her face he said, "I want to ask a question, Polly."

There was a breathy pause as she smiled and waited for the question.

"What did you and Steve talk about at the wedding?"

Up to that moment there had been no reference to Polly's brief fling with the trainer, nor had the subject of his arrest been mentioned.

Taking a moment to collect herself and rearrange her facial expression, she said, "We talked about horses, and my interest in books, and the *Stablechat,* and his allergy, but mostly horses. Shirley had told him about you, and I elaborated on the generous things you and the K Fund have done for Moose County. When I heard about his arrest, I wondered if he had been using me for an alibi on the night of the murder."

"No, the timing was off. More likely he was trying to establish a financial connection. The Amberton Farm is looking for an angel."

"When did you first suspect him, Qwill?"

"When he came to the barn to talk about the farm last Wednesday. He asked what happened to my trees in the orchard. If he hadn't been there before, how would he have known the orchard had been cleaned out? Also, it looked as if some work had been done on the righthand side of his van, at the approximate height of my mailbox, but I couldn't be sure. Nothing really clicked until Koko found a file of VanBrook's personal papers. There were two wills: one dated recently, naming Pickax as the beneficiary, and a prior will naming Steve's stableboy as the sole heir."

Polly frowned. "Stableboy?"

Qwilleran helped himself to another brownie and described the principal's curious relationship with his housekeeper and her son. "It was Steve's idea to eliminate VanBrook before he could change his will, but it was too late. When I saw those two wills, I had a hunch that the gun used to kill Koko's cardinal had also killed Cardinal Wolsey." He patted his moustache.

"Look!" cried Polly. "I believe that's a female black-throated green warbler!"

"If you say so, I believe it . . . Would you like to come up and see my tapestries?" he asked as they started packing the picnic things.

Polly said she would be delighted.

"Just don't sit under the apple tree," he warned her.

On the way to the apple barn he apologized for his bad humor before lunch. "I'd had a hair-raising experience with Yum Yum," he explained. "She won't walk on a leash, the way Koko does. The first time I buckled her harness, she played dead. The second time, she froze. This morning she galloped up the ramp and disappeared. We found her on one of the radiating beams that meet in the center of the barn. She'd been up there before, but this time her harness snagged on a bolt. She couldn't get loose. I had to go after her."

"Heavens, Qwill! It's forty feet above the floor!"

"Yes, Polly, that thought occurred to me. And the beam was only twelve inches wide. I had to crawl out there and dislodge her and then back up all the way to the catwalk, clutching her in one hand. It seemed like half a city block! She enjoyed it! She was purring her head off all the way."

"And what was Koko doing?"

"Trying to help—by crouching on my back. He thought it was a steeplechase! . . . Why did I ever get involved with *cats?*"

They had a seven o'clock reservation at the Old Stone Mill, and Qwilleran took Polly home to feed Bootsie, take a nap, and dress for dinner. Back at the apple barn Koko was on the desk, sitting on *Watership Down*.

"Okay, we have time for one chapter," Qwilleran said, sinking into his favorite leather chair. Yum Yum settled down on his lap slowly and softly like a hot-air balloon deflating, ending in a flat mound of virtually weightless fur. Koko perched on the arm of the chair, sitting tall with ears alert, whiskers bristling with anticipation, and eyes bright with intelligence.

Qwilleran shook his head in wonder. "I never know what's going on in that transistorized brain of yours. Did you know VanBrook was going to get it in the back of the head? Did you know Redbeard was the murderer? Did you know something vital was hidden behind the books in VanBrook's office?"

Koko shifted his feet impatiently and waited for the reading to begin. Qwilleran had to answer his own questions. No, he thought; it's all coincidence, plus my imagination. He's only a cat . . . But why did he keep twisting his tail like a horseshoe? Why did he twice tear up *Stablechat*? Why did he sink his fangs in every one of the red jelly beans?

"Don't just sit there; say something!" he said to Koko. "Read my mind!"

"Yow!" Koko said, a yowl that ended in a cavernous yawn.

Qwilleran opened the book to page eight. "Chapter two. This is about the Chief Rabbit . . ." He closed the book again. "One more question: Was your sudden interest in rabbits supposed to put the finger on Mr. O'Hare?"

Koko stiffened, turned his head, swiveled his ears, leaped impulsively from the arm of the chair, and bounded to the front windows. And from the berry bushes came a whistle, loud and clear: *who-it? who-it? who-it?*

THE CAT WHO SNIFFED GLUE

Lilian Jackson Braun

A JIM QWILLERAN FELINE WHODUNNIT

Jim Qwilleran, prize-winning reporter turned novelist,
shares his bachelor apartment with two of Moose
County's most notorious felines. Naturally suspicious,
the Siamese – Koko and Yum Yum – share their patron's
insatiable curiosity, but do they really have the talent for
detection that Pickax lawman Andrew Brodie suspects?

Pickax's sedate calm is occasionally disturbed by random
acts of vandalism, but nothing more serious than paint
daubed on civic property. Until, that is, the cold-blooded
murder of the young banker Harley Fitch and his new
bride Belle, which is altogether more shattering.
Qwilleran's moustache twitches in anticipation of
mystery and Koko develops a fascination for all things
glutinous. Just what is the attraction of the musty old
books under the guardianship of softly-spoken Edd
Smith; of Harley Fitch and his intricately detailed marine
models; of Wally the taxidermist? Koko is sure to sniff
something out . . .

'Mrs Braun has a breezy style; the cats are really smart'
New York Times Book Review

'Great fun!' Lawrence Block

'The new detective of the year!' *New York Times*

FICTION / CRIME 0 7472 3325 X